"SO THIS IS YOU SPEECHLESS?" he mused. "Mmm, I think I prefer the feisty Rachel more, but at least I know for future reference."

He took a step into my personal space, allowing the heat of his body to roll over my already too-hot skin. "For the record, I didn't sleep well at all. Want to know why?"

I found myself nodding without thinking.

He lifted his hand to tuck one of my blonde strands behind my ear and lightly brushed the back of his knuckles down my neck to my collarbone, then back up. "It took considerable effort to stay in my room last night, more so than usual." His palm slid to the back of my neck. "And seein' you look at me like that right now, darlin', won't make tonight any easier."

I shuddered as he brushed his lips against mine in the lightest of caresses. It wasn't nearly hard enough, or long enough, and did not at all live up to my expectations of how he would kiss me the first time.

"You let me know when you want more," he whispered, his nose briefly touching mine as he started to pull away. I grabbed his wrist, and he cocked a brow. "Yes?"

Words were still an issue, so I responded by closing the small gap between us and looping my arms around his neck. He didn't hesitate. His mouth claimed mine in a kiss so carnal that I felt it down to my toes.

Mershano Empire Series

THE CHARMER'S *Gambit*

♥ A MERSHANO EMPIRE NOVEL ♥

LEXI C. FOSS

This is a work of fiction. Names, characters, places, and incidents are either the product of the authors imagination or are used factiously, and any resemblance to actual persons living or dead, business establishments, events or locales, is entirely coincidental.

The Charmer's Gambit

Copyright © 2017 Lexi C. Foss

No part of this book may be reproduced in any form or by any electronic or mechanical means, including information storage and retrieval systems, without written permission from the author, except for the use of brief quotations in a book review. This book may not be redistributed to others for commercial or non-commercial purposes.

Content Editing by: Twitching Pen Editing

Line/Copy Editing by: Bethany Pennypacker

Cover Photography: RLS Model Images Photography

Cover Model: Nathaniel Bell

Cover Design: HWCC Author Services

Published by: Ninja Newt Publishing, LLC

Print Edition

ISBN: 978-0-9993709-3-3

This one is for my readers… I'm humbled beyond words by your support and kindness. Thank you so much for allowing me to entertain you with the voices in my head.

I hope you enjoy Rachel & Will <3

THE CHARMER'S
Gambit

A little over four months ago. . .

My best friend had lost her mind.

A contract.

To stay on a reality dating show that she never wanted to be part of anyway.

For money.

I still couldn't believe it.

Oh, the terms were straightforward: pretend to date "The Prince of New Orleans" and refuse his proposal during the last episode, and then he would fund her private marketing firm. An easy bargain, sure, except it required her to give up her job and livelihood for a man she hardly knew on the promise that he would follow through in the end.

Okay, so the agreement his attorney drafted was solid, but a billionaire like Evan Mershano could easily find a way out of it. And then my best friend would be left picking up the pieces of a broken life, while he walked away unscathed.

And what was worse, Sarah Summers's involvement

with said billionaire had introduced me to his overconfident, sexy-as-sin cousin, who refused to leave my apartment.

"You." I pointed a finger at Will Mershano and narrowed my gaze. "Get off my bed."

"Yes, ma'am." He planted his feet on the floor and stood to his six-foot-whatever height and flashed me an amused look. "I can't say that's ever happened to me before."

"Happy to be your first." I cringed. That was the second time tonight I had said that to him. The damn man had followed me home from the office after showing up unannounced with a Mershano-stamped legal contract. One Sarah had requested I personally review. As her best friend, and the only attorney she knew, I was the obvious choice. Much to my chagrin.

"Shouldn't you, I don't know, be leaving? There is a Mershano Suites a few blocks over." And his cousin, the same one propositioning Sarah, owned it.

"There is, but it's much easier to stay here." He moved past me to the kitchen, where he started going through my wine collection.

"You're not staying here." If *he* found out, there'd be hell to pay, and I really didn't need to give him a reason to bother me. Not now. Not ever.

Will pulled a bottle from my fridge and eyed the label. "Not a bad brand." He found the corkscrew in a drawer and started opening it without permission.

"Did you not hear a word I just said?"

He opened a cabinet to pull out two wine glasses. How he found them on his first try was anybody's guess, but it seemed to fit his personality perfectly. He expertly served the wine while I stared at him in shock.

Who is this man, and why is he in my personal space?

Oh, right. My best friend sent him to me.

I picked up my phone and started typing an angry message, when a generous pour of red wine appeared in my peripheral vision.

"Hint of apple. Nice," Will murmured after a sip from his glass. "I prefer my personal reserve, but this will do for the evening." He padded barefoot over to my couch and made himself at home.

"Are you hard of hearing?" I asked. Because that would be lovely. He needed some sort of flaw to detract from his thick blond hair, perfect jaw structure, high cheekbones, and muscular stature.

He kicked his feet up onto the cushion as he rotated to face me. "So what contract amendments does Sarah want you to make?"

I folded my arms. "Is that why you're still here? Because I think your supervising my work all day was quite enough, don't you?"

"I promised Evan I would oversee this entire exchange personally." His chocolate gaze danced appreciatively over my blouse, pencil skirt, and stockings. "And I take my job very seriously."

My tongue hurt from biting it so hard. Less than twelve hours of knowing this overconfident, sexy-as-sin billionaire, and I wanted to kill him. He ruined an otherwise perfect day by showing up unannounced, and then he followed me home like I couldn't be trusted. "I already signed the nondisclosure agreement."

He shrugged. "That means little to me. You could still violate it."

"And risk my job in the process? No, thanks." This might be a personal favor for a friend, but it could still hurt my career if I violated any of the terms Evan's private legal team drafted. Garrett Wilkinson was not an attorney I wanted to piss off. "I don't require a babysitter, Mister Mershano."

He eyed me over the rim of his glass. "Oh, I'm well aware of what you require, Miss Dawson."

I snagged the crystal stem from the counter and took a healthy sip of wine. It felt like heaven against my throat and helped calm some of my nerves. "You're not going to leave, are you?"

"Not until we're done," he confirmed. "As I said, I take my job seriously."

"I bet you do," I muttered, rolling my eyes as I snuggled into the oversized chair beside the couch with my laptop and wine. If he was hell-bent on finishing this contract tonight, then I'd stay up as late as he wanted, so long as it meant he'd leave sooner.

"You know, Mershano Vineyards is in the market for a corporate attorney to help with some international acquisitions. It'd be a big job, I think, and would require overseeing a legal team."

"That's nice," I replied as I pulled up the legal document Garrett sent over an hour ago to review the edits I requested earlier this afternoon.

"Someone with your skill set might be a good fit," he continued.

"You'd need someone with a lot more experience than my four years, Mister Mershano." My experience qualified me to join the team, maybe, but not lead it.

"I think that's for me to decide," he murmured. "And I think you'd be a good fit, darlin'. We should work together."

I couldn't help the laugh that bubbled out of me. "Yeah, that's not going to happen. Ever."

He cocked his head to the side and rubbed a thumb over his bottom lip as he considered me in a manner that sent a shiver down my spine. *Oh, that look is trouble…*

Challenge oozed from him, thickening the air around us. "Hmm, we'll see, Miss Dawson, won't we?"

1

THE BUSINESS PROPOSAL

"Didn't we just do this?" I asked, studying all the boxes in my guest room. All of them were marked "Sarah Summers," just like last time.

"Yep." Sarah made a popping sound on the *p* and flashed me a brilliant smile. "But we don't have to carry them this time."

"Thank God for that." Moving my best friend in last month had been a bit of a nightmare. We lugged everything from the third floor of her building to the ninth floor of mine. A truck helped us out for part of the journey, but everything else was a generous balance between the stairs and elevator. "I love you, but I never want to do that again."

She scrunched up her nose. "Yeah, that sucked."

The wince that followed wasn't so much a result of the move as the reason behind it. My best friend had lost everything after her idiot twin sister, Abby, auditioned for a reality show under Sarah's name as a prank. Instead of suing her idiotic sister for fraud, she chose to go on the show and then struck up a ridiculous contract with the show's "prince." Their agreement didn't go according to plan, but somehow they worked everything out in the end, despite a few misconceptions along the way.

Still… "I'll kick his ass if he screws this up again."

"Duly noted, Miss Dawson." The murmur came from Evan Mershano, also known as "The Prince of New Orleans." He had his shoulder braced against the doorjamb, his dark eyes on Sarah. The adoration in his gaze placated me a little.

"Rachel," I corrected. Only my clients called me *Miss Dawson*.

He grinned. "Rachel."

We met last week for the first time in person, and his love for my best friend showed in every move he made. The fact that he supported her career raised him a peg in my book, and he didn't seem to be a scoundrel. Still, he had money—a lot of it—and in my experience, powerful men like that could not be trusted. To be unsupportive would be an insult to Sarah's intelligence, so I kept my mouth shut and silently vowed to be here if she needed me.

"Right, I think that's everything." Sarah wiped her hands on her jeans after taping the last box, and Evan added it to the growing pile. His fitted white T-shirt stretched over his biceps as he moved, hinting at what lay beneath his clothes. Yeah, I could admit, he was a fine specimen of a man. My girl had chosen well. The curl of her full lips said she agreed.

"Does that mean it's time for La Rosas?" That was the payment I requested for helping today.

"Oh yeah." Sarah loved the cute little Italian place more than I did. "Did we decide on getting takeout, or are we eating there?"

"Don't look at me," Evan replied. "You know I'm always up for a challenge, Miss Summers."

"You just want to get caught, Mister Mershano," she accused, grinning. The reality show they starred in two months ago was about to air, which meant they couldn't be seen in public together.

He shrugged. "It would make things easier."

She trailed her fingers up his shirt as he grabbed her hips. "For you."

"For both of us." He bent to nuzzle his nose against hers, making me roll my eyes. I was all for budding romance, but these two needed to get their own room. Outside of my apartment.

"I vote we eat there. Otherwise, you two might come up with some kinky food games in my living room." I left their resulting laughs behind me as I went to change for dinner. My rumbling stomach kept me from worrying too much about my appearance. I threw on a pair of jeans and a tank top and pulled my blonde hair up into a messy bun. It was a stark contrast to my usual lawyer garb, but I didn't have any clients to impress tonight.

Sarah and Evan met me in the foyer, both dressed similarly in jeans and wearing matching grins. "You two are starting to look like each other," I observed. "Evan just needs a better tan and some curves."

"I rather like his lack of curves," Sarah murmured, pinching his ass.

"Yeah, yeah, let's go." I shooed them out the door and into the elevator. The walk to La Rosas was quick but hot, thanks to the Chicago humidity. Mother Nature wanted everyone aware that June was here. I picked at my tank top, hating the way it clung to my clammy skin, as we entered the restaurant.

"Air-conditioning is…" I trailed off as my eyes landed on the casually dressed man waiting by the hostess stand. "Oh, you've got to be kidding me right now!" I spun around and glared at the grinning couple. "I hate both of you."

The warm chuckle behind me made my stomach flip. It

always did that in his presence, against my better judgment. Seduction seemed to ooze from Will Mershano, wrapping everyone in the room in his alluring web. Including me. And I despised it. I had my doctorate in turning down men, yet this one maneuvered around each of my denials with the skill of a professional athlete. And his sport of choice was flirting.

"Hello, Rachel," he murmured.

I ignored the shiver traversing my spine and further narrowed my gaze at Sarah. "This was not what I had in mind for dinner."

"He insisted," was her excuse.

"Oh, I just bet he did," I snapped.

The millionaire playboy redefined the meaning of the word persistent.

I turned to meet his dark eyes, so similar to Evan's, but with a hint of deviousness. Their familial relation showed in their height and broad shoulders, but Will's nose had a slight bend to it and his jaw was dusted with fine blond hairs as opposed to dark ones. Both men possessed an aristocratic air, screaming wealth and superiority, but there was a playfulness to Will that Evan seemed to lack. Carefree seemed to be Will's persona of choice.

"No," I said in greeting. A word I seemed to say a lot in his presence. Of course, he never listened—just took it as a challenge to change my mind. We'd been playing this game for months, ever since he first showed up in my office with that damn contract that Sarah requested I review on her behalf.

"No?" He cocked a dark blond brow. "But you haven't even heard today's proposal yet."

"I don't need to." There was no way in hell I would work for him. First, it required leaving Chicago and living in North Carolina. Which, right there, was a deal breaker. Not because of my love for the city, but because of something, or rather, *someone*, who would never let me leave. And second, it meant joining Will's staff. Not necessarily a negative, except I would report directly to him. My hormones could not handle short bouts of time with the man, let alone a long tenure of employment.

"The answer will always be no." He could try to entice me with food and charm all he wanted, but I would never agree.

"How about we discuss it over dinner." Not a question, just a statement underlined with a hint of demand. Typical Will.

"Are you paying?"

"Naturally."

I gestured for him to lead the way. "Then after you, Mister Mershano."

"I'll keep him in line," Evan said as he trailed along behind us.

"That's a tall order," Sarah said, putting in her two cents.

I snorted. "Please. I've got this." There was a reason I became a lawyer. Winning an argument ran in my blood.

Will held out a chair for me, so I took the one opposite him. His dimples flashed in response, and he sat beside me while Evan and Sarah looked on in amusement. If that simple act entertained them, then they were in for a treat.

When the waiter arrived, I ordered a bottle of the restaurant's most expensive imported wine and one of each appetizer for the table. "Oh, and I won't be sharing the wine, so just one glass."

Sarah coughed to cover her laugh while the waiter jotted everything down. "And for you, sir?"

Will didn't miss a beat. "Hmm, I'll take an extra order of calamari and a glass of the Reserve Mershano Cabernet Franc, please."

The grin slipped from my face as the waiter beamed. "Ah, excellent choice, sir. We just received our first shipment, and the customers love it. I promise you won't be disappointed."

"Oh, really? It's an unknown brand in these parts.

What is everyone saying?"

I rolled my eyes as the waiter gushed over the positive feedback and reviews.

"The best they've ever had, huh?" Will mused. "Interesting. Did you hear that, darlin'? Maybe you should give it a try."

"No, thank you," I replied sweetly.

"We'll take a bottle," Evan murmured, handing his menu to the waiter. "And I don't think I'll need a main course with all the appetizers." He cast an amused glance my way before looking at Sarah.

"Oh, I want lasagna. And if you try to steal any, I'll divorce you."

"That requires you to marry me first, sweetheart."

She shrugged. "Semantics."

"I'll have lasagna as well," Will added before smiling at me. "Do you want a main course with all those appetizers?"

"Chicken Alfredo, please. And can you add lobster and shrimp to that?"

The waiter gave me an appraising look, as if to ask, *Where are you planning to put all this food?* I might be a tall woman at five feet ten, but I was on the thin side thanks to my morning workout regimen and genetics. My mother's Irish heritage paled my skin, while my father's German side gave me the blonde hair and blue eyes. They were both on the slender side naturally and passed those traits on to me and my brother, Caleb. Although, he seemed a bit bulkier the last time I'd seen him, and not with fat.

"Of course, ma'am," the waiter said after he finished checking me out. "I'll be back with your wine." His parting words had me turning to the arrogant blond beside me.

"You shipped a case of Mershano Vineyards to the restaurant?"

"No, I shipped several cases. Sarah said it was her favorite place in Chicago, and I figured the beautiful clientele might appreciate some decent wine."

I huffed out a breath. "You're unbelievable."

"Why, thank you, darlin'. The feeling's mutual. Now, would you prefer to hear my proposal while you're sober or after you've had a few drinks?"

"Wine won't make me say yes, Will."

"My wine might."

I batted my eyelashes at him. "Care to wager on that?"

I half expected him to take me up on it, but instead, the businessman peeked out from behind his playful mask. He usually bantered with me for a few more minutes before this side appeared.

Uncertainty settled in the pit of my stomach.

No more teasing.

His expression boasted confidence as he prepared for a new round of negotiations.

This was the part of him I feared, the persona that made me feel inferior. He had no way of knowing this, nor was it something he did on purpose. On a logical level, I understood that, but I couldn't help my knee-jerk reaction to run.

Powerful, rich men always won, no matter the cost. I knew that better than anyone.

"Why are you so adamant against working for me, Rachel? It's a stable position with excellent benefits, and I've already offered to triple your current salary. What more do you need?"

"I don't want to move."

"I've offered to let you work remotely in Chicago."

I shook my head. "There's no way I could hire and manage a team of a dozen lawyers from here. What you're asking me to do is nowhere near as simple as whipping up a contract."

"I know that, which is why I want to hire you."

"What I did for Sarah and Evan is nothing like an international acquisition, Will. That was a simple contract."

"Right, one written by Garrett Wilkinson that you shredded."

The famous name made my heart skip a beat, as it always did. He was the prime example of what an expensive education and inherited contacts could do for a lawyer. It helped that he was brilliant and also good-looking. I'd never actually met the man, but I knew I stood absolutely no chance against a man of his reputation.

"I didn't shred anything. I just rewrote part of it," I muttered.

"And impressed the hell out of him in the process."

I almost laughed. "Doubtful. You should hire him instead."

"He's an estate attorney, not a corporate lawyer. Besides, I want you." Those last three words warmed me in a way they shouldn't. He said them to me every time we debated his proposal. I should be used to them by now, but I couldn't shake the giddy sensation that blossomed deep within. Which was precisely why I kept saying no. I refused to allow this attraction to grow between us. Whether he intended to act on it or not remained a moot point. I'd sworn off men like him a long time ago, and I wasn't about to break my rule now.

"I'm flattered, but I'm not interested." *In working for you, or otherwise.* "I like working for Baker Brown. They're one of the top firms in Chicago, and I have no intention of leaving them anytime soon."

The waiter chose that moment to return with our wine. Excellent timing. I needed a drink, or twelve, to calm my nerves. Will always did this to me, even in the beginning. Men rarely flustered me, but he found a way each time. And he kept sweetening the offer, making it nearly impossible to refuse.

The opportunity itself was a dream job. Mershano Vineyards needed an attorney who specialized in corporate law to lead an international acquisition project. My education and experience tied nicely to the requirements, and managing a team of lawyers would look great on my resume. But there were other, more qualified candidates out there, and Will had to know that. Which was why I suspected he wanted me for the wrong reasons.

Will was the type of man who enjoyed a good game of cat and mouse, and I refused to sleep my way up the corporate ladder. When he finally realized that, he'd lose interest, and I'd be without a job. A harsh train of thought, sure, but realistic.

Maybe there was more to his offer, but I refused to let myself read into it. Because I knew if I found any truth in it, then I'd be more likely to accept, and I couldn't risk it.

"Tell me about your firm," Will said after the waiter finished pouring our drinks.

I finished half my glass before I gave the usual spiel reserved for potential clients. Not that he was one, but because it was easier. He listened patiently, asked all the right questions, and continued the discussion while we indulged in way too much food. He didn't make me another offer, for which I was thankful, but I knew he hadn't given up. Not by a long shot.

Evan and Sarah busied themselves with talking about a work-related trip and the nuances of the move for tomorrow. He had hired a company to pick up the boxes in the morning, and they planned to meet their belongings in New Orleans. I offered to oversee the move from my apartment so they could head home early, which meant I would be going home alone tonight.

"I'm going to miss you," Sarah whispered as she hugged me tight.

"Me too." And I would. Maybe not as a roommate, because I liked my space, but she was my best friend. I loved her like a sister.

"I'll call you every day."

"You better. And you better visit too." Because I wouldn't be able to visit her very easily. She would assume work was the reason, but it had nothing to do with my job and everything to do with my past. My former fiancé didn't like me to travel, and he had abnormal resources at his disposal to keep me in Chicago.

"Definitely," she promised. "Love you."

"Love you too."

Evan opened the door of a waiting car for her, and she slid inside. "You two behave," he said, his gaze on Will.

"I always behave," he replied, smirking.

"Right." With a shake of his head, Evan joined Sarah in the back seat.

I smiled as they pulled away. My best friend had finally found a man worthy of her. His wealth and stature concerned me a bit, but if anyone could handle an influential man, it was Sarah.

"Let's go, darlin'." Will, the forever gentleman, insisted on escorting me home since I'd finished half my bottle of wine by the end of dinner. He didn't touch me but walked close enough for me to catch his spicy scent. I hated that it made my nostrils flare.

He was potent and he knew it. Every flash of a dimple, the confident way he moved, and the constant taunt in his gaze made for a toxic combination.

That, coupled with the alcohol, and I could admit he was downright attractive. And so not coming into my apartment tonight.

"Still no?" he asked as we paused at my door.

"I'm slightly buzzed, not drunk, so yep. Still no."

"Good thing I didn't take that bet," he replied, grinning that cocky grin of his. "But I have hope, Miss Dawson. We'll work together."

"Uh-huh." I patted his muscular chest and immediately regretted touching him. He radiated a heat that left me feeling so cold. I couldn't even remember the last time I let a man entertain me. It wasn't that I disliked sex. Quite the opposite. I loved it. But after the last time, I swore never to take a man to my bed again no matter how much I desired him. I refused to let anyone else get hurt as a result of knowing me.

Will cocked his hip against the wall while I slid my key

into the lock. "Have a little faith, darlin'. We'll get there."

I stepped inside and turned to face him. "You really don't know when to quit, do you?"

He braced his arms over the door frame and stared down at me. His pupils dilated as they dropped to my lips and slid back up. "Evan's father once called my desire to own and run a winery a 'pipe dream' and insisted I give up. Now that 'pipe dream' is worth eight figures, and you know why? Because I didn't quit."

He dropped his arms and stepped just over the line into my personal space. I had to look up to hold his stare, which put our lips a few inches apart at best. This was a new tactic, and it halted the air in my lungs.

"I never quit when I want something, Miss Dawson." He pressed even closer, his breath feathering over my parted lips, but still not touching me. "And as I've said, I want you." He stood like that a moment longer, lingering, taunting, and making me wonder what he would do next.

Will he kiss me? Do I want him to?

Maybe…

But he pulled back and flashed that dimpled grin at me. "Have a good night, darlin'. I'll see you soon." He turned away with a playful wink.

Well, hell.

I stood gaping after him as he strode down the hall, hands in his jean pockets, his shoulders straightened with confidence. *Arrogant man.*

"I'll still say no!" I called after him.

"I wouldn't have it any other way, darlin'," he returned.

I shut the door with a shake of my head and a smile on my face. This game, or whatever it was, had started out as annoying but seemed to be heading into entertaining territory. As long as I kept refusing him, of course. Once I gave in, the fun would end.

I took two steps toward the kitchen, when a knock sounded behind me. "Oh, good grief. I am not ready for another round, Mershano," I said as I opened the door.

"My answer…" My smile died as I met a pair of icy blue eyes that were nothing like Will's dark ones.

"Ryan," I breathed.

"Hi, baby girl."

2

POLITICAL ASPIRATIONS

My eyes darted to the chain on the door. I had it installed for moments like this, but being with Will had put my guard down. I didn't even think to check before I opened the door either.

Ryan didn't ask if he could come in. He never did. Just pushed the heavy wood forward and me backward along with it. He looked immaculate in his designer suit, his brown hair styled to perfection and his demeanor intimidating. It used to be a look that made my mouth water. Now all it did was push ice through my veins.

Six months.

We went six months without seeing each other. No calls, no notes, no nasty emails or unexpected late-night visits. I had taken it as a sign that maybe, finally, he was letting me go.

I walked away from him three years ago. It took considerable effort and help from an old friend to do it, but it happened. Ryan had tried for weeks to force me "home," showing up every day at my friend's apartment with a new taunt. It'd been the hardest months of my life, but I'd survived.

Because of Mark...

If he hadn't been home that day...

But he was.

The memory of that afternoon elicited a grimace, as it always did. I hated that I couldn't escape Ryan on my own, but I also acknowledged that reaching out to Mark for help was what empowered me. It gave me back my freedom. Or at least a semblance of it.

But Ryan had it in his head that he was the one who proposed a temporary break, which happened several months *after* I originally left him.

"You focus on your career, baby girl. I'll be back when we're both ready." It'd been a taunt and a promise all wrapped up in one, and it haunted my nightmares.

Because he did, in fact, show up when and where he wanted and contacted me at least once every other week in some shape or form.

Then he vanished around the holidays, and I thought maybe, just maybe, he'd moved on or found someone else to obsess over.

But no.

It was a naive notion.

And I knew better.

Ryan Albertson did not simply forget about the things he deemed to be his property. He gave them space on occasion, but he always came back to check on what he considered to be his.

He didn't waste any time in searching my apartment, checking my bedroom first, the bathroom, and then the guest room. The words, *Get the fuck out*, lodged in my throat, unable to escape. Standing up to him always made it worse. Playing along worked best. My hand trembled as it slipped into my pocket to find my phone. Two clicks and it would dial Sarah. I waited to see his expression before I made my decision. He might hide behind a mask of handsome perfection for the outside world, but he never hid from me.

"Is Sarah coming or leaving?" he wondered, noting the boxes.

I cleared the emotion from my throat. "She's moving out." Lying was only a short-term solution. He always checked what I told him, and the repercussions for a lie were far worse than the truth. Ryan's political connections were vast and terrifying. He'd threatened to have me disbarred more than once, and I had no doubt he could do it.

"Good. I never liked her." He smoothed a hand down his tie as he turned toward me with an adoring look that made my insides churn. How many times had he used those eyes on me and won?

I'm sorry, Rachel.

I love you.

I'll never do it again. I promise.

Those eventually turned into something much worse.

I own you.

You would be nothing without me.

Shut up, or I'll do it again.

I shivered at the onslaught of memories. They felt so fresh despite being several years old. I barely survived him once, but sometimes I wondered if I ever really did. He seemed to think this separation was temporary. That I would eventually be his again and just needed time to grow my career first.

He called it an experiment, to see how it would help his already prestigious position to date around and build politically favorable relationships. But I was still his *girl*, the one he would wed one day when the time was right. And I didn't have a say in it.

Most days, I wondered who left whom, because I could swear I was the one who broke off the engagement. Granted, I never did say the words. That would have required Ryan to be there the day I woke up alone on the floor.

"I've missed you, baby," he murmured, cupping my cheek. I caressed my phone, debating whether or not to dial Sarah. This close, he would hear it ring. And that would infuriate him. I had too many meetings this week to risk one of his *lessons*. Walking in with a black eye never impressed anyone. "What have you been up to?"

"Working." I tried to swallow but couldn't. Not with him touching me. "A lot."

"Mmm, I think you work too hard. Always have."

Yes, that was a point of contention between us. He wanted me to be a Barbie doll stay-at-home wife who attended his political functions and looked pretty on his arm.

It didn't start that way. He used to encourage my studies and even applauded my high marks. We went out to celebrate the day Baker Brown offered me a position after I graduated from Northwestern.

Then things started to change.

The signs were always there, but I didn't understand them. He showered me with love and affection, and I thought it was the rigorousness of law school keeping me from seeing my friends and family. But it was him. Always him. And when I finally broke and told him I couldn't take it anymore, he punished me. Severely. After I regained consciousness, I called the only person I trusted to help. *Mark.*

My neck ached just thinking about that day.

Three years ago, I swore never to be that weak woman again, and I'd avoided powerful, high-handed men ever since.

Until Will.

The thought of him sent a chill down my spine.

Did Ryan see us together? Is that why he's here now?

He always found out about my dates in the past, which was one of the reasons I stopped going out with men. The one time I tried a one-night stand, it also ended badly, hence my vow of celibacy.

I wasn't entirely sure how Ryan knew so much, but I suspected he had someone following me. Or maybe he used electronic means to monitor my movements. Both alternatives unnerved me and left me in a constant state of caution. I thought twice about every email I sent, and I refused every come-on regardless of whether I wanted the man or not. Sarah understood more than most, but I never told her everything. Not even close.

His hand slipped to the back of my neck as he tried to pull me in for a kiss. My palms went to his chest, holding him back. The fact that he let me was an indicator of his mood.

"Ryan," I managed, throat dry. "Sarah will be back any minute." A complete lie, one that would surely cost me later if he ever found out. "It's her last night in the city."

"Ah, girls' night in, then?"

"Yes."

That seemed to appease him, which indicated he didn't know about dinner at La Rosas. Not yet, anyway.

"Well, I suppose I can allow that. But I want to see you later this week. There's a fundraiser on Friday night, and I need a date."

I barely suppressed my snort. "We're not dating, Ryan."

"So come with me as a friend." His reasonable tone was one he used often with his colleagues. Not me. Which was why I hesitated before replying. *What are you up to?*

"I'm not sure that would be a good idea," I said slowly.

His brow furrowed. "Why?"

Because I hate you.

Because you ruined my life.

Because you scare the shit out of me.

If there was a door separating us, I would say any number of those things. But we were both standing in my apartment, alone. And face-to-face. He wouldn't hesitate to hurt me, and calling the police wasn't an option. Ryan had too many friends in high places.

"Because I'm not ready," was my lame excuse.

He sighed and dropped his hand into a fist at his side. "Not this again. You're not getting any younger, Rachel. When are we going to move past this?"

I bristled a little at that but managed to bite my tongue. Years of experience dealing with him kept me in line.

"I'm only thirty, Ryan."

If anyone is getting older, it's you. Though, he still looked the same as he did twelve years ago when we met during my freshman year at Northwestern. He was a senior at the time.

"And," I continued, "I don't know if I'm ready to start things up with you again. You're busy with work, right? It's been a few months since I last saw you."

I kept a hopeful note in my voice, encouraging him to talk about his political aspirations instead of us. It worked, as he dove into a fifteen-minute diatribe about his campaign schedule for the US Senate. The current republican in office was stepping down in two years, and Ryan seemed the obvious choice. It chilled me how many people couldn't see through his pretentious facade, but then I remembered I used to be one of them.

"Okay, baby girl. If you're not ready for this Friday, then fine. I understand that it's short notice. But I need you to start attending functions with me." He tucked a strand of hair behind my ear. "You understand, right?"

I hated those three words. Especially from him.

I didn't understand why he seemed hell-bent on destroying my life. What did I do to deserve it? But I nodded anyway and bit my lip to keep it from trembling.

It was amazing how I could go from having a mostly fun evening, to torment, in the span of seconds. What would have happened if I let Will in before Ryan arrived?

Nothing good.

"That's my girl," Ryan murmured, kissing me on the

forehead like I was five. "I'll call you later this week or have my secretary send you an agenda, okay?"

I nodded again, but I had no intention of following through with anything. And knowing Ryan, he'd forget to call me anyway. He usually did. Then he'd show up again in a month or two, demanding the same thing.

But something was different about the way he looked at me this time. The way he gently brushed his fingers down my cheek to the base of my neck. He usually tried to kiss me now, but instead, he trailed his nails down to my hand and gave it a light squeeze.

"Soon, baby. Soon."

I didn't like the sound of that. I opened my mouth to tell him, but as always, the words clogged in my throat. I hated how inferior he made me feel, how childish and alone.

My stomach knotted as heat caressed my neck. I faced men like him every day and always held my ground, but Ryan crumbled my resolve with a single look. Maybe it was because I let him inside my heart and allowed him to dampen my fire and crush my dreams. No one else ever came close, a defense mechanism I put in place after picking up the pieces of my life. But the second he waltzed through the door, I went back to that place he left me in, and quivered like a little girl. *His little girl*.

He brushed my cheek once more and let himself out. I stood shivering in the foyer, staring after him with a mix of fury and fear. My fists curled, and my desire to break something took over. I picked up the closest thing to me, a vase filled with flowers Evan bought Sarah earlier this week, and shattered it against the door.

"Fuck you," I managed, seething both at myself for my weakness and at the man who put me here. Just when I thought my old self had finally resurfaced, Ryan tore it down.

This was why I couldn't say yes to Will's proposal. No matter how much he sweetened the deal, I would never work for him. I already had one dominant man ruling my life. Two would absolutely destroy me.

3
COFFEE WITH CREAM & SUGAR

I studied my blue eyes in the compact mirror at my desk. They didn't look as tired as I felt, thanks to my morning date with the makeup bag. I hated foundation but needed it to cover my sleepless weekend.

Ryan's unexpected visit, coupled with Sarah's surprise goodbye visit early Sunday morning, meant I hadn't rested at all. My ears were acutely tuned to every single noise in my apartment building, causing me to jump at the oddest of sounds.

Like the dinging of the elevator down the hall.

I closed my door when I entered my office, but the damn binging went off every minute as my colleagues arrived. If my assistant hadn't called me about the last-minute meeting on my calendar this morning, I would have opted to work from home. The vagueness of the invite made me frown.

Urgent Meeting: All Hands on Deck.

Not a useful title, but at least I had a location and a time.

I slipped on my black pumps and grabbed my jacket from the hanger behind the door. Skirt suits were pretty, but I preferred comfort while I worked. Hence my habit of kicking off my shoes and wandering around in stockings. Not exactly work-appropriate attire for a meeting, though.

The conference rooms were located on the top floor with the executive offices, a place I rarely visited. Baker Brown LLP was one of the largest firms in the country with over 1,500 attorneys, and offices all over the world. They only recruited from top-tier law schools—including my alma mater, Northwestern—and had a reputation for being one of the top firms in the United States. Meetings on this floor with fourth-year associates were rare at best.

I stopped by the receptionist's desk to check in and was met by Janine Lawson. I recognized the petite redhead immediately as Jeff Dower's assistant. I shook her hand as a cold sensation trickled down my spine. *Why is a partner's assistant greeting me like she knows me?*

"This way, please, Miss Dawson," she murmured.

I wiped my suddenly clammy hands against my black skirt and followed her down a hallway of windows overlooking the Loop. When we arrived at a set of glass doors, my stomach flipped. Janet Bishop, another of the firm's partners, stood on the other side, chatting with Jeff. Her white suit popped against her ebony skin, and her teeth were equally bright as she flashed us a welcoming smile.

"Are you sure this is the right meeting?" I whispered.

"Yes, Miss Dawson. They're expecting you." Janine gestured for me to enter.

Right. Okay. I'd operated on less sleep before. I could handle this. They probably had a brief question about an existing client, and then I'd be sent back to my office to hide. All my cases were up to date or ahead of schedule, and no one had ever complained about my work. No need for concern.

I entered with the calmest demeanor I could muster. It wasn't every day I met with the most powerful attorneys in the country, but confidence was key.

"Ah, Rachel, thank you for joining us this morning."

Holy shit. Jeff Dowers knows my name. "Good morning, Mister Dowers. I'm happy to be here." *I think.* "Miss Bishop."

"Good morning," she replied, shaking my hand. It was firm and exactly what I expected from a woman in her position. "I believe you've already met Will Mershano."

The smile slipped from my face as she motioned to the man sitting at the head of the table. His hands were clasped in front of him as he observed the exchange with an amused expression. I had been so consumed with the partners that I hadn't noticed the third person in the room, which was a bit of a miracle considering his attire.

Holy cow, the man cleaned up nicely. I'd only ever seen him in jeans and T-shirts, even on the days he visited my office. Those were nice, but this suit... Wow. Talk about tailored to perfection. He smoothed his dark tie as he stood and walked around the table to shake my hand. His palm smoldered against mine, a feat considering the warmth radiating across my skin.

"Miss Dawson," he greeted. "A pleasure as always."

My mouth opened, closed, and then reopened. *What the hell are you doing here?* were the words I wanted to say, but, "Mister Mershano," popped out instead. At least my brain had the wherewithal to remember our audience. I frowned at that last bit.

Hold on...

His eyes danced with mirth as he watched my sleep-fogged mind catch up with my surroundings. A meeting on the executive floor with two partners and Will Mershano dressed in a suit... *Oh no.*

"Shall we get started?" he asked before I could

comment. His focus had gone to the partners behind me.

"Of course," Jeff replied.

Will tugged on my hand, reminding me that I had yet to let him go, and flickered his gaze to a seat beside the one he just vacated at the table. A cup of coffee and a doughnut rested in front of it. Given he had his own travel mug next to his leather portfolio, I guessed he had procured the breakfast items for me.

How thoughtful. Or maybe not. Because what the hell was he thinking setting up this meeting?

My feet moved on autopilot to the spot he saved for me, and my hands wrapped around the hot mug. *Oh, caffeine, how I love thee.* I took a fortifying sip and fought a groan. He had added just the right amount of cream and sugar.

The man's memory when it came to my preferences astounded me. After I first refused his employment offer, he showed up at my apartment holding a bag of my favorite Chinese cuisine. He only knew about my love of Szechuan chicken because it was what I ordered the first night we met, and yet he remembered. No wonder the man owned a multimillion-dollar winery.

"Thank you again for meeting with me on such short notice," Will started. "As I mentioned over the phone, Mershano Vineyards is in the market for a firm to advise on some international acquisitions and manage the relations going forward. It's my understanding that Baker Brown's corporate and securities practice is one of the best." He flashed me a grin as he repeated my words from the other night before returning his focus to Jeff and Janet. "So I'm here to learn more."

My heart dropped to my stomach. That grin, coupled with the way Janet eyed me now, confirmed that Will had told them who he took his advice from on setting up this meeting. Meaning I would be either thanked handsomely after this or sacked, depending on whether or not Will moved forward. But maybe his hiring the firm would be a good thing. They could pair him with a more appropriate lawyer, and he would get his legal advice and then leave me alone.

I expected to smile with the realization, but my mouth curled in the opposite direction. An odd reaction to something I thought I wanted.

Jeff launched into a presentation reviewing Baker Brown's history and statistics, focusing mostly on the handling of acquisitions and client satisfaction. The spiel had been tailored to Mershano Vineyards since he discussed cross-border deals and industry-specific issues related to Will's business, like alcohol trade laws. Our marketing team had done an amazing job, and Jeff's delivery was phenomenal.

"Excellent," Will said after the last slide. He launched into a set of technical questions that surprised me. Someone had done his homework. This business-savvy side of him was one I had only caught glimpses of during our discussions, but I knew it existed beneath the surface.

Evan was the one the family groomed for the Mershano Suites legacy, while Will went off on his own to create his own empire. And from what I'd seen, the man had done one hell of a job. Of course, he had all the right connections through his last name, not to mention whatever inheritance he received, but still, seeing him in action proved that his determination and intelligence played a big part in his success.

"And if I went with your firm," he continued, "who would be Mershano Vineyards's primary point of contact?"

"Likely myself or Janet," Jeff replied, his fingers lacing together on the table. His expression remained all business, but a hint of excitement shone in his hazel eyes. Will's name alone made him a huge client, but it was his connections to Evan that really intrigued the Baker Brown partners.

"I see." Will tapped his chin and looked to me. "I was

rather hoping to work with Rachel, given she's the reason I'm sitting here today."

My lips parted in shock. What the hell was he thinking? He had to be crazy coming in here and requesting an associate for a project that deserved a partner-level attorney. My experience paled in comparison to the two people sitting opposite us. I met their surprised gazes and fought the urge to cringe. Apparently, I wasn't the only one astonished by Will's request.

"That's certainly something we can discuss, but our associates are not typically assigned as the point of contact; however, they might work on aspects of the project as a team." Janet's smooth response was well practiced and far more eloquent than the words rolling around in my mind.

"I can appreciate that, but I've seen Rachel in action. Unfortunately, a nondisclosure agreement keeps me from going into the details, although I can say that she impressed not only me but my cousin Evan and our family attorney, Garrett Wilkinson."

That statement had Jeff breaking his composure and lifting both eyebrows at me. "Which project was this?"

Oh, shit... Attorneys helped friends all the time, but seeing as Baker Brown paid my malpractice insurance, they would not appreciate *knowing* about it. Especially considering who had been on the other side of the table.

I cleared my throat. "It, uh, wasn't a project, but a favor for a friend. I can't go into the specifics because of the NDA, but I read through a few things on her behalf. Nothing company related, just a personal agreement."

Jeff scratched the salt-and-pepper beard lining his jaw. The term *silver fox* suited him well. "That's how you two met?" he asked.

"Yes." No point in elaborating.

More massaging of his chin as he studied me. "Hmm, well, we typically frown upon our associates doing work outside of the firm, even as favors for friends, but considering it brought Will to us, I guess we can let this

30

slide."

I swallowed. The words "for now" hung in the air. Which meant that if Will went with a different firm, we'd be having a more serious discussion, but if he chose Baker Brown, they'd ignore it.

No pressure.

Will and his fucking mouth were going to cost me my job.

"So what would it take to have her be my primary point of contact?" Will asked, lacing his fingers over his leather binder, completely at ease. "Or at the very least, be my on-site legal representation as needed?"

My jaw threatened to unhinge. This wasn't the same as asking me to move to North Carolina, but it certainly came close to it. Except I wouldn't have to live there. Nor would I be working directly for him. *Clever bastard.* He found a loophole around both of my reasons for turning him down, and he went over my head. If the firm assigned me this project, I would have to accept or commit career suicide.

His high-handedness made me sick to my stomach. This deal would force me into a corner with no way out and place him in a position of power over me. I should have expected this tactic. A man like Will got what he wanted, just like all the other rich men in this world.

You're nothing but a puppet…

I shivered as Ryan's voice slid through my mind. *Not now.*

"As I said, typically a partner is the primary contact, but if you prefer to work directly with Miss Dawson, we could assign her as the lead attorney on the project. She would need to work with one of us, at least in terms of advice and general management, but could serve as your lead counsel. And we could arrange for her to be on-site as needed, whether that be in North Carolina or internationally." Janet looked at me. "We would need to clear your workload and meet off-line to review the details."

My teeth were clenched too tightly to verbalize a response, so I simply nodded. I could not believe this was happening. Will Mershano was going to win. What a great way to start a business relationship, with me saying no and him forcing me to comply anyway.

This was why I hated wealthy men. They always won in the end and didn't care who they hurt in the process.

"That sounds amenable to me," Will murmured. "When your team draws up the formal proposal, I would like those terms included."

"Of course," Jeff replied as he switched presentations on his computer to a financial report screen. I tried to listen while he reviewed the proposed hourly rates and general project-resource needs, but a roaring sound had taken over in my head. I'd gotten so caught up in Will's game of cat and mouse that I never considered he would take it to this level.

You were starting to trust him, my conscience accused. A stupid thing to do considering my history. I just never thought he'd go over my head and force my hand. Yet here we were, sitting in a conference room while my fate was decided for me. Ryan already dictated my personal life, and now Will would own my professional world. Where did that leave me?

By the time our meeting ended, my blood was boiling. I wanted to punch something, preferably the arrogant son of a bitch standing beside me, but my employers would frown upon that. When he reached out to shake my hand, I squeezed a little too hard and gave him a tight smile. I thought a hint of concern deepened his brown eyes, but it was gone in a flash as he focused on Jeff's inquiry regarding lunch.

"Sure," he replied.

As they started to discuss lunch location prospects, I politely excused myself. The meeting only on my calendar until noon, and it was half past that already. I murmured something to Janet about needing to finish a contract by the end of the day—which wasn't a lie—and she let me go with a pleased grin.

I didn't bother saying goodbye to our "future client." He could eat dirt as far as I was concerned. Besides, I'd be seeing more than enough of him over the coming months. If he thought I'd be thankful or cheery about that, then he had another thing coming.

Will Mershano was about to meet a whole new side of me. And he wouldn't like her one bit.

4

FAMILIAR RINGTONES

I threw myself into work mode the moment I entered my office. There was too much to do, and thinking about this morning's meeting made me want to vomit. Reviewing contracts always put my mind at ease because it forced me to focus. I was on the second to last page when someone knocked on the door. Unlike the top floor, mine was made of wood and not glass, so I couldn't see my intruder.

With a sigh, I sat back in my chair and called, "Come in."

Will Fucking Mershano entered in that carefree way of his, holding a plastic bag in one hand and a drink in the other.

"Lunch?" he asked as he closed the door with his foot. He had lost his jacket and tie somewhere and rolled up the sleeves of his white shirt to expose his muscular forearms. My damn hormones did a little jig at the walking male advertisement, while my eyes narrowed.

"Are you fucking kidding me?" The words escaped me

before I could swallow them. His brow dipped down, which only further infuriated me. "You couldn't even give me a few hours of peace after forcing my hand? Unbelievable."

He set the items down on my desk and stuffed his hands into the pockets of his slacks. "Not the reception I expected—"

"Oh, I'm sorry." I stood up to be more on his level. He still had half a foot on me, but it was better than looking up at him from my desk. "Do you want me to fawn all over you now? Say how thankful I am that you don't understand the word *no*? My bad, Will. Thank you for forcing me to work for you after I repeatedly said I didn't want to. I truly appreciate it. Is that better?"

His eyebrows hit his hairline. "Okay, you have this all wrong—"

"Do I?" I stepped into his personal space and hit him with my best glare. "Did you not just open negotiations with my firm to hire them? All so you can force me to work with you? Because you know I'll have no choice. It's either I accept the project or forfeit my career, especially after you so beautifully brought up how we met. You do realize law firms frown upon their employees taking on pro bono work for friends, right? Of course you do; who am I kidding? Is this how you win all your games? By backing women into corners they can't fight from?"

My tone was semi-hysterical by the end, but I didn't care. After Ryan's surprise visit, and now this, it was a miracle I could formulate words. Fury and fear fought for control inside of me, and right now the former was winning.

Will said nothing for a long moment, his dark eyes clouded by shock and an emotion I didn't recognize. Regret, maybe? No. That couldn't be. Men like *him* didn't understand the meaning of the term, let alone feel it.

"Are you done yelling at me?" he asked, voice soft.

"Probably not." I folded my arms and ignored the heat

radiating from where they brushed against his abdomen. Maybe standing this close to him was a bad idea, but I refused to let him intimidate me.

"Your reasons for not wanting to work with me on this project were that you didn't want to move to North Carolina or leave Baker Brown. And, although you didn't quite admit it, I've gathered that you don't want to work directly for me. Did I capture all that correctly?"

"Okay, so it's not a hearing issue; it's just you misunderstanding the word *no*." We'd discussed this enough that he knew his summary was accurate. Why confirm it?

"By hiring your firm, I have agreed to all of your terms. You don't have to move, you will continue to work for Baker Brown, and you will not be reporting to me as your direct supervisor. What am I missing?" Genuine frustration colored his tone, causing me to blink. I expected a smirk or a backhanded statement about how I should be grateful, or something manipulative. Not this logical explanation.

"But you're still forcing my hand."

"In what capacity?"

"Hiring Baker Brown under the pretense of working with me leaves me with no choice but to accept the project, or they'll fire me. Hence, you win. Because I need my job."

He studied me intently before releasing a long, drawn-out sigh. His fingers raked through his thick blond hair before trailing down to palm the back of his neck. The carefree man seemed to have disappeared behind a veil of uncertainty. *That's new.*

"Rachel, I only approached your firm because I considered it a win-win scenario. It met your requirements and granted me the opportunity to work with you. If you truly despise the prospect of helping me with the project this much, then I'll walk away. It was never my intention to force you to accept this position."

All my fury and hurt dissipated into a cloud of confusion. "You would turn down the proposal?"

"Yes." No hesitation. "Or, with your permission, I would accept and work with a partner as they suggested."

"With my permission?"

"Yes. And since my admitting how we met could be an issue for you at Baker Brown—something that I didn't know would be a problem, by the way—then I'd recommend this route, if that's what you want." Uncertainty and a touch of chagrin touched his gaze, and his voice lowered.

"Rachel, for what it's worth, I would never purposely jeopardize your employment. I really do respect what you do, which was why I mentioned our history and also why I want to work together. I would never intentionally corner you, even if it has come off that way."

I blinked. Will never did what I anticipated, and this was no exception. He floored me at every turn. I recounted the meeting from this morning and the moment I'd let fury take over. His high-handedness reminded me of Ryan, except his intentions were entirely different. While my ex-fiancé strived to control me, Will only wanted the opportunity to work with me. Despite his flirty nature, he'd yet to initiate a relationship.

Had I gotten this all wrong? Did he do all this to hire me rather than to sleep with me? It was the opportunity of a lifetime, not to mention a fantastic way to impress the partners. If I did well on his project—which I would—I'd be a prime candidate for an early promotion. And the bonus I would get in leading this project would handsomely increase my salary for the year.

"Look, I won't have the proposal until tomorrow or Wednesday. And I can ask for the weekend to think on it, which gives you a week to let me know how you want me to respond." The somber note in his voice wiped away all traces of his Southern drawl. Not that I'd heard much of it today. His accent only seemed to come out during playful moments, leaving me to wonder whether it was intentional or an indicator of comfort with his audience. Did that mean I no longer made him comfortable?

My phone dinged with a chime I hadn't heard in months. A cool breeze swept down my spine.

Ryan.

When it pinged again, I cringed. I blocked his number once. It ended with him showing up unexpectedly at my office. Why did he choose now of all times to reenter my life?

I walked around my desk without a word to look at his messages.

My assistant made reservations for us at Provinos for 8 tonight. I'll pick you up at 7:30. x

The next message had my free hand curling into a fist at my side.

Wear something appropriate. You know what I like, baby. x

"Everything all right?" Will asked, reminding me of his presence.

I swallowed and flipped the mobile over. "Yeah. Yeah, I'm fine." I had to shake my head to clear it. "I'm sorry. I've completely lost my train of thought. What were you saying?"

Concern seeped into his expression as he looked me over. "I said I could stall the agreement for a week. Are you sure you're all right?" His dark eyes went to the phone, then back to my face.

"Yeah, it's nothing." Just my ex-fiancé acting like we're together again. "What are you doing tonight?"

His eyebrows crept up his forehead. "I need to make a few calls, but otherwise, I have no plans. Why?"

"How much information did you bring to Chicago? About the acquisition, I mean."

"Almost everything is on my laptop, so I have the majority of it with me."

I bit my lip to keep the words from spilling from my mouth. If I said them, there would be no taking them back. I chewed on my tongue, thinking through my options, and eventually sighed. My mind was made up when I realized I'd blown this morning's meeting out of proportion and nearly chased away one of the best opportunities to ever reach my desk. There was only one thing left to do.

"I'd like to review it with you to get a head start, but I'll need permission first. It's not a typical situation, but we're already behind, and I'll need to pull several all-nighters as it is to catch up, so they should be agreeable. But you're not technically a client yet, so that could pose an issue." I stopped rambling as all the air left my lungs. *Holy hell, he has a fantastic smile.* It creased at the sides, creating a pair of adorable dimples that could captivate a room. I hadn't realized I'd missed it until it appeared again. Frowning did not suit Will Mershano, but smiling? Oh, that suited him just fine.

"You're saying yes." Not a question, but a statement.

"Yes."

Somehow his happiness seemed to increase a notch. "Oh, how I've longed to hear that word cross your lips."

I rolled my eyes but felt my mouth curling in amusement. "Don't get used to it, Mershano."

"I wouldn't dream of it, darlin'." That devilish glint returned to his gaze. "I'll call Janet to expedite the contract and see if I can't sweet-talk my way into starting early. What time should I come over?"

I looked at my phone, my grin slipping. "Uh." I paused to clear the frog from my throat. "Yeah, let's meet at your hotel instead. I assume you're staying at Mershano Suites off Michigan Avenue?"

"My cousin would kill me if I didn't."

"Right." Another message sounded from the mobile, solidifying my resolve. "I'll be there at seven."

5
FRENCH FLIRTATION

I texted Ryan the excuse of having to work tonight, and he never replied. Experience told me that wasn't a good sign, so I went straight to Mershano Suites instead of stopping by my apartment, which left me dressed in my skirt suit and carrying my laptop bag.

I planned to phone Will when I arrived, but it wasn't needed. He stood at the bar just off the ornate lobby, chatting with three women in dresses that hugged every curve and displayed their long, shapely legs. Two brunettes and a blonde. It sounded like the beginning of a bad joke, which he apparently found amusing, because I could hear his warm chuckle from the hotel entrance. Manicured fingers danced over his button-down shirt as I approached, darkening my already sour mood.

Catching my gaze—or more accurately, my glare—the millionaire playboy grinned. "My apologies, ladies, but my seven o'clock just arrived. Thank you for entertaining me while I waited."

Three sets of female eyes turned to look me over, all of them narrowing in annoyance, as Will finished his glass of wine. He signaled for the bartender, who ran over to greet him.

"Yes, Mister Mershano?"

"Please charge this to my room, as well as anything these lovely ladies desire for the evening." He flashed his dimples at the *lovely ladies*, which transformed their severe expressions into ones of adoration. I rolled my eyes.

"Are you sure you can't stay?" Blondie trailed her red nails down the buttons of his shirt to his belt, where he caught her wrist and brought it up to his lips.

"Another time, darlin'." He murmured, his dark eyes on mine as he nipped the woman's palm and dropped it. "Enjoy your evening, loves."

The women around him seemed to sigh as a collective unit as he pushed away from the bar. If he heard them, he didn't acknowledge it, just kept his burning gaze on mine as he sauntered up to my side.

"We can reschedule if you have other things to do," I said by way of greeting. "Or should I change that to 'people'?"

Laughter stared down at me. "My only plans tonight are with you, darlin'. Shall we go upstairs?"

"You sure you don't want to invite your new friends?" They seemed to be mourning his loss and planning my untimely demise.

"Maybe later." He tugged the bag from my arm and slipped it over his shoulder. I opened my mouth to inform him I could carry it myself, but my throat constricted around the words.

He nodded his head toward the elevator bay in a *follow me* gesture and led the way while I trailed along behind him.

Maybe later. Those two words were a kick to the stomach and weighed heavily on my thoughts as we headed up to his room.

Why do I care? Will had every right to play the field and probably did frequently. As a wealthy, handsome bachelor, he likely attracted countless conquests, hence the harem at the bar.

This just happened to be the first time I saw him hitting on a woman other than me, which meant my earlier thoughts about his flirtation being harmless were right. The man didn't need to offer a woman a job in exchange for some midnight company. A little bit of wine and his charming self did the trick just fine. I'd seen the look in their eyes; all three of those women would have accompanied him upstairs if he asked.

To live a life of leisure...

That thought took on a whole new meaning when Will opened the door to his presidential suite. Not the penthouse, but pretty damn close.

"Holy wow," I breathed, taking in the floor-to-ceiling windows overlooking Lake Michigan. I slipped out of my shoes, leaving them by the door, and padded over to admire the view. The lake glistened in the evening sun, taking on an endless appeal that stole the air from my lungs. I loved this city, but sometimes it suffocated me. This view reminded me of the world beyond it, giving me a sense of hope.

Will's reflection appeared in the window as he wandered up behind me with two glasses of wine. I considered refusing on principle, but I loved a good red. Besides, it'd been a long few days and I could use the drink. "Cabernet Sauvignon?"

"Yes, with black cherry notes and a splash of plum."

I shook my head as I turned to accept a glass. "A simple yes would suffice."

"What would be the fun in that?" He tapped his drink against mine. "To new partnerships."

Sure. "Cheers." I took a sip and fought a moan. Dear God, the man knew his wine. "This is delicious."

"I know."

I grinned over the rim at him. "Cocky."

"I prefer 'confident.'" He took another sip, eyes smoldering as they danced over me. "Did Janet follow up with you about getting started?"

"She called me around six to say I could do a preliminary review of the materials, but that's it." Until he signed on the dotted line, I couldn't offer any legal advice or start researching on his behalf, but I was allowed to look over whatever documents he wanted to share.

He gestured toward the living area I ignored in favor of the view. It was twice the size of my apartment's common room and had a full kitchen off to the side that overlooked a dining area with a table set for eight. A hallway trailed off to the right, leading to a few bedrooms and bathrooms.

I folded my legs under me on the oversized couch while he took the chair and swapped his wine for a laptop. He hadn't changed out of his business attire yet, leaving him in black slacks and the same white shirt with the sleeves rolled to his elbows.

His exposed forearms flexed as he typed, alluding to the ample muscle beneath his clothes. Those long legs were all strength, and the way his belt cinched around his lean waist suggested his familiarity with the gym. Or maybe he acquired his figure after long hours at the vineyard. He had the hands of a man who worked hard, not that of an aristocrat. I noticed that the first day we met. His palm had felt rough and masculine against mine, not soft and satiny. It didn't match the charming persona, or the entitlement attached to his last name.

"All right, this should be enough for you to get started." He set the laptop on the table between us. "I'm going to order some dinner. Any preferences?"

"Not really." I hadn't eaten much all day—a side effect of stress and not sleeping well. That made nearly finishing this glass of wine dangerous, but I couldn't bring myself to care. I set the glass aside and picked up his computer to review the contents on the screen. "What am I looking at?"

"The property in France that I'm acquiring. There are a few others, but this is the most imminent, as they want an in-person meeting in just over a month."

"Where are the others?" I asked more out of curiosity than anything else.

"Various places, none of which are set in stone yet, so let's focus on the French vineyard first."

"You're the boss." I regretted it the second I said it. Grimacing, I met his amused gaze.

"Client," he corrected. "But feel free to address me as 'sir' anytime, darlin'."

I snorted. "Not going to happen."

His pupils dilated as he studied me. "We'll see," he murmured in a tone that lacked his usual teasing quality. It was low and alluring and touched me in all the right places. Oh, I liked that voice far too much, as well as the look that came with it. Confidence smoldered in his chocolate irises and curled his lips into a seductive smirk that had me clenching my thighs.

Shit.

Maybe meeting in his suite was a bad idea. I always seemed able to ignore my attraction to him when in the comfort of my own space, like the apartment or the office. But here, in his space, with his spicy scent seducing my senses, I felt hypnotized by his presence, by the way his thumb swept over his bottom lip as he studied me, by the heat flaring in his eyes.

Look away.

I focused on the website he pulled up, and started reading in French. It was all gibberish, not due to a lack of understanding, but due to my brain forgetting how to read. Each word sounded wrong in my head. I couldn't even translate the company name.

Yes, this is a great start.

Pull it together, Dawson.

I peeked at Will and found him leaning against the wall,

with an ankle crossed over the other, as he played with his phone. Completely unaffected. Meanwhile, my cheeks burned with a fervor.

The man was potent. If a few glances and words set me on fire, what could his hands do?

So not thinking about that.

Except I was. A very vivid image of what I would like his hands to do to me flashed through my thoughts. I bit my lip to keep from moaning. This was what forced celibacy had debased me to. And the lack of sleep wasn't helping.

Focus, Rach.

I started rereading the vineyard's history, and the words semi-clicked in my mind. I'd gotten about halfway through a paragraph when Will's warm tones distracted me again.

"Evenin', Vanessa." A pause, then his trademark chuckle caressed my senses. "You know me so well. Uh-huh. There will be two of us dining tonight. Yes." Another deep laugh. "No, she's a colleague. Exactly. Thank you, darlin'." He slipped the phone into his pocket with a shake of his head and pushed off the wall to sit across from me again. "I ordered us a pizza."

"Didn't hear anything about food in that conversation." It was the second time tonight I sounded like a jealous girlfriend. First with the women downstairs, and now with his phone call. *So unprofessional.*

He brought his ankle up to rest on his knee. "Vanessa knows what I like." *I just bet she does.* "So what do you think of the vineyard?"

"Uh, I'm not done reading about it yet."

He arched a brow. "I thought you spoke French fluently."

"*Bien sûr que oui, mais je suis fatiguée.*" *Of course I do, but I'm tired.* Not the full truth, but true nonetheless.

"*Très bien, ma chérie.*" *Very good, sweetheart.*

His accent blew mine out of the park. Why was that so sexy? "What other languages do you speak?"

45

"Italian, Spanish, and I know enough German to be dangerous."

Impressive. "I only know French and English."

He shrugged those broad shoulders. "You weren't groomed to work for an international hotel chain. I'd argue your law degree from Northwestern is far more impressive."

"Don't you have an MBA from Stanford?"

"Are we measuring our resumes, Miss Dawson?"

"Just pointing out your impressive qualifications, Mister Mershano."

He waggled his eyebrows. "You find me impressive, do you?"

I rolled my eyes at the innuendo in his tone. "Stop distracting me. I need to read."

"Now I'm a distraction?"

Picking up the throw pillow beside me, I hefted it at his head. He caught it with one hand and laughed.

"Careful, darlin'. You don't want to start a pillow fight with me unless you intend to finish it." His deep baritone elicited a shiver from deep within me. The man affected me like very few men ever had, and his gaze said he knew it. My decision to meet him here escalated from *maybe* being a bad idea to *definitely* being a bad idea. I clearly couldn't keep my mental faculties in check around him in such an intimate space. Next time, we would meet in my office or in a conference room. Or in a crowded café.

Ryan's ringtone filled the air, dousing cold water over my hormones. *It must be after seven thirty.*

Will hopped up to grab my purse, forcing me to scramble off the couch. I nearly dropped his laptop in the process but managed to set it on the table and reach him just in time to snag the phone from his hand.

"Whoa, darlin'. I wasn't going to answer it."

The ringing stopped, then started again a second later. I closed my eyes and breathed deeply through my nose. Ryan wouldn't stop until I answered. If I turned off my phone, he'd show up at my office tomorrow. Or worse.

"Is there somewhere I can take this?" I asked without looking at Will.

"Sure, down the hall is the master bedroom. I'll stay out here to wait for the food."

I swallowed. "Thank you."

My stocking-covered feet slid a little as I wandered down the marble-floored hallway to the open door at the end. I passed two doors along the way but wanted to be as far away from Will as possible when I made this call. The last thing I needed was for Ryan to hear a male voice in the background.

Shutting the door behind me, I moved to the oversized bed in the middle of the room and leaned against it. The dimming sun cast the room in eerie shadows, befitting my mood. When the phone rang again, I answered it.

"Hi—"

"Where are you?" he demanded.

I cleared my throat. "I told you I'm working."

"Don't lie to me, Rachel."

"I'm not." Silence settled over my shoulders and scattered goose bumps down my arms. He wasn't even breathing. "Ryan—"

"You know, when you mentioned having to work, I actually felt bad. I picked up a nice dinner for us to enjoy in your office, so imagine my surprise when I opened the door to an empty room."

My heart dropped to my stomach. Not because of the darkness coloring his tone, but because of his words. Baker Brown resided in a secure building. Keycards were required after hours, and they were programmed by floor. I also locked my door before I left. It was possible a security guard let him up, he knocked without an answer, and he jumped to assumptions, but I doubted it.

He has a key to my office…

"Where are you?" he repeated when I said nothing.

My legs started to wobble, forcing me to sit on the bed.

"I'm with a client," I managed.

It seemed that whenever my confidence started coming back, Ryan chased it away with a simple appearance or a tone. How many times would I allow him to do this to me? Why did I put up with it?

Every time he showed up or called, he acted like we were still together. It didn't matter what I said or how many times I refused, he still *owned* me.

And I hated him for it.

I hated myself for allowing it.

"You're with a client?" he repeated, incredulous.

"A potential one, yeah." I coughed to dislodge the cotton balls coating my throat. "I'm reviewing their portfolio and assessing the scope of their project." I purposely avoided a male pronoun. "Baker Brown is drawing up a proposal, and if it's accepted, I'll be the primary point of contact." I stopped explaining. *Too much information.*

He said nothing for too long. "What's the project?" I listed a few financial statistics, and he let loose a low whistle. "And they want you to lead it?" He sounded not so much surprised as impressed.

"Yes." I didn't elaborate.

"Wow, that's great, baby! Why didn't you say anything?"

I shivered at his swift change in demeanor. *Hello, Doctor Jekyll.* "I didn't want to jinx it." It was the best excuse I could come up with on the spot. *Because it's none of your fucking business,* was what I wanted to say, but the words sat heavy in my chest.

"Are you out with clients right now?"

I didn't correct his use of the plural. "Yes."

"So that's why you didn't answer. Okay. Sorry, babe, I thought…" He trailed off on a breath, and I sensed him shaking his dark head. "Hey, we need to celebrate."

Or we could not and say we did. I bit my lip, considering. "Well." *Think faster, Rach.* "Assuming the proposal is accepted, I'll have to drop all my current tasks to get caught up. There's a lot of work to do, and they want me to travel, so I have no idea what my schedule is going to look like or when I'll be free." It all came out in a rush, a habit when my nerves took over. *He's going to think I'm lying.*

"Yeah, no, I totally get that. Of course. We'll figure it out, though, baby. We always do."

You mean you always figure it out. "Right." A female voice floated down the hallway, telling me the pizza had arrived. Or maybe Will's friends from the bar. I frowned. "I've gotta go." My voice sounded stronger. Irritated, even.

"Of course. Go woo the client, baby girl. You've got this."

Those last three words used to empower me. That was before I understood their purpose. "Thanks," I forced out, my temporary strength forgotten.

He blew a few kisses through the phone before hanging up, and I threw myself into the pillows behind me. I pulled one over my face and fought the urge to scream. It was that or throw my mobile across the room. I'd done that before. My bank account hated me for it.

"Fuck!" The feathers muffled my yell, so I did it again. And again. Over and over, while my body trembled with rage.

"You know, darlin'." The deep male drawl chased away my unease, replacing it with a hotter emotion. One that slid over my body like a forbidden caress, causing all my limbs to lock in place. "A man might get the wrong idea after finding a woman lying in his bed and screaming, 'Fuck,' over and over again."

6

CURSING IN BED

I pulled the pillow away from my head and stared up into a pair of amused brown eyes. Will's hands were in his pockets, his stance casual. The desire to grab a fistful of his shirt and yank him down hit me hard in the lower abdomen. It'd been far too long since a man touched me.

Time seemed to stand still as his gaze dropped to my mouth. Intensity replaced amusement, causing his pupils to flare. Suddenly he didn't seem so relaxed, and I didn't feel nearly as tense. What would he do if I grabbed him? He stood less than a foot away. It wouldn't be difficult.

Heat fluttered across my skin as my breathing shallowed. Will's innate sexual confidence seemed to fill the room, making my hormones go to war with reason. My attraction to him was never a question, but I knew better than to follow through on it. That didn't stop my nipples from hardening against my lacy bra. He must have noticed, because he glanced down, then continued his survey in a slow motion that felt like a caress against my skin.

This is it. After weeks of what felt like verbal foreplay, he was finally going to make his move and prove the real reason for wanting me on this case. Relief mingled with disappointment. I wanted him on a base level and would certainly enjoy a night in his bed, but a small part of me hoped he considered me more valuable than just another conquest. *Oh well, at least he'll end my bout of forced celibacy, and help—*

Will cleared his throat and took a step back.

"Pizza's here." His tone lacked the usual teasing quality I'd come to associate with him. "I'll be in the living area."

I stared after him as he sauntered out of the room. *Wait, what?* Had I misread his body language? No. No way. I knew what desire looked like, and it practically radiated from him. But he'd walked away. Without even an inkling of hesitation. He had to have sensed my acceptance, right?

I frowned. Sarah teased me about my constant cold shoulder, a habit I developed to thwart male advances. Was it so much a part of me that I'd let it follow me into the bedroom? A glance down at my exposed legs sent heat crawling up my neck. No. Definitely not a cold-shoulder issue. If anything, my hiked-up skirt lent a desperate appearance, and my hair probably looked like a hot mess thanks to the pillows.

I pinched the bridge of my nose and grimaced. How unprofessional did I look sprawled out on a client's bed, screaming, *Fuck!* on repeat? On top of that, in my mentally tired state, I misread Will's expression. I shook my head to clear it.

The calm, collected, confident version of myself settled over my shoulders as I rolled off the bed. The bathroom mirror confirmed the bird's nest on my head. I ran my fingers through the unruly blonde waves and used the hair tie around my wrist to pull it all back into a messy bun. Not the most professional, but better than before. Tucking my blouse back into place, I smoothed my hands over my wrinkled skirt, grabbed the phone I'd left on the bed, and headed back into the living room.

Will was seated at the dining table, reading something on his laptop, when I entered. The pizza box sat untouched, with two plates off to the side and our wine glasses. Mine appeared to be full again. I picked it up by the stem, took two fortifying sips, and busied myself with serving the pizza while he studied his screen.

After a minute, he shut the lid. "Your firm sent over the proposal," he murmured as he accepted the plate I held out for him. No sign of awkwardness or acknowledgment of what just happened in the bedroom. *Maybe it was all in my head?*

"Do you agree to the terms?" I asked, voice professional.

"Most of them. I'll need to confer with Garrett on a few items." His forearms flexed as he sliced through the monstrosity of sauce, cheese, and crust in front of him. Who knew eating Chicago-style pizza could be sexy? He made it look like a work of art as he popped a bite into his mouth and waggled his brows.

"Not bad for a Southerner," I teased before following suit. *Mmm.* There were pepperonis hiding beneath the cheese. Always a delectable surprise.

"Not my first time," he replied. "So who was on the phone?"

I almost choked on the food in my mouth. It took a minute to remember how to chew and swallow. I followed it with a healthy sip of wine. "Uh, no one important." *Yeah, that's convincing.*

"'No one important' makes you scream profanities, huh?" Incredulity colored his tone, but his expression remained playful as he devoured another masterful bite of cheesy goodness. "The proposal lists you as the primary contact but Janet as the project lead. How do you feel about that?"

The change in topic was jarring. I expected him to press harder, but he dropped it. Because he recognized my discomfort, or because he didn't actually care?

"The firm considers you a lucrative client," I replied. "It makes sense to assign a partner as the lead."

"But you'll be doing all the work."

I shrugged. "That's how the business operates."

"That's not how I run my company."

"Yes, but you have what, a hundred employees? Baker Brown has significantly more."

"Mershano Suites has hundreds of thousands, and Evan always gives credit where it's due." He paused to inhale another bite before fixing me with a look. "And Mershano Vineyards has closer to five hundred employees."

"Really?" My preliminary assessment of his company a few weeks ago wasn't as thorough as I thought—a result of not taking his offer seriously, something I regretted now. I could have gotten a head start on this project. Instead, I would be playing catch-up for weeks.

"And I expect to add more with these acquisitions overseas." He finished his pizza and pushed the plate aside. I expected him to want more, but he rebooted his laptop instead.

"Once the contract is signed by me and your firm, I'll send you everything I have on the pending merger and the other properties I'm interested in pursuing. Plus you'll have access to Mershano Vineyards's records, financials, and other key components. In the interim, you can read up on the terms the vineyard in France has requested. That should keep you busy this week and allow you to properly introduce our first project to your team next week."

Sounded about right. I polished off my pizza and glass of wine while he composed an email filled with project materials. My pocket buzzed a minute later to let me know his message had arrived. Walking back to the living area, I pulled my laptop from my bag and fired it up on the couch.

It dawned on me a few minutes into reading that he

may have wanted me to leave, but a glance at him said he wasn't in a hurry to kick me out. He was engrossed in his own work, or maybe the proposal, and didn't seem the slightest bit irritated that I'd taken over his couch.

With a yawn, I went back to translating the website on my screen and read all about the vineyard he was acquiring in the South of France. The pictures were gorgeous, and the winery's reputation was solid. I wondered idly why they were selling, then stumbled upon a photo of the elderly owners. It seemed they were childless and looking to retire. Interesting.

I started reading through the terms he'd forwarded, and stretched my arms over my head. Every muscle along my shoulders and neck seemed to ache. I considered packing up to leave, but Will's comments about preparing for next week rattled around in my mind. If I wanted to prove to the partners that I had what it took to lead a project of this magnitude, then I needed to be prepared. Arriving with all the high-level background details would be a healthy start.

My eyes drooped a little as I continued reading in French. It wasn't so much boring as exhausting. The weekend was definitely catching up with me. When the words started to blur, I pinched the bridge of my nose and let my lids fall closed. This happened all the time in college. I just needed them to reset, and I'd be right as rain. Stifling a yawn with my opposite hand, I laid my head back against the soft cushion and relaxed.

Just for a minute.

* * *

I breathed deeply, inhaling the alluring scent surrounding me. Peppermint cloves and something decidedly masculine.

Delicious. It made my mouth water.

I burrowed deeper into the heaven surrounding me, luxuriating in the satiny cotton and plush pillows. My limbs felt well rested, my chest warm and content, but my feet felt constricted. I wiggled my toes against the suffocating fabric and frowned. *Why did I wear pantyhose to bed?*

My eyes opened as I shot forward. "Oh no." The curtains were drawn over the floor-to-ceiling windows, masking the light pouring in from outside, but a sliver was all I needed to see. My head fell to my hands on a curse as I started shaking it back and forth. "Fuck."

"You do seem to enjoy saying that in my bed, darlin'."

I flinched and peeked at the well-dressed blond leaning against the door frame. He had traded his white button-down and black pants for a light blue dress shirt and charcoal slacks. Even in the dim lighting, I could see his dimples.

"What time is it?" Sleep clung to my throat, softening my voice.

"Just after ten in the morning," he murmured, amusement coloring his tone.

"Fuck!" My phone must have been in the other room or dead, because I'd missed my six o'clock alarm. Being late was a pet peeve of mine, and I never arrived for work after nine.

I jumped out of the bed, only to have a warm body halt me in my tracks. Will's hands went to my hips, steadying me before him when I would have fallen backward. "Whoa there, darlin'. Didn't mean to startle ya."

My head spun, trying to catch up with my body's too-quick movements, and I clutched his biceps for support.

"I spoke to Janet this morning," he continued, "and told her we were meeting over breakfast to review some of the materials. No need to rush about."

I palmed my forehead with one hand while the other gripped his arm tighter. A variety of words fought for precedence in my mouth, leaving me mute. I had no idea where to start.

I'm sorry.

I can't believe I fell asleep.

I can't believe I slept.
I have way too much work to do.

Will pushed me back a step, causing the back of my knees to connect with the mattress. I sat on instinct and let go of his arm. Both hands went to my roaring head. How much wine did I drink last night? Because I could swear I felt hungover.

"Be right back."

I barely registered his murmur over the tribunal going on in my head. Talk about unprofessional. First the odd moment in his room yesterday, then me falling asleep in the middle of reading up on his merger, and now this? I bit my lip and shook my head. This could be the biggest moment of my career, and I was well on my way to blowing it.

The curse word caught between my teeth as Will reentered the room. His expression said he knew what I'd been about to say and that he wanted to laugh but refrained. "Here." He handed me a glass of orange juice, making my nose wrinkle. "Trust me. It'll help."

"What a mess," I whispered, more to myself than to him, and took a drink. The thick pulp told me it was freshly squeezed, and yeah, it felt heavenly against my throat. I finished half of it before saying, "Thank you."

"Of course," he replied. "Feel free to use the bathroom to freshen up. We can swing by your place on the way to the office so you can change."

I winced. "Nothing like doing the walk of shame with a client."

"No shame here." His chocolate gaze snagged mine and held. "I suspect we'll be pulling a lot of long nights together over the next month or two, Miss Dawson. And I'm looking forward to every minute." With that suggestive statement hanging between us, he turned and softly closed the door behind him.

7
A DONE DEAL

None of my previous hotel rooms came equipped with the amenities I found in Will's en-suite bathroom. Toiletries were typical, but the variety of hair brushes and dental supplies were not. I took advantage of them and fully showered and groomed myself before re-dressing in my skirt suit. It helped me feel somewhat human again and also granted me the time I needed to gather my bearings.

At least until I stepped in the living area and found Will chatting with a dark-haired man of similar height and stature. His crisp suit screamed elegance and wealth, as well as good taste. It clung to his torso, tapered at his waist, and highlighted the strength of his thighs. His cuff links winked in the light, platinum, not gold, and his grin was all arrogance.

"Miss Dawson," he greeted.

His suave tones sent a chill of familiarity down my spine. One late night of endless debate left him unforgettable. "Mister Wilkinson."

His striking blue eyes held a hint of menace that made my pulse race, but when he held out his hand, I reciprocated. His firm grip screamed dominance, but it wasn't bone-crushing or cruel. Just an alpha confirming his presence. When I returned the gesture subtly, his lips curled and he flashed a look at Will that was too quick for me to read. Approval, maybe?

"Nice to finally meet you," he murmured as he dropped my hand. "Will tells me we're stopping by your place on the way to the office?"

The knowing way he said it made me cringe. "Yes, or you both can head to the office and I can meet you there."

Garrett glanced at his watch. "No, we have time."

I frowned. "When is your meeting?"

His responding smile hinted at his nickname. *The Devil indeed.* "Oh, sweetheart, the tricks I could teach you…"

"We don't have a meeting time," Will elaborated, amused. "Garrett prefers the element of surprise."

"Which you just ruined."

"Rachel won't say anything."

I cocked an eyebrow as some of my personality returned. "Do you speak for me now?" What was with rich men and constantly throwing me off my game?

"I wouldn't dream of it," Will replied as he hefted my bag over his shoulder. I hadn't even noticed it sitting beside him on the table. "But as I have your laptop and phone," he continued, "I feel rather confident in my assessment."

My jaw unhinged. "Some would call that stealing."

"I call it safeguarding. Shall we?"

I parted my lips to argue, but the fight left me on my next breath. I didn't want my phone back. Not after last night. Ryan always chose random times to reach out to me, but something about his approach was different this time. It felt more urgent, which concerned me. Desperation made him even more dangerous, and I couldn't afford for him to escalate his advances right now. Not when it was so clear I still lacked a backbone around him.

"Rachel?" The concern etching Will's brow was the last thing I needed.

"For the record, I'm only letting you hold on to my stuff because I don't feel like carrying it." The snarky tone felt forced to my ears but seemed to appease him enough to smooth the lines on his forehead.

"Whatever you say, Miss Dawson."

"Can I get a recording of that?" Because those words would definitely come in handy over the next few weeks.

He pressed his hand to the small of my back to propel me forward. "Not a chance, darlin'."

* * *

"He talked you into it." The laughter in Sarah's voice came over the phone loud and clear. "I can't say I'm surprised. That man is all kinds of insistent."

I relaxed into my office chair and sighed. "It's not like I had a choice. He's hiring my firm." I'd left Will and Garrett in the elevator, wishing them both the best as they headed upstairs to surprise the partners. After listening to their male banter over the last ninety minutes, I knew Jeff and Janet would have their hands full. Part of me pitied them, while the rest of me was relieved to have some space. Too much arrogant male for one day, thank you very much.

"Uh-huh. Admit it. You're flattered."

I snorted. "I'm really not."

"I've known you what, almost twenty years now? You're totally flattered."

"I'm going to hang up on you. Bye, Sarah." I pretended to put the phone down, then brought it back up to my ear and waited a beat. "Okay, so I'm a tiny bit flattered and a whole hell of a lot annoyed."

"Aha! And there it is, ladies and gentleman, my best friend admitting defeat. You do realize I'm recording this conversation, yes?" Her teasing tones forced me to smile. Sarah would have no idea what this small gift of normalcy meant to me. The last few days had been a whirlwind of insanity. I felt like I was losing myself in the process, but a few words from her grounded me in reality.

"You know, the next time you need a contract reviewed, try calling your other lawyer friend for help. Oh wait, you don't have one…" Sarcasm hung from my every word.

"Yeah, yeah." I pictured her waving her hand around while she spoke. "So tell me everything."

"There isn't much to say other than he arranged a meeting with Baker Brown first thing yesterday morning, invited me, and then insisted on making me the lead contact for the case. He's up there right now with Garrett discussing the proposal my firm sent over last night."

"Garrett is there?"

"Yeah, apparently, he flew in first thing this morning, which tells me Will is playing hardball over something in that proposal." Why else would he invite The Devil to come out and play?

"Is Garrett as pompous-looking as he sounds?"

I laughed. "He wears arrogance well."

"That good-looking, huh?"

"I couldn't even begin to do him justice," I admitted. "He gives Will a run for his money." Perhaps literally if that suit was anything to go by.

"So the three of them in a room… ?"

"Would make me consider looking twice," I replied, knowing she meant Evan, Will, and Garrett.

"Nice. We should make this happen, although I think you've already looked more than a few times at Will?" A question lingered in her voice, as it always seemed to lately when we discussed Will.

"You know he's not my type." Except for maybe physically.

"Actually, I'd argue he's precisely your type."

"I don't date men like him."

"Which again, I'd argue isn't true," was her soft reply. "You can't let Ryan control you forever, Rach."

The mention of his name wiped the grin from my face. Emotion burned a hole in my throat, thwarting my ability to snap out a reply to that too-accurate assessment.

"He's not Ryan, Rach. You have to see that," she continued, knowing she'd struck a nerve. "I worried you might liken his persistence to that of your ex, but you have to see that he would never actually force himself on you, right? I mean, aside from hiring your firm, which, I suppose, could be seen that way…" I sensed her frowning. "Remind me to kick his ass for that."

"He gave me a choice," I murmured. "Yesterday, I mean. After the meeting, he brought me lunch and told me he would walk away if I really didn't want to work with him." I should have let her kick his ass—because that would be fun to watch—but part of me felt the need to defend him. Because he *did* offer me a choice and then proceeded to prove my instincts wrong at every turn.

"Ryan would never have given you a choice," was all she said in reply, her point made.

"He came over Saturday night." I winced at the weakness in my voice but felt a surge of strength for finally admitting it to someone. It was when I kept him a secret that things were worse for me. I knew that, but each time, it felt like ripping off a Band-Aid and exposing my soul.

"What?!" Sarah exclaimed. "That fucker! Is it because he knew I moved out?"

"No, but he knows now after seeing all the boxes."

"Jesus, Rach, why didn't you say anything Sunday morning? Never mind, I know why. You knew I wouldn't leave." I pictured her pinching the bridge of her nose as she let out a long sigh. "You need to get a restraining order."

"The last time I tried that, he showed up with the paperwork and burned it two inches away from my face." I shivered at the memory, both in fear and rage. "You know it's not that easy with him."

"Maybe Will or Garrett—"

"No." I didn't know what she planned to suggest, but my answer was adamant. "I'm not involving them, or Evan. You might trust them, but I barely know them."

"But—"

"No. We're not having this discussion."

She was quiet for a long moment. "Do you need me to come home? Because you know I will."

"No, no, of course not." The last thing I wanted was to take her away from happiness. Ryan was my issue. "I can handle him." I fought the urge to laugh hysterically at that pronouncement. As if I'd ever been able to handle him.

"Have you ever considered talking to Caleb's friend? You know, the sexy fed?"

My brow pinched at the mention of my brother's name, then my heart sped up.

"You mean Mark?" I never told Sarah how much he already knew about Ryan, and her dropping his name out of the blue made me wonder what she suspected.

"Yeah, he's FBI right?" she asked.

I swallowed roughly. "Uh, yeah." Except I didn't think that was true. I suspected Mark was really involved in black ops of some kind, maybe the CIA or something even more elusive. Half the time I called his cell phone, it went straight to voicemail and he replied a week or so later with a vague "Sorry, work trip." But he always called me back. And he was always there when I really needed him. Like three years ago.

Shoving the memory from my mind, I switched focus to a more comfortable topic. Something a little more fun. Revenge.

"Actually, that reminds me, did you still want me to reach out to him about pranking that twin of yours?" After Abby forced Sarah to participate on *The Prince's Game*, we discussed a few ideas for payback. If anyone could pull off an elaborate ruse, it was Mark Kincaid.

"Yeah, I do, but I want to plan it for next year. I'm currently punishing her by letting her think I'm still suffering from a broken heart. Once I admit to dating Evan again, then I'll need to lull her into a false sense of contentment before really getting revenge."

I laughed. "I approve." Abby deserved it, and worse. "Just let me know when to talk to him."

"You could talk to him about Ryan."

My insides churned at the reminder of why she'd brought up Mark.

Sarah had no idea how her words affected me, how they dragged up memories from a moment I'd prefer to forget. The moment I broke and called for help. Mark hadn't asked any questions, but he had to know. It was written all over my face and neck in bruises. Yet he showed up, helped me move, and never demanded a reason. Just handed me a business card with a mysterious phone number and told me to call it if I ever found myself in a similar situation.

To this day, it sat idle in my wallet. I couldn't bring myself to discard it despite knowing I would never use it. I made a personal vow that afternoon to always take care of myself first and to never end up in a similar situation again.

"Rachel?"

I cleared my throat as I tried to remember what sent me down the rabbit hole. Talking to Mark. About Ryan. Right. "Uh, yeah, maybe."

"Come on, Rach. You know you want to let the sexy fed kung-fu Ryan's ass."

My lips curled. "That is a fun image." Mark would take his pompous ass down with a single punch.

"He could dispose of the body too, right? I like this plan. Let's call the fed."

I rolled my eyes. "If only it were that easy." Sarah only knew small details about Ryan, and I intended to keep it that way. A ding on my computer drew my attention to an incoming email from Janet. Will's name was in the subject line. "Uh, I gotta go."

"Work?"

"Yeah. Looks like Will just became our client officially."

"That was fast."

"Yeah, something tells me Will doesn't know how to take things slow."

She laughed. "Too true. All right, good luck. Let me know when you fall into bed with him."

"That's not..." My voice trailed off when I realized she'd hung up after that parting sentence. "Not fair, Sarah. Not fair at all." I sent her a text with my heated rebuttal, then switched gears. *Time to work.*

8
CONVOLUTED
CONVERSATIONS

Janine stood by the receptionist's desk, just like earlier this week, waiting for me. I half expected to be escorted to the conference room, but instead, she led me to her boss's office, where Jeff and Janet were waiting for me. They wore matching smiles, something I took as a good sign, and the redheaded assistant closed the door behind me.

"Well, I guess you know why we've asked you up here." Janet's knowing look left me a little unsettled, but I rolled with it.

"Will?" Because why else would I be here?

"Yes. He's quite charming," Janet said as she took over a plush chair. She gestured for me to take the other, so I set my portfolio on the table and joined her.

"I can't believe you kept him from us all this time." Jeff gave a little laugh with the words as he popped his hip against the mahogany desk behind him and folded his arms. "You know I need to say something about how the two of you met, though, right? Now, Will assured us it wasn't Mershano Suites related, but it walks a very thin line, Rachel."

I cleared my throat. "Yeah, I'm sorry. It, well, I can't talk about it, but it wasn't business related at all." Not to mention the entire thing was null and void now anyway since they'd gone and fallen in love.

"I'm willing to overlook it because you brought us Will, but you do realize there are conflicts of interest here, right? With your history and relationship, I mean?"

"Um." I bit my lip. Sarah's being my best friend and dating Will's cousin could be considered an issue, especially if their relationship went sour. "I'm not worried. My professionalism comes first and foremost." Besides, no way would Evan let Sarah walk away from him now. I'd seen the way he looked at her. He was a man in love, and no way would he let her go without one hell of a fight.

"You're absolutely sure?" Janet pressed. "Will's already given his side, of course, but seemed confident that the circumstances wouldn't impact the project."

Of course he wouldn't worry about it. He'd proclaimed Sarah and Evan soul mates from the very beginning. "I'm not concerned," I said with finality. "It won't be an issue."

"Excellent." Jeff popped up to shuffle some of the documents on his desk. "Did you want to review the agreement?"

"Uh…" Was he asking because Will requested me as the project lead? "Is there anything unique about it?"

He shook his silver head. "No, just what we've discussed."

"Then I'm okay. I trust it's all in order, but thank you." Reading the financial figures they'd agreed to would be interesting, but I preferred not to know. Whatever agreement Will had come to with the firm was his business. I would just be here to support the project.

Jeff's smile reached his ears. "Fantastic. Then I have

nothing else right now. Will said he left you with materials to review this week, and we'll start scheduling project calls next week."

"You and I will meet once a day until you feel more comfortable with the assignment," Janet added. "Will plans to conference in as well."

Right. Because he already left Chicago.

He'd called last night to say, "I trust you, darlin'. Call me if you need me." Other than an email this morning, I hadn't heard another word from him. It left me wondering if he really did only want to work with me, but now wasn't the time to consider that.

"Sounds great," I said, forcing a smile. "I need to delegate a few of my assignments, and then I'll be one hundred percent focused on this one."

"I bet," Janet said with a twinkle in her eyes.

Okay. "Well, thank you so much for trusting me with this opportunity. I promise not to let you down." I sounded like a corporate robot, but their responding grins said it worked. We all shook hands, and I escorted myself back down to my office and poured a giant cup of coffee.

I'd just sat down when a knock sounded. My heart did a little flip-flop at the prospect of it being Will. He couldn't be here to surprise me with a late lunch again, could he? It seemed like something he would do…

Except he's in North Carolina.

A girl can dream.

Those hopes died as a tall man in a suit with too-dark hair and icy eyes stepped into my office without permission and closed the door behind him.

My heart sunk to my stomach. "Ryan…"

"I see you have time for a coffee break, but not to call me back. And here I was worried." He shrugged out of his jacket and hung it on the door before walking around to sit on my desk with his legs right beside me. "You know I don't like being forced to come over here, Rachel."

"I… I didn't mean…"

"You mean you didn't think." He gripped my chin when I dropped my gaze, and forced me to look at him. "You owe me a dinner date, baby. We need to be seen in public together."

"Why?" I whispered. Why after all these months of silence was he insistent on harassing me again now? I called off our engagement three years ago. It'd taken every ounce of willpower I owned to ask Mark for help, and then to leave that day, and there'd been a thousand times in the months following that I considered going back, if only to make life easier. Those were my darkest days, the ones where I forced a smile at work and curled into a ball each night, terrified of doing it all over again the next day.

The threats nearly killed me, and then he'd stopped. I naively thought he was moving on, but no. Photos started arriving of him out with other women—his way of "playing the field to secure more political connections," as he'd so eloquently put it. The entire charade was all a game to him. He never considered me a person, but his property. And he did not like it when his *baby girl* stepped out of line.

"Do I need a reason to take my fiancée on a date?" He sounded deceptively sweet as he traced his thumb over my lips.

"We're not engaged, Ryan." It came out hoarse rather than strong, and it caused him to grin.

"I love when you tease me, baby girl," he murmured. "You may have taken off your ring, but that's just symbolism. I know what we are, and soon the public will as well."

My throat closed off any opportunity for a response. Not that I had one. He hadn't acted like this for so long that I didn't know how to interpret his change. It reeked of desperation, and that scared me more than anything else.

"Oh, before I forget, I spoke to the wedding coordinator." He pulled his phone from his pocket and started typing a message. "She wants to meet with you on

Saturday to look at venues. I told her we prefer a summer wedding, and she's looking at July of next year. Apparently, thirteen months doesn't leave us a lot of time for wedding planning, so we need to decide on a location and a date immediately. I realize this isn't great timing with your big work project, but our nuptials are more important. Especially since you won't be working afterward anyway."

My lips parted, but nothing came out.

He was delusional.

Completely insane.

And if I protested right now, he'd create a huge scene, thus guaranteeing I wouldn't have a place to work by this time next week. Which explained why he decided to drop all this on me at the office.

He *wanted* me to react. To scream, to rant, to make a general scene, just so he could play the wounded hero and gain sympathy from my coworkers. The man knew how to play this game far better than I did, but I'd memorized his manipulative ways. It was the only way to survive our volatile relationship.

My phone dinged as he finished typing his message, and I found the wedding planners' name staring back at me. *Becky McGraw*. Lovely.

"She wants to have brunch Saturday," he continued. "I suggested Francine's for memory's sake."

Right. The place he proposed.

I was going to be sick.

"Ryan, this is all rather sudden…"

The hand on my chin tightened to a painful degree. "Sudden? I've given you three fucking years, Rachel. Most would say I've been more than patient with your antics."

Tears sprung to my eyes, not from his words but from the grip on my jaw. He knew exactly where to press to evoke the most pain. "I'm sorry," I whispered. "You're right." I had to say the words I hated most to appease him, or I'd end up with bruises I couldn't explain. And screaming in the middle of my office would get me nowhere. Sure, he'd let me go, but his reaction would worsen once we had an audience, and somehow I'd be the guilty party. It'd happened before outside of work. I had no reason to believe my coworkers would react differently.

"Of course I am, baby girl." He finally loosened his grip and bent to place a kiss against my jaw, then my lips. It took everything in me to respond just enough to make it believable, and then he brushed the tear from beneath my eye. "I'm willing to take a rain check on dinner, but you will be at brunch on Saturday."

This was the Ryan I knew, the one who pretended to negotiate, when in reality, nothing he said qualified as a concession. *I'll let you skip the date, because I love you, but you'll be at the wedding planning session.*

I couldn't respond to that.

My livelihood relied on my ability to argue, and yet no words presented themselves in my thoughts.

I sat mute in my chair, staring up at him with resignation. The word *okay* hung unspoken between us because I refused to let it slip. It was my only defiance and one he allowed as he swept his lips over my forehead.

"Francine's at ten thirty sharp, Rachel."

Another tear fell as he sauntered out of my office without another word.

My fingers fluttered to my tender jaw to rub the imprint he'd left there. It ached more from clenching my teeth than the pressure he applied, but together they left me feeling ill.

Marriage.

The man had lost his fucking mind.

I couldn't marry him.

Why couldn't he find someone else to obsess over?

And where the hell had he been these last six months?

My head spun with confusion. Two visits in one week, plus the failed one Monday night, and all the calling... It reminded me of the weeks after we broke up. Except, rather than be violent and cruel, he'd taken a different approach. One that presented his suave side with just a hint of the lethality beneath.

A chill slithered down my spine.

I couldn't go through this again.

What choice do you have?

I studied the number on my screen. Calling to cancel would piss Ryan off, and I couldn't deal with him throwing a fit in my office.

Have you ever considered talking to Caleb's friend? Sarah's words from the other day drifted through my mind.

Mark...

My eyes went to the drawer holding my purse. The card he handed me three years ago sat inside. Who knew if that number was even still valid?

No.

I could handle this myself. I had to. Ryan had escalated his efforts, but it wasn't out of my control. Not like the night he strangled me...

My jaw clenched, causing me to flinch as I recalled the pressure he'd just applied to my chin. "Bastard."

I hated him.

No way in fucking hell would I marry him.

But there were other ways to play this game. Maybe.

He wanted a wedding? Then I'd plan one. And then I wouldn't show up. *Game on, asshole.*

I hit dial before I could talk myself out of it.

The wedding planner answered on the second ring. "Hello, Miss Dawson."

Oh, good, my *fiancé* had given her my number. "Hi, Becky. Please call me Rachel."

"Of course," she replied, her voice businesslike. This I could handle. "Did Mister Albertson tell you about our meeting on Saturday?"

"Yes, that's actually why I'm calling." I leaned back in my chair and closed my eyes. This had to work. But I needed to remain calm. I could do this. Stealing a deep breath, I jumped feet first into the deep end.

"So you're aware of our timeline, right? And Ryan wants a big wedding. Given our timeline, I really don't think waiting until Saturday is a good idea, so if you're open to discussing options over the phone earlier, I wanted to let you know I'm available." *Then you can go off and plan whatever the hell you want on Saturday while I work.* Hopefully, she used Ryan's credit cards in the process.

I crossed my fingers and waited. Her fingernails clicked against a keyboard over the line as the seconds ticked by. "Okay, Miss Dawson. How about now?"

My gaze went to the clock. "Sure," I managed. It was going to be a long night anyway; I might as well spend it at the office. "Let's discuss it now."

9

NORTH CAROLINA

My conversation with Becky placated Ryan enough that he'd given me a temporary reprieve of sorts to focus on work, but I suspected that was about to end.

First, because I'd denied his dinner requests four times now, claiming meetings as a repetitive excuse.

And second, because I'd just left the state without telling him.

I pressed my palm against my skirt as I dragged my suitcase along behind me and stifled a yawn. These last few weeks were working hell. Not just managing Ryan's persistent calls and random visits, but also working long days, followed by longer nights, and spending weekends at the office. Baker Brown had assigned a dozen lawyers to Will's case, marking it with high urgency given the timeline, and threw ample funding behind it.

I hadn't seen Will since the day he finalized the agreement with my firm three and a half weeks ago. We'd talked a few times over the phone since, but always professionally and only about the project. It left me feeling a bit empty and confused and a tad bit disappointed. Which wasn't fair. I wanted him to hire me for my work, not for my body, yet I missed his easy candor and flirting—a conundrum that left me walking at a clipped pace toward the exit.

I didn't want to be excited at the prospect of seeing him outside those doors, but the jumping jacks going on in my belly told me the truth. I'd missed him. Ridiculous. Idiotic. Annoying.

When I spotted a man in a suit holding a placard with my name, the gymnastics in my stomach halted, leaving behind a queasy feeling.

This is what I wanted. To be treated like a professional. *Pull it together, hormones.*

"Miss Dawson?" the man asked, his drawl reminding me a little of Will.

"That'd be me."

"A pleasure, ma'am." He tipped his hat, revealing a touch of his salt-and-pepper hair at the sides, and opened the back door of his black town car. "I'll take your bag."

"Thank you, Mister... ?"

Another tip of that hat. "You can call me Rudy, ma'am."

I grinned. "Thank you, Rudy."

"Careful, he's a bit of a flirt," came a voice from inside the car. My heart kicked up a notch as I bent to find Will sitting in the back seat, dressed in khakis and a blue polo shirt. "Mornin', darlin'."

"Hi," I managed. He looked tanner, probably from the North Carolina sun, and his hair seemed a bit brighter. But his grin was the same—all male confidence—as I slid into the car beside him. "You didn't need to pick me up."

He shrugged. "I figured we could get a head start on our meeting."

"Oh, that makes sense." All business as usual. Except the disappointment radiating through me wasn't professional at all. Of course he wanted to discuss the acquisition. That's why we were working together. I'd let my ego grow to unhealthy levels, because I could swear he wanted to sleep with me in the beginning, which sounded ridiculous now.

He'd been nothing but the perfect client for weeks, and even before that, he'd really only been politely flirtatious. The whole thing was wishful thinking on my part because of my innate attraction to him. I assumed our feelings were mutual, but given the foot of distance between us now, no way did he find me nearly as appealing as I found him. And wasn't that a kick in the gut?

Ignoring the ache in my chest, I focused on him and tried to figure out what he was talking about.

"Which is why I think we should leave Friday night instead, just to acclimate and be prepared. Thoughts?"

I squinted at him. "Uh, sure." *Leave Friday night for what?*

"Excellent. I'll ask Miranda to book it, and she'll send the itinerary to you."

"Great." *I can't wait to see it and find out where I'm going.*

Wow, I needed to pull it together, and fast. Both Janet and Jeff had mentioned how impressed they were with my work on this project, and it seemed five minutes in Will's presence was long enough to derail several weeks of hard work.

Awesome. Nothing like allowing a silly crush to ruin a career.

And I shouldn't even be attracted to him in the first place. So what if he had a perfect square jaw covered in attractive stubble, alluring dark irises dusted in long blond lashes, and a head of thick hair. Looks didn't mean everything. Neither did all that muscle he was packing beneath that fitted shirt, nor did the strong thighs and impressive package in those khaki pants. My gaze flew upward when I realized where it'd gone, and found Will grinning.

"You all right, Miss Dawson?"

I had to clear my throat twice to speak. It did nothing to hide the heat overwhelming my face. "I, uh, it was a long flight." Lamest. Excuse. Ever. And he knew it too.

"Was it, now?" The amusement in his voice only made me hotter. "If you thought ninety minutes was bad, wait until Friday."

My jaw loosened. "What?"

He laughed. "Darlin', you haven't heard a word I've said since gettin' in this car, have you?" He shook his head. "Well, to teach you a lesson, I'm going to make it a surprise. But don't worry; I'll make sure Janet is aware so you don't get in trouble. You do have your passport, right?"

"Wait, no, I mean, yes. I mean…" Oh my dear God, I'd never been so tongue-tied in my life. I pulled the passport from my purse to wave at him because that was easier than speaking. "But I want to know where we're going."

"Then you should have paid attention." His taunt, accompanied by those dimples, helped ground me a bit.

"I can refuse to get on the plane."

"You most certainly could, but how would you explain that to Baker Brown?"

"I…" Well, crap. He had me there. I opted for a new route. "A gentleman would tell me where we're going."

"And a lady wouldn't be caught checking out her client in the back seat of a town car, yet here we are, Miss Dawson."

"I wasn't…" Okay, yeah, no way around that. Any lie I could even consider would just get shot down. So I shrugged. "Fine. At least tell me what to pack."

"No need. We'll shop when we get there."

"Excuse me?"

"You would understand, had you been listening."

I shook my head. "My suits will have to do, then, and no way did I miss *that* much of the conversation."

His chuckle was a velvet caress over my skin. "Perhaps

not, but needling you is becoming one of my favorite pastimes. In addition to you checking me out, of course."

I rolled my eyes. "Well, I hope you enjoyed it, Mister Mershano, because it won't be happening again."

"Oh, we'll see about that, Miss Dawson. I give it an hour."

"Cocky." I shifted my focus to the rolling landscapes outside the window. Apparently, we'd left the city.

"Confident," he corrected.

"Uh-huh." Taller mountains appeared in the distance as we continued our drive, stealing all my attention. Born and raised in the Midwest with a minimal budget left my travel experience rather lacking. Ryan took me on a few trips while we dated, but those always involved a beach and me in a bikini.

I knew from my research that Will's headquarters was located north of Charlotte, closer to the Virginia border, but he owned vineyards throughout the southern states. "Why North Carolina?" I wondered out loud.

"What do you mean?" His voice warmed me in a way few voices could.

"What made you choose North Carolina for Mershano Vineyards?" I finally looked at him, and found his brow creased. "You own several other properties in South Carolina, Georgia, Alabama, and Louisiana, right?"

"I suppose that detail wouldn't be in the corporate files I sent over." He ran a hand through his hair. "Well, in short, my family is from here."

I frowned. "I thought the Mershano 'empire' was headquartered in New Orleans?" I used finger quotes around "empire" since it was a term coined by the media.

"Sure, but that's Evan's family dynasty, not mine. A lot of people like to say we're brothers since I essentially grew up with him, but we're cousins. I was born here, where I lived with my parents until the car crash." His gaze grew distant at the mention of what had to be a painful memory, and I reached for his hand on instinct.

"I'm so sorry," I said, feeling like an idiot. Of course I knew that about his parents. Not necessarily that they were from here, but that they'd died. Sarah had mentioned it once when she explained his familial relation to Evan. Most would assume them to be brothers due to their similar eyes and statures.

He twisted his hand, palm up, and wrapped his fingers around mine to give a gentle squeeze. "It was a long time ago," he murmured with a small smile as his thumb drew circles against my wrist. "But I always wanted to come back, and I did."

I opened my mouth to reply, when my phone buzzed a familiar ringtone. *Ryan.* Dropping Will's hand, I fiddled through my purse to silence the tone and then sent him a quick message.

With my client.

In North Carolina? he returned not fifteen seconds later.

I shivered. His text confirmed all my suspicions about him keeping tabs on me. The thought of it had always bothered me, but the reality was so much worse. Because now I *knew* he had the connections to monitor my travel.

This was why I couldn't move. Ryan would know. Just like he knew about my business trip, one that was planned two days ago. Which also meant he knew I didn't have a return ticket booked yet because we didn't know how long this next round of reviews would take.

"Are you all right?" Will asked. He couldn't see the screen but could surely see my expression.

I forced a smile. "Yeah, fine. Just—" The phone dinged again.

How is the weather in Charlotte? was his follow-up message.

It's hot. I'm with my client. Which he already knew. Not that he would care.

Don't forget our engagement photos this weekend.

I blinked at the message. He never mentioned anything about photos but did say something about an announcement.

I won't be home this weekend. I hit send before I could delete the words and held my breath. I couldn't believe I'd just done that. A version of no in a text. *I can't talk,* I quickly added before he could call or respond, and silenced my phone before shoving it back into my bag with more force than necessary.

Oh God... He was going to lose it. Would he find me in Charlotte? My hotel wasn't part of the itinerary, but I doubted he'd let a thing like that hold him back.

Fuck. My shoulders seemed to lock in place as the scenery passed by in a blur. What would he do the next time I saw him? Hit me? Choke me again?

And when he realized I had no intention of going through with his wedding, then what? Would he force me down the aisle?

I pinched the bridge of my nose and blew the air from my lungs, then jumped when a warm hand brushed up my arm to my tense shoulder.

"Rachel," Will murmured. "You know you can talk to me, right?"

"Oh, it's nothing." My voice shook with the lie, so I cleared my throat. "Everything's fine." Just my insane stalker ex knowing my every move. "How much longer is the drive?" Was Ryan tracking my phone? I had no doubt he already knew the name of my client, which made the location easy to find as well, but that didn't make it any less creepy.

"Another twenty minutes or so. You sure you don't want to talk about it?"

"Yep." That wasn't a lie in the slightest. I flipped to the first topic change that sprung to mind, which, of course, was work related. "So I've been wondering about why you want to expand internationally. Why Nice?"

His gaze searched my features for too long, then he sighed and dropped the hand that was still on my shoulder, leaving me feeling cold. "This vineyard grows a unique variety of grapes only found in that region."

"Which means it'll be different from your existing brand, right?"

"Very."

I tried to think like a businessman, to understand his vision. "Okay, so you're acquiring a new variety to add to your collection, right?"

"Yes, I'm expanding my collateral." He turned toward me as he continued. "As you've seen, the French vineyard has required the family name remain on their product. As they've already established a clientele, I have no problem adhering to that. Mershano Vineyards will essentially operate as a silent owner, which gives me more bargaining power with retail chains and restaurants. Instead of offering only Mershano brands, I'll be able to offer international brands with reputable backgrounds."

He settled into his seat and cast me an unreadable expression. "I also like the challenge of learning something new, and the Mediterranean region offers a different variety of grapes."

I nodded. "Makes sense. I'll admit that I was surprised you agreed to not tying your name to the product."

"It'll be there on the label in small print, but the original family name will be what consumers notice."

"It's smart. But the property in Greece you want to own." I phrased it not as a question but as a statement. He hadn't started negotiations with that one yet but planned to at a later date.

"Right, because it's run-down and not being cared for properly. My advisors are calling it a gamble because it's a major renovation that may prosper, or fail. But as I said, I like a good challenge." His gaze darkened on that last bit and dropped briefly to my lips before trailing back up to my eyes. "The harder the fight, the sweeter the reward."

I swallowed. I wasn't so sure we were talking about wine anymore. The car pulled off the highway, which momentarily distracted me and saved me from having to answer. But then we continued down a road that appeared to lead to nowhere.

"Is your office out here?" Because it seemed off the beaten path.

"My office, yes, but I think you mean my headquarters, which is not."

I looked at him. "I thought we were meeting the team."

"We are, but at my home. It's an easier location for my employees who work remotely. Our main office is in a building just north of Charlotte, but I only stop in there once a week at most. It's a location for our sales and marketing team to meet with prospective clients, but not much else. You'll find that the majority of us prefer to work near the product."

"So where am I staying this week?" I noticed my itinerary didn't include the hotel, but I assumed it was just missing from my documents.

"I have plenty of open rooms at my estate, if you're comfortable staying with me. Otherwise, there's a motel about five minutes from the primary vineyard."

"Is it typical for you to host an employee at your home?"

He chuckled. "Actually, yes. Several live on my property."

The way he said it had me frowning. "How big is this house?"

"Oh, darlin', let's talk after you meet the team."

10
PLAYING DOCTOR

Will's amusement made a hell of a lot more sense now that I stood in the center of his property. I spun around in a circle, awed by my surroundings. Vineyards sprawled to my left, going on for what looked like miles from my standpoint. Mountains decorated the landscape beyond it, giving the area a wilderness feel that was belied by the small community at my back.

"That's the original winery." Will pointed to the large building to our right. "We still use it for these vineyards, but most of what I produce out here is aged for long periods and kept within the family."

"So this was your original investment." I couldn't keep the shock out of my voice. Talk about impressive.

"Yep, but it didn't look like this when I bought it. See that tree about fifty yards out?" He waited for me to nod. "Everything beyond it was dead, and the winery had seen better days. They used to pick all the grapes with this old machine that has long since retired. I prefer to gather by hand, hence all the necessary employees for the various vineyards. It's more expensive, but the wine is better for it."

"Interesting." I was too fascinated to come up with a better word. This was nothing like I imagined. All the millionaires I knew dressed in fancy suits and lived in boardrooms, yet here was Will, standing in the middle of a field, explaining his world.

"Anyway, that home over there"—he pointed to a house with a long front porch directly across from the vineyard—"is the newest and houses the Greggory family. Sam Greggory manages this vineyard for me now, so it's helpful to have him live close by. The home on the other side of the winery over there is for employees during grape harvest season. Those can be some grueling shifts, so I like to keep everyone safe. Most of my estate staff reside in the lodging over there." He gestured to what reminded me of apartments down the road away from the winery.

"And the home way over there, up on that hill, is mine. That's where we're meeting everyone for dinner."

"I see." Millionaire. Right. Got it. "You own a lot of land."

His grin held a touch of boyishness. "I've expanded as needed."

"Uh-huh."

He glanced at my feet. "I would recommend we walk up the hill to my place, but you're not properly dressed for it."

"I walk Chicago in heels every day."

"Not the same, darlin'."

My eyes narrowed. "I can handle a hill." It didn't look that far away. Maybe three blocks, tops. Easy.

He folded his arms over his broad chest. "Care to make it interesting?"

"As in a bet?"

"More like a challenge with rewards."

The competitor in me stepped up to the plate and

cocked a brow at him. "Go on."

"A race. If I win, you stay at my house the entire week."

"Hardly fair considering you live here and are wearing"—I studied his shoes with a frown—"...not necessarily sneakers... But men's footwear still has a leg up on women's heels any day."

"I promise to walk the entire way, but you can run."

I scoffed at that. To assume I would have to run to beat him? "Yeah, because that's not arrogant at all."

"You were the one who stated male footwear trumps heels any day."

Okay, he had me there. "So I can run, if I want, but you have to walk. And if you beat me up there, I have to stay in your house all week. What do I get if I win?"

He spread out his hands. "Whatever you want."

I took in my surroundings and what appeared to be a gorgeous home up on that hill. Staying there would not be a hardship in the slightest. But... "What if I want to stay in your house while you sleep at the motel?"

His laugh was unexpected and charming. "Kicking the client out of his own home? Surely Janet wouldn't approve." His light tone said he wasn't offended, so I rolled with it.

"Well, she's not here, and this little wager is between you and me." I waggled my finger between us. "Unless you're afraid you might lose."

"Oh, darlin', I know I won't."

"Then game on."

"I'll even give you a head start. Just follow the road." He pointed to the long driveway ahead of me where Rudy had stopped the town car. The older man stood leaning against it with a smirk on his face. Seemed Will wasn't the only one who expected me to lose.

"You're going to regret underestimating me, Mister Mershano."

"Likewise, Miss Dawson." His cocky grin hit me square

in the lower abdomen. Confidence was definitely one of his sexier traits, not that I would ever admit it out loud.

"I hope you enjoy motel rooms!" I shouted as I started up the hill at a brisk pace. No way would I run up the hill in these two-inch heels. They would break in the gravel. But a quick walk? No problem. I spent most mornings at the gym, though I'd taken a bit of a hiatus thanks to this giant project. Still, it couldn't be that hard. I walked over a mile in heels every day to work, and back again.

My feet started to complain about a quarter of the way up, mostly because the point of my stiletto kept catching between rocks. Will's knowing chuckle slid up my spine as he followed, his steps silent on the gravel. I almost looked over my shoulder, but I caught myself. Knowing he was there, closing the distance with every step, pushed me harder.

The sensation of being stalked sent a chill down my spine, and my pulse kicked up a notch. It had nothing to do with exertion or the desire to win, but with the thrill of the chase. His game evolved in my head, causing me to lengthen my strides as I felt him nearing. I considered kicking off my shoes and running, but the gravel would destroy my stockings, and I was rather fond of them. And as athletic as I was, no way could I pull off running in these heels. I'd break my ankle.

"I'll admit"—his breath was warm against the back of my neck, eliciting a yelp of surprise—"you're doing far better than I anticipated, but we're only halfway there, and even with the five-minute lead I gave you, I'm about to pass you."

I turned around to smack him on the chest for scaring the shit out of me and caught my heel on a rock instead. His hands caught me before I could fall and yanked me back against his chest to steady me. My limbs shook so hard from the adrenaline coursing through my system that I couldn't move. *Caught*, my body seemed to say. *Submit*. I shivered as that word traversed my thoughts.

"Do you want another head start?" he whispered. "Or do you surrender?"

I trembled at the word *surrender*. Why did that sound so alluring on his lips? I'd given up control once and it hadn't ended well, yet something about this man made me want to consider trying again. "Giving me another head start would be cheating."

His hands seemed to tighten on my hips as he inhaled deeply, pressing his chest hard into my back. "I wouldn't mind catching you again." The words were hot against my ear. "Unless you forfeit, in which case I can call for the car."

I stared up at the house. *Halfway*, he'd said. Exhilaration swam through my blood, exciting every nerve. The idea of a chase floored me in a way I never could have anticipated. A fun reprieve from reality, maybe? In any case, the idea of pushing Will sounded like an excellent diversion. But it would mean ruining my stockings. Oh well. I had a suitcase full of them. What was one pair for a little fun?

"Forfeiting isn't in my nature," I told him as I kicked off my heels and took off at full speed up the hill. Rather than stick to the gravel path, I took to the grassy field and heard him shout something behind me. Maybe a curse or a word about his future stay at the motel. Grinning like a lunatic, I bounded up the hill, my sights on the house above, and felt triumph bubbling to the surface just as my foot nailed a sharp rock. It sent me flying forward into a grassy mound that softened the blow, but my left ankle throbbed. Will's face hovered over me a second later as he fell to his knees, his hands on my leg.

"Right. That backfired badly," I said through gritted teeth.

He said nothing as he examined my ankle, rotating it and making me wince in the process. "I don't think it's broken, but very likely sprained." His warm touch drifted up and down my lower leg before he met my gaze. "I tried to warn you about the rocks."

I tried to smile and failed. Instead, I ended up biting my lip and lying back in the grass as my pain receptors caught up with my ankle. The adrenaline coursing through my system had weakened the impact, but now that it'd worn off, a flood of sensation rushed through my limbs and brought tears to my eyes.

Will took one look at my face and sighed. "Yeah, bad idea on my part. I'm going to need to carry you."

I grabbed his wrist before he could wrap it beneath my shoulders. "Just help me up." I paused to take a deep, steadying breath because, fuck, my ankle hurt. Dizziness hit me next, causing me to forget what I'd been about to say. Will twisted easily from my grip and slipped his arms beneath me. I didn't get a chance to argue as he lifted me with ease and began the ascent up the hill. The lawyer in me who loved a good fight fled as I wrapped my arms around his neck and gave in to his strength.

"Ice and painkillers ought to do the trick," he murmured.

I nodded, eyes closed. Focusing on his spicy scent and sturdy hold kept me from thinking about my ankle. Of course, it awoke a myriad of other, more pleasurable sensations deep down. He felt every bit as hard as I imagined, his muscles flexing as he climbed the hill with the ease of a man who exercised daily. His introduction when we arrived confirmed my suspicions about his work habits. Will was a man who liked using his hands. Unlike most men in his position, he preferred to take on the tasks himself, even the laborious ones. Respect tightened my chest. Sure, his influential family helped him purchase this property debt-free, but he'd built it up with his own sweat and tears. *Impressive* didn't begin to cut it.

"I'll get that," Rudy said as he rushed past us. I opened my eyes to see we'd arrived at the main house. It seemed modest for a man of his wealth but was still larger than the average home. Definitely bigger than anything I could afford in Chicago or the nearby suburbs. Will carried me inside through the open two-story foyer, past what appeared to be an oversized living area, to a staircase that went up to a landing overlooking the gathering areas of the home. He walked up with ease and strolled down a hallway with five doors, giving me an idea of what he meant about having extra bedrooms to spare, to the end where Rudy stood waiting.

"Thanks," Will murmured as we passed him at the threshold. Bold, masculine colors assaulted my senses as we entered what had to be the master bedroom. Open doors leading to a balcony overlooking the back of the house greeted me on one side, while a massive bed and mahogany furniture greeted me on the other. More windows, including a skylight, told me Will was a fan of the sun. He laid me gently on a quilt meant for cuddling and left me gaping at his backside as he disappeared through a pair of French doors at the far corner of the room. He returned a minute later with a glass of water and a bottle of painkillers.

"Take three of these; they're anti-inflammatories. And drink this whole glass of water. I'll be back with ice."

I didn't argue, just did as he asked before making myself more comfortable on the bed. It wasn't easy with the throbbing ankle, but I managed to pull myself up to the pillows. When Will returned, he set the ice aside and looked over my legs.

"Your stockings are ruined," he murmured. "And I think that skirt might be too."

I hadn't even bothered to look, but a glance down made me grimace. Yeah, I looked like hell. "Good thing we're shopping for new clothes," I joked, earning a brief grin from him.

His fingers danced over my ankle. "We need to remove these so I can look at the cut on your foot and the scrapes on your knees."

"Cut?" I repeated. I'd been so consumed by my ankle, I hadn't noticed the stinging until he mentioned it. A glance down had me starting to roll off the bed, but a hand on my hip kept me in place. "I'm bleeding on your quilt."

"Like I care," he chastised. "No moving unless it's to help me get these stockings off."

"Yes, sir," I grumbled, sarcastic. "I'll have to unhook them from the garters." Yes, I had a fetish for lingerie. Not that anyone ever had the pleasure of enjoying it except me.

His eyes darkened as I lifted my skirt to fiddle with the stockings. I wasn't nearly as gentle as I should be, but they were going directly into the trash anyway. When I lifted to undo the back, pain shot up my leg, making me wince.

"Here," he pushed my hand away and deftly unfastened the fabric at the back of both thighs. I should have known he'd be skilled at that. He lifted my uninjured leg first and placed my foot against his solid abdomen before dipping his fingers into the lacy top. My breath caught as I met his gaze. The pain had dulled the intimacy of the act, but watching him slowly roll the stocking over my thigh, then my knee, and down my calf sent a jolt of desire right to my core. I fought the urge to clench my thighs, knowing he would feel it if I did.

When he started on my other leg, the desire to squirm overwhelmed me until the fabric slipped over my knee. I'd apparently gone down on this leg first because my other one was unmarred. I hissed out a breath as he continued exposing my leg and another scrape I hadn't realized was there. Pain and pleasure seemed to war inside of me, sending mixed signals to my brain. I didn't know whether to moan or to cry. He took particular care as he rolled the silk over my ankle and injured foot. When he didn't drop it right away, I risked a glance down and found him surveying the cut.

"I don't think you need stitches, but we definitely need to clean it up and put a bandage on it."

"Great." I fought a whimper as he set my foot down.

A knock at the doorway had Will lifting his head.

"Maeve is here," Rudy said. I started to shift, self-conscious at all the skin on display, but Will caught my hip again and flashed me a dark look that froze me in place.

"No moving," he reminded me, making me shiver. I knew he was dominant, but this was new. "Tell Maeve we're going to be a few minutes."

"Yes, sir." Rudy never walked into the room, much to my gratitude, but I still narrowed my gaze at Will.

"Excuse me for not wanting the world to see me like this."

He snorted. "Rudy is hardly the world."

"Still, it's my body, and I'll move if I want."

"Not in my bed, you won't."

My lips parted on a gasp. He had to be joking. But the look in his eyes said he wasn't. He held me for a second longer—to drive home his point—before heading back to the bathroom.

I blew out the breath I hadn't realized I'd been holding and shivered. It went against the grain to be turned on right now, but my nipples were as hard as rocks against my lacy bra, and my panties were more than soaked.

What the heck is wrong with me?

Powerful men had always fascinated me, hence my involvement with Ryan. He was the epitome of formidable, with all his political connections and domineering attitude, but he took it to unhealthy levels. And his version of control in the bedroom involved him getting off whenever he wanted and leaving me high and dry.

Something about the way Will looked at me just now said that was not his idea of dominance. And unlike Ryan's, Will's alpha tendencies were more subtle—charming, even.

Except for his comment about moving. Which I did now just to spite him. He caught me in the act of shuffling up the bed and cocked an eyebrow as he walked out of the bathroom.

I didn't bother stopping and returned his look with one

of my own. *What are you going to do about it?*

The smile he flashed at me said, *Oh, darlin', wouldn't you like to know?* But he didn't comment out loud as he sat on the bed beside me and started doctoring my foot.

"This is going to sting," he warned as he started cleaning the cut. I bit my lip to keep from squealing, then let it go with a pop when he bent to blow on my foot. When he did the same thing to the cut on my knee, I shivered. Okay, maybe this doctor thing wasn't so bad. And the feel of his rough hands on my bare skin? Yeah, I liked that too.

"All right, you need to elevate this for at least twenty minutes with ice. While you're doing that, I'll grab your suitcase from the car so you can change." His lips quirked up. "Just because you decided to cheat and run through a rock-infested field does not mean you get to skip this afternoon's meet and greet with my team. Nice try, though, Miss Dawson."

My eyes narrowed. "Are you accusing me of slacking off?"

He reached over me to grab two pillows and paused with his face a few inches from mine. "No, I'm accusing you of cheating. Which, by the way, means I won, and we'll be sharing this house for the week." He waggled his brows. "I think we've gotten off to a fabulous start, don't you?"

Will arranged my foot on the pillows, then draped a towel, which I hadn't realized was there, over my ankle before pressing the ice pack to the most tender area.

My resulting wince killed whatever retort I had lined up on my tongue. I couldn't even remember what we'd been bickering about. How stupid had I been to run through that damn field? All for what? To win a silly game? Or was it darker than that? I'd enjoyed him chasing me. Deep down, I'd hoped he would catch me. Part of that fantasy came true, since I'd landed in his bed, but not nearly in the way I desired.

He leaned over to tug at the edges of the quilt from the opposite side of the bed and yanked it closer. "In case you get cold," he explained as he left the corner beside me. His hand went to my hip. "Now, I mean it, Rachel. No moving." That dark look was back, sending a shiver across my skin.

Why is that so sexy?

Because you've lost your marbles.

"You realize orders don't work on me." I couldn't help throwing that out there. He had to know this about me by now, and if he didn't, then we had another conversation coming.

He grinned and dropped his lips to my ear. "Oh, I do, darlin'. But I also know you enjoy them." His teeth scraped over my neck in such a brief caress that I wondered if I'd imagined it. And then he was gone.

11

A FRESH DYNAMIC

Will's doctoring helped with the swelling, but my ankle hurt like hell during the meet and greet in his oversized living room. I forced myself to ignore the pain as I shook hands with all his senior staff members and matched names with faces.

My feet were bare, something no one seemed to notice since they'd all discarded their shoes at the door, but I felt naked wandering around without my usual stockings. I caught Will looking at my exposed legs more than once. Each time, he flashed me a grin that sent heat rushing to all manner of inappropriate regions. It left me questioning his attraction all over again, especially when he maintained a purely professional demeanor. The way he handled the meeting and deferred to me for the legal updates were with the utmost respect. Never once did he make a suggestive comment or look.

And then there was that nibble. Every time he smiled, whether seductively or amusedly, it reminded me of his teeth against my neck and elicited a shiver. Like now as he chuckled at something David said. The financial analyst seemed to be the joker of the group. He had a light air about him that kept everyone laughing.

Will shook his head. "You're trouble, man."

"So my wife tells me," the redhead replied. "Speaking of which, she'll kill me if I come home late tonight after pulling all those hours last week."

"Can't have that," Will replied, still grinning. "I think we've all done enough for today. Next week is shaping up to be a success, and it's thanks to all the hard work in this room and also to Rachel's team at Baker Brown."

There was a round of cheers and excited claps, then each member of Will's team came up to shake his hand before leaving. Maeve, a slender woman with auburn hair, was the last to leave. Her lips curled into an adoring grin as she placed a kiss on Will's cheek. The woman's sharp suit fit her like a glove, leaving little to the imagination with all her curves and long legs.

"We need to review the Francis presentation," she murmured.

"Send it to me and I'll take a look."

She glanced at me with a curious look, then back at him. "Or we can review it now."

Will grinned. "Maeve, go home. You've worked far too hard already."

"You know I don't mind."

"Pretty sure Robbie does, though."

She sighed. "Yeah. Doesn't matter how many times Mia explains our friendship, Robbie still worries." Her kind brown eyes met mine and crinkled at the edges. "Have you met Mia yet?"

The name didn't ring a bell. "I don't think so."

"My cousin," Will explained. "Evan's little sister."

"Oh, the doctor?" Sarah briefly mentioned her to me. "She's moving home soon, right?"

"December," Maeve replied, her excitement palpable.

"She's Mia's best friend and practically grew up at the Mershano family home."

"Hence the reason Will hired me."

Will cast her a fond look that was more brotherly than romantic. The competitor inside me relaxed at that expression, while the sane part of me cringed.

Getting protective over a man who isn't even remotely yours. Smooth, Rach.

"We both know that's not why I hired you, darlin'. Your resume more than qualified you. Now seriously, get out of here before Robbie calls me to complain again."

"Yeah, yeah. I can handle him." She winked at me like I understood the dynamic between them all, then grabbed her bag. "I'll send you the presentation when I get home."

"Thank you, Maeve."

"Nice to meet you, Rachel. I look forward to working with you more in the future."

"Uh, me too," I answered slowly, narrowing my eyes at Will. "What have you been telling people?" I asked after Maeve disappeared into the foyer.

"That you're an amazing attorney whom I wanted to hire," he answered with a shrug. "But you already know that."

My brow crinkled in confusion. "We've been working together for weeks."

"Sure, through your firm. That doesn't dismiss the fact that I still wanted to hire *you*." The intensity in his gaze matched the one I'd seen upstairs in his bedroom. My thighs squeezed at the memory, forcing me to take a step back to relieve the ache building there. Pain replaced desire as I stepped too hard on my injured foot. I'd spent most of the afternoon unconsciously balancing on one leg, and my other was quick to remind me why. Will's hand snagged my hip, keeping me upright when I would have staggered back.

"I think it's time for more elevation and ice," he murmured as he guided me over to the couch. "I did recommend you stay seated for the meeting, and not stand up."

I snorted. More like he ordered me to remain in my chair, which was why I ignored him. "I like to be on equal footing with clients," I muttered as I fell into the plush cushions. They felt like clouds, which was the only reason I didn't argue as he nudged me onto my back. Those clever fingers drifted down my leg as he snagged a pillow with his opposite hand.

"Yes, I've learned that about you." He gently lifted my ankle and propped it up on a pile of fluff. "Your assertiveness is sexy, if a little dangerous."

"Dangerous?" I repeated, incredulous. "Why, because it intimidates you?"

"No, darlin'. Because it excites me." The grin that accompanied those words had me swallowing my tongue.

Wolfish didn't even begin to describe *that* look. It was the kind of expression a woman wanted to see in the bedroom. The type filled with promise and confidence, and screaming, *I know what you need.* It scattered goose bumps down my arms and caused delicious sensations to coil tightly in my lower abdomen. It usually took a man several minutes of foreplay to entice that sort of reaction, but Will managed it with a wicked curl of his lips.

He let the moment simmer, heightening my arousal with each brush of his thumb against the hem of my skirt. My fingers twitched with the need to reciprocate, to touch him, to do *something* other than curl tightly at my sides. But I couldn't move, captivated by that look, entirely at his mercy. I'd never felt so completely floored in my entire life, but I luxuriated in it. Ryan's control left me quivering in terror, while Will's subtle dominance thrilled me. It was utterly fucked up, yet I had no desire to fight it.

"No more standing," he murmured as he stepped away.

I glowered after his perfect ass, irritated that he broke the intimacy between us. "Or what?"

His response was a low chuckle that stoked the flames

higher inside. How did he do that? It was both enthralling and infuriating. I considered standing again just to piss him off, but my ankle protested the idea. He returned a few minutes later with another towel and a bag of ice, as well as a glass of water. "Too soon for another anti-inflammatory, but hydration helps. You finish this and rest while I go figure out dinner."

"You're going to cook?" I hadn't meant for it to sound so dubious, but from my limited experience, most men did not know their way around the kitchen. Ryan considered it a place for his staff, or the occasional woman, like me.

"Any vegetables you're particularly averse to?" he asked, ignoring my question.

"Brussels sprouts." I detested them.

"Noted," was all he said as he disappeared down the hall. I hadn't been to the back of the house yet, but I imagined it contained a large kitchen and dining area and maybe another entertainment-style room. This one lacked a television but did contain a few bookshelves and a myriad of seating. It had housed his team of twelve comfortably while we all introduced ourselves and reviewed various documents. Considering everyone's comfort, it seemed obvious they met here often.

Savory notes tickled my nose after what felt like a lifetime of staring at the ceiling. I considered asking for my phone, but I didn't want to see how many missed calls I had from Ryan. He likely wanted an update on my business trip, which was not his concern. Those words were on the tip of my tongue every time we spoke, but I could never force them out. Yet I had the sudden desire to send him a message stating just that. Maybe it was the security of being in Will's home that left me feeling so bold. Ryan couldn't touch me here, but he could the minute I left. That latter thought was what kept me from following through on the notion. He'd be waiting for me, and then all hell would break loose.

The last time I tried to stand up to him had not ended

well. My sprained ankle had nothing on that experience. I rubbed my healed ribs as the memory assaulted me.

No. Never again.

Shoving it away, I pushed off the couch and grabbed the ice pack. The scents wafting in from the hallway were far more appealing than the recesses of my mind. I hobbled toward what I assumed to be the kitchen and found myself staring at a wall of windows overlooking the wooden deck outside. Mountains littered with trees sprawled beyond it, causing me to pause. I was a city girl at heart, but I couldn't deny the tranquility in this view.

"Wow," I breathed.

A chuckle had me glancing left to find Will leaning against a marble counter, arms crossed. He glanced at his watch and tsked. "Fourteen minutes of rest is not going to help your ankle."

"That was only fourteen minutes?" Shit. It felt like closer to an hour. I did not do idle well.

"Thirteen and some change, to be precise." He pushed away from the mahogany cabinets and crooked a finger at me. "You can sit at the table while I finish dinner."

"I'd rather sit outside," I admitted, surprising myself. Bugs and nature were not my thing, but the lounge chair on his deck appealed to me, as did the small pool beyond it. I didn't wait for him to agree, just ambled over to a set of glass doors and slipped outside with the ice still in my hand.

"Oh yeah," I murmured as I folded myself into the cushioned chaise outside. I placed the ice on my ankle and sighed in contentment, only to jolt upright when warm fingers wrapped around my calf. "What are… ?" He lifted it with ease and settled a pillow he'd procured from God knew where beneath my heel. The reproach in his gaze did not go unnoticed, but he said nothing as he returned to the house.

Our dynamic seemed to be shifting to a new phase that combined flirtation, professionalism, and something *other*.

He wasn't admitting his attraction, but he wasn't necessarily hiding it either. Instead, he left it out there like an open door inviting me to enter at my own risk. I sensed myself faltering just outside, lingering and waiting for the inevitable desire to run in the opposite direction, but it never came. On the contrary, the only pull I felt was the one drawing me closer, enticing me to take a chance and see what Will had to offer. Which was ludicrous because I knew what to expect—fantastic sex, followed by awkwardness as we continued to work together on the merger.

Or maybe the sexual affair could last for the duration of the project...

My hormones piqued at the thought. Pleasure without remorse, and since it would happen away from Chicago, Ryan would never know.

"Do you want to eat out there?" Will called from inside the house. He'd left the door open, something I noticed was also the case upstairs on the balcony. The air in the mountains was cooler than I expected for North Carolina but was still warm enough to warrant the abundance of fans decorating each room of his home. There were also a few built into the ceiling covering his deck, including the one directly over my head.

"I definitely want to stay outside," I replied. Eyeing the glistening water a few yards away made me regret not packing a swimsuit. Stones decorated the edges, giving it a lagoon-style appeal that seemed to invite sunbathing. I would float in the center with a book and a margarita and wish to never leave.

"Bon appétit," Will murmured as he sauntered outside with a tray.

I eyed the offerings with trepidation, but I needn't have worried. "Stir-fry. Nice." I accepted the food with a grin. "Thank you." He even gave me chopsticks and paired it with a glass of wine. This was much better than a motel down the street.

He joined me a minute later with his own tray and kicked back in the opposite chaise under his own fan. We ate in companionable silence, my foot resting on the pillow and my stomach rolling in contentment.

"You know, I think this is the first Mershano white I've tried." I savored the fruity notes on my tongue and licked my lips. "Which one is this?"

"It's a Pinot Grigio with apple notes from one of the South Carolina vineyards."

He deftly plucked a piece of chicken from his plate and popped it into his mouth—such a subtle thing that he somehow managed to sexualize. Or maybe that was just my hormones talking.

I focused on my plate and enjoyed the sautéed zucchini. "So you can cook," I finally conceded after several more delicious bites. "Like, you can *really* cook." Because this meal was restaurant quality, maybe even better.

"I considered opening a wine bar and restaurant about a decade ago but decided preparing food for customers wasn't really my passion. I much prefer dividing my time between the vineyards and business tasks. But I still enjoy cooking for myself."

At first, I thought he was joking. But nothing about his expression or tone suggested humor, just fact. "Well, my stomach thanks you for the experience."

He raised his glass in a mock salute. "Cheers."

I lifted mine in response and took another savory sip. "I'm almost glad I lost earlier, Mershano. Not so much about the ankle, but I could get used to living like this for a week."

An emotion teased the edge of his lips, but it disappeared too quickly for me to catch. He stood a few minutes later and glanced at my tray. "Done?"

"Yeah, but I can—"

"Your only job right now is to rest that ankle," he stated, effectively cutting my offer to help clean the dishes.

"Bossy," I accused with a roll of my eyes.

"You have no idea." Wickedness touched his gaze as he tugged the tray away from me. "I'd tell you to stay put, but we both know how you'll respond to that."

I grinned. "You're learning."

"Oh, we're just gettin' started, darlin'," he drawled. "I'll be back in a minute to take you to bed."

12

A TASTE OF LUXURY

Will's words after dinner last night left me hot and bothered for hours, just as he likely intended. His version of taking me to bed meant showing me to my room, which happened to be right next to his suite.

"I noticed you admiring the balcony in my room earlier, so I thought you might like this room. It shares the same space outside, just through those doors over there." He'd pointed them out last night, and I'd stupidly slept with them open thinking he meant to come through them later. Nope. Didn't happen.

I scowled at the curtains blowing with the morning air. It soothed my overheated cheeks but did nothing to calm my racing pulse. Visions of Will sneaking into my room for a midnight rendezvous kept me tossing and turning until the early hours, and when sleep finally visited me, it was in the form of dreams that left me panting. The cold shower I took thirty minutes ago did nothing. My pencil skirt felt oddly suffocating, as did my blue blouse. I wore these clothes every day, yet all I wanted was to rip the offending fabric from my body.

With an irritated huff, I stepped out onto the balcony, hoping the cool air would help soothe my aroused skin. Closing my eyes, I leaned against the railing and inhaled the crisp morning scent. Sweet and clean, with a hint of spice. The latter I associated with my sensual torturer. I glanced toward his open doors and gasped.

Oh, of all things holy…

Will sat lounging on a chaise, reading the newspaper, in nothing but a pair of black boxer briefs. Ripples of tanned muscles assaulted my senses, leaving me momentarily brain-dead. Even though he was sitting down I could tell he had those little indentations right by the hip bone, and, oh, those thighs were mouthwateringly delicious. All strength and steel and happily on display for my viewing pleasure.

"Enjoying the view?" he asked, drawing my attention to his full lips. They curled into one of those seductive grins that were becoming impossible to ignore. My tongue thickened in my mouth, rendering speech impossible. All I could do was nod. Let him make of that what he wanted. He obviously knew I found him attractive. No point in denying it.

When he stood and stretched his long arms over his head, my head spun. Oh yeah, definitely had the full package. Those boxer briefs left nothing to the imagination. It took more effort than I thought possible to drag my eyes up to meet his as he strolled over to me on the balcony.

"Did you sleep well?" he asked, voice low and intimate.

My lips parted, but my vocal chords weren't ready, so I closed my mouth. I had no idea where my dignity went, but surely it would return as soon as he put on some clothes. Maybe. He dragged his fingers through his artfully messy hair and flashed one dimple at me in the process. Those muscles flexed with each move, highlighting his power and well-earned confidence.

"So this is you speechless?" he mused. "Mmm, I think I prefer the feisty Rachel more, but at least I know for future reference." He took a step into my personal space, allowing the heat of his body to roll over my already too-hot skin. "For the record, I didn't sleep well at all. Want to know why?"

I found myself nodding without thinking.

He lifted his hand to tuck one of my blonde strands behind my ear and lightly brushed the back of his knuckles down my neck to my collarbone, then back up. "It took considerable effort to stay in my room last night, more so than usual." His palm slid to the back of my neck. "And seein' you look at me like that right now, darlin', won't make tonight any easier."

I shuddered as he brushed his lips against mine in the lightest of caresses. It wasn't nearly hard enough, or long enough, and did not at all live up to my expectations of how he would kiss me the first time.

"You let me know when you want more," he whispered, his nose briefly touching mine as he started to pull away. I grabbed his wrist, and he cocked a brow. "Yes?"

Words were still an issue, so I responded by closing the small gap between us and looping my arms around his neck. He didn't hesitate. His mouth claimed mine in a kiss so carnal that I felt it down to my toes.

This was what I anticipated. All dominance, strength, and passion packed into a powerful meeting of tongues as he vied for control of my mouth. I moaned in response, unable to hold back the need brewing deep inside, and rubbed against him in the most inappropriate of ways.

His arm slipped around my back to hold me there as his thick arousal hardened against my lower belly. A tear leaked from the corner of my eye at the feel of it. I'd never wanted something, *someone*, so bad in my entire life. If his goal had been to undo all my hard-earned self-restraint, he'd done it, because I came apart in his arms. Whatever he wanted, I would do, so long as it meant a night in his bed.

He nipped my lower lip, eliciting a yelp from me, before plundering his tongue so deep that I forgot how to breathe. My knees threatened to buckle, which he must have sensed because his arm tightened around me as his opposite hand knotted in my hair and tilted my head to the angle he preferred. I held on to his shoulders, my fingers digging into the thick muscle there, as he took what he wanted.

My hips hit the balcony as his groin fought for purpose against my lower belly, or maybe that was me trying to find friction. The juncture between my legs throbbed with a need far more painful than my ankle last night, but my skirt kept me immobile. No matter what I did, I couldn't get the right angle, and his chuckle told me he knew it, yet he did nothing to help me. When I went to fix the issue, I found both my wrists captured in one hand. He nipped my bottom lip, then traced it with his tongue.

"You're not ready yet, darlin'," he murmured.

I opened my mouth to protest that theory and was silenced by another deep kiss. By the time he pulled back, I couldn't remember my own name.

"Mmm, I do love that look on you, Rachel." He nuzzled my neck and licked a path up to my ear. "But you're not coming to my bed until you agree to stay there. For good." His teeth scraped over my jaw as he nibbled his way to my mouth for one final mind-destroying kiss. "I'm going to take a long, very hot shower," he murmured. "I'll meet you downstairs in an hour to go over the Francis proposal."

I grabbed the balcony to steady myself as he walked away without a care in the world. If I thought his ass looked fine in slacks, it looked sexier now in those very tight boxer briefs. *Fuck*. What the *fuck* was that? He kissed me like his life depended on it, just to saunter off with what I knew was one hell of a hard-on. Which he clearly planned to take care of in the shower. Alone. Or was that some screwed-up form of an invitation.

You're not coming to my bed until you agree to stay there. Replaying his words in my head sent a shiver down my spine. *For good.* As in forever? He couldn't possibly mean that. A man of his wealth and stature was destined for a life of bachelorhood, right? But despite the occasional flirtation, I'd yet to see any indication that he enjoyed playing the field.

I'd shamelessly researched him right along with his company and didn't see any reports of his dating life, casual or otherwise, from the last few months. The most recent article I found was from a fundraiser last year where he brought a model. All the events from this year recorded him as a single attendee. I had tried not to think too hard about those dating-life clues, but coupled with his words, it was hard not to speculate.

I touched my swollen lips. Did he want more from me than just a few nights of pleasure? It seemed impossible, but he had gone to great lengths to secure me for this project. An elaborate ruse to date me, or because he respected my professional skills? Or both?

My clammy hands tightened on the railing. Short term I could give him, but long term would never happen. I might be able to hide from Ryan for a few weeks, months even, but beyond that? No. He'd come after me, and Will would suffer. My insane ex always found ways to take down the men in my life. He taught me that lesson early on, which was why I avoided dating.

I couldn't let Ryan anywhere near Will. There was no telling what he would do, especially since Will presented a more significant threat than any of the previous men in my life. Because I actually liked him. A lot. Too much.

I brushed my sweaty palms against my skirt and squared my shoulders. Time to get my shit together, and I would start by throwing myself into work. That's what I did best, and it would be to the benefit of this project. At least I could please Will in one way. Being a good lawyer would just have to be enough.

13
PRUNING

No awkwardness.

No reaction.

No comments.

Nothing.

That summed up the last two days. It was business as usual between us, with the occasional heated glance and demand for me to elevate my foot. Oh, and freshly prepared dinners both nights. I tugged on the curtain beside my balcony door and frowned when I found it empty. Aside from the first morning here, he hadn't greeted me outside. Always downstairs, fully dressed, with a cup of coffee. It seemed today would be the same.

It pissed me off despite it being for the best. But I wanted to know I affected him at least a little. He had me questioning his intentions all over again. Had I misunderstood his bed requirement? The one where he said I could only join him there when he knew I wouldn't leave?

My head spun with possibilities that threatened to derail my composure as I walked down the stairs. The pain in my ankle had subsided substantially, telling me it wasn't so much sprained as bruised.

"Mornin'." Will greeted me with a cup of coffee fixed just the way I liked it and a plate loaded with eggs.

"This is new," I remarked as I took one of the stools at the breakfast bar.

"You're going to need more than a banana today," he replied, referring to my preferred breakfast. "And you're going to need to change."

I eyed his jeans and fitted gray T-shirt. "Why?"

"We're going on an adventure."

"Uh, elaborate please."

He grinned that charming grin of his. "Not a chance, darlin'. You'll need jeans, boots, and a tank top or T-shirt."

"I didn't pack anything like that."

He hummed something under his breath as he left the kitchen. I stared after him unashamedly. His ass was created for those jeans, as were his thighs. And that fitted shirt showcased all those back muscles nicely.

"I approve of casual day," I murmured to myself before scooping some eggs into my mouth. "Oh," I moaned. "Okay." Will could change my mind about breakfast with food like this. "Did you add cheese or something?" I called to him after swallowing.

"Vermont white cheddar," he replied as he strolled back into the kitchen with a shopping bag. "And bacon grease."

"Healthy," I joked around another bite.

"Delicious," he corrected. "Now, I had a feeling you didn't bring the right clothes, so I ordered some for you. Boots, size nine." He set a box on the marble counter beside my plate. "Jeans, size six, and a medium tank top. Did I get all that right?"

I gaped at him. "It's a little scary how you do that." And sexy as hell.

"Let's just say I have a vivid imagination, Miss Dawson." He folded his arms on the counter to lean in close. "And your clothes fascinate me more than they probably should."

My mouth went dry at the insinuation in his tone and the heated look he gave my lips. But just when I hoped he'd kiss me again, he pushed back and wrapped that damn professional blanket around us again. "We leave in twenty minutes, so I suggest you finish that and change. I'll meet you outside." He picked up a cowboy hat I hadn't noticed on the counter and plopped it on his head. "Ma'am," he said, tipping the rim at me.

Oh, not fair. Wealthy businessman I could handle, even dressed-down millionaire, but sexy cowboy? A midwestern girl had her limits. And coupled with that Southern drawl?

"Yeah, I'm in so much trouble," I whispered.

* * *

The clothes fit perfectly. Not that I was surprised. Will gave me a once-over and stared at my injured foot. "How does your ankle feel?"

"Secure, actually. The boots are a lot better than my heels."

He nodded. "Good, that was my hope." He pulled open the door of an oversized pickup truck. "Hop on in, darlin'."

"Okay, now I'm officially in the South." I accepted his hand to help me up into the passenger seat. "Let me guess," I continued when he climbed in beside me. "Country music is next?"

He waggled his brows. "Worried I might covert the city girl in you?"

"Not a chance," I replied as I pulled on my seat belt.

"So confident," he murmured. The engine roared to life, and with it came the soft sound of a strumming guitar accompanied by a deep male voice. Definitely a country drawl, but not the folksy tune I expected. It was rather pleasant. Not that I would ever admit that out loud.

Will fastened his belt as well and put the car in drive. "There's a cooler of bottled water in the back in case you need something to drink. You'll thank me later."

"I take it we're not going to the office to review the final proposal."

"Nope, we'll do that on the plane tomorrow, or Saturday."

"In France," I added. Because I'd figured out that's where we were headed first.

He grinned. "Glad to know you learned how to focus, darlin'."

Oh, I didn't know about that. The way his forearms flexed as he handled the car was one hell of a distraction, as were those illegal jeans. But it was his voice that fried my brain. He started by humming along to the music, which I enjoyed more than I cared to admit, and then he started to sing. Not loudly, but softly, and in perfect pitch. My lips parted and refused to close, and no amount of admiring the scenery around us could distract me from the deep tenor of his voice.

I'd developed these expectations in my mind about him, and Will continued to break them at every turn. His last name and wealth influenced my initial assessment, something one might refer to as stereotyping, but in my experience, the men in influential circles tended to act the same. Except for Will. Dressed down in his T-shirt, jeans, cowboy boots, and hat, he resembled an ordinary man. And this truck wasn't anything expensive or flashy, just a convenient vehicle created to master the bumpy road we were now driving down. Fields crowded us on both sides, but a ranch-style home stood at the end of the gravel road.

A man dressed in overalls and a floppy hat walked out onto the porch and waved as Will parked beside another truck. "That's Joe. He maintains this vineyard," he explained before hopping out and meeting me by my door.

His hand was warm in mine as he helped me step down onto the uneven driveway. My ankle didn't protest when I put my weight on it, which I took as a good sign.

"Howdy, Mershano," the older man welcomed as he rounded the truck bed.

"Hi, Joe," Will replied. "This is Rachel."

"Ah, lawyer lady, yep." He held out his hand, and I shook it.

"I prefer Rachel over lawyer lady, please," I told him with a smile.

"Ya prove to be as helpful as Mershano says ya are, and I'll call ya whatever ya want," was his reply.

"Careful, Joe. She'll take you up on that."

I didn't correct him because he was right. "So what are we doing?"

"Prunin' and hedgin'," Joe replied before fixing hazel eyes on Will. "You gonna help me with some of the nets while she does that?"

"Yep, but I need to show her how to prune first."

Joe nodded. "Good luck with that. Those purdy hands tell me she's not gonna be too great at it."

I put my "purdy hands" on my hips. "Hey now, don't judge a book by its cover."

Will draped his arm over my shoulders and gave me a half hug. "I'm not worried, darlin'." He let me go to retrieve some gloves and two pairs of scissor-like gardening tools from the truck bed. "Pruner," he explained, catching my scrutiny. He attached them to his belt via some crafty method I didn't catch, then tucked the gloves behind his back. "You'll see."

"You're the boss," I told him, knowing it would make him grin. It did.

"Still waitin' for you to call me 'sir.'"

"You'll be waiting a long time."

His eyes danced over me in a lazy fashion. "Hmm, no, I don't think I'll need to wait too much longer." He opened the passenger door again. "Almost forgot your hat, darlin'." The item in his hand when he turned around was not part of the earlier bag of clothes and not something I noticed on the back seat.

"You can't be serious."

"About you? Very." Much to my chagrin, he plopped it on my head. "Trust me, gorgeous. Your face will thank me later."

Uh, what? He used *darlin'* so often that *gorgeous* shocked me into silence. I'd never heard that word or term of endearment from him.

He wrapped his arm around my shoulders again. "I'll meet up with you in thirty, Joe."

"You know where I'll be," he replied.

"Okay, so what am I doing, and why am I doing it?" I asked as Will guided me around the house toward the vineyard behind it. Several heads popped up as we approached.

Will cupped his free hand over his mouth to holler a "Howdy, y'all!" Several variations of the greeting floated back to us, making my companion chuckle.

"To answer your question, we're here to help Joe pamper the vineyard. He's having some issues with birds, so we have to put up some nets to keep them away from the berries. But you're going to help prune some of the vines. As to the why, hard work is good for everyone. Besides, being part of the environment will help give you a better understanding of why I do what I do, which will be important as we go into these negotiations."

I frowned at that. "You don't think I respect what you've built." Not a question, but a statement. Because why else would he feel the need to show me all this?

He shrugged. "I think you're under the impression this was all handed to me because of my family name, and I believe in showing rather than telling."

"Right, but you already showed me the original vineyard and explained how you turned it around." What more was there to understand? I already harbored respect for him and his accomplishments.

"Correct, and now you'll get an appreciation of what that actually meant." He guided me down an empty row and stopped at a random place in the middle. "Keep in mind that this is a healthy vineyard you're about to prune, not a ruined one, *and* you have over a dozen people helping. I had two."

"Okay, but for the record, I do respect what you've built."

He grinned. "Maybe so, but you'll have even more respect by the end of the day. And as I said, you'll have a better understanding for our meetings next week. Trust me, the families who own those vineyards will appreciate your knowledge and experience, even if brief."

Ah, okay, now I understood the purpose of this activity. "They're afraid of a corporate buyout," I translated. And he wanted to assure them that wasn't what he intended. "Got it."

"Yes, but it's more than that." All teasing left his features as he dropped his arm to his side. "I love what I do, Rachel. I care about this industry, and they know it. That's why they're agreeing to work with me. They need to know I surrounded myself with employees who care just as much, if not more."

I brushed my knuckles over his cheek without thinking. Before I realized what I'd done or why that'd been my instinctual reaction to his words, he caught my wrist and brought my palm to his lips. He gave it a nibble, evoking a shudder from deep within.

This man is going to break down every protective barrier I've ever created…

"You look awful cute dressed as a cowgirl," he murmured. "It's giving me all sorts of new scenarios to consider later."

Heat climbed up my neck. I had no idea how to reply to that, so I focused on his earlier comment about the negotiations. It was a safer topic, more professional, because, yeah, that's how I was feeling at the moment.

"I might not share your knowledge, but I understand passion. Show me how to use those scissor things so I can impress the people in your world."

He grinned against my palm. "Pruners."

"Sure."

He clucked his tongue. "Oh, darlin', you have so much to learn."

"Then you better start teaching me."

"Already am," he murmured with another tender bite. "You just don't realize it yet." He tugged a glove from his belt and slipped it over my hand, then repeated the action with my other, minus the nip. When he was satisfied with the fit, he put on his own pair and handed me a pruner. It was much heavier than a pair of scissors. When I said that out loud, he laughed.

"They're sharper too," he said. "All right, so I chose this spot because it looks like someone pruned up until this point. So you can start here and work your way back toward the entrance. If you finish before lunch, then you can start on the other side of the row and work back to this point. Good?"

"Yep. Question, though. How can you tell the others pruned until this point?"

"Shading. See how thinned out this vine is compared to the one next to it?"

I studied it with a frown. "Not really, no. I mean, they look almost the same."

"That's because Joe has done a good job maintaining the vineyard, but you can see where this one was freshly pruned here to maximize shading over the grapes here. And it looks like two clusters sprouted off this shoot, so someone trimmed the excess." He gestured to something light-colored on the ground.

"And you noticed that just by walking down the vineyard?"

He chuckled. "Experience, darlin'."

"I'm nowhere near that good."

"We'll get you there. How about I demonstrate on this first one, and then you can try the next one while I watch?" He grabbed what he referred to as a shoot. "See how there are two clusters? We only want one, and it's best to trim the excess in the summer to help the grapes grow. So I'll trim the smaller one, which will allow the bigger one to grow."

"And when they're fully ripe, you pick them all by hand?" He mentioned the other day that he didn't use machines to pick grapes during the harvest.

"Yup."

"Wow."

"Now you're getting it," he replied as he snipped the smaller cluster. "All right, shading…" He continued his spiel by going into a diatribe about the sun and where it hit the vines in this row. By the end, I had enough understanding to repeat his actions on the next set and only managed to make one mistake.

"It's the smaller cluster, but it'll be fine," he murmured. "You'll get it. Next time we'll master rounding, but this will work for now."

"What's rounding?"

"It's where you snip the bottom of the grape cluster to make them round. It improves the size of the fruit."

That sounded complicated. "Uh, if you say so."

He grinned. "I do. All right, I think you've got this. I need to help Joe with the netting, but I'll be back to check on you in an hour or so. Okay?"

I focused on an overgrown leaf and clipped the stem. "Yep."

"One more thing." His bare palm slipped to the back of my neck before I realized what was happening, and his lips captured mine. I stood frozen with my gloved hands out to the side, worried I might stick him with the pruner. He tilted my head to the angle he preferred and gently slipped his tongue into my mouth. This wasn't like the hungry mating of mouths on his balcony, but that didn't make it any less potent. Because this man knew how to deliver a kiss. It left me shaking as he pulled back to stare down into my eyes. "Did I mention how much I like this outfit?" he whispered.

I swallowed. "Maybe once or twice."

"Thank you for helping today."

"If this is my payment, then consider me willing to help anytime." The words were out before I could catch them. Oh well. That didn't make them any less true.

He smiled against my lips. "Duly noted." His mouth took mine again in a brief kiss before he pulled back. The palm on my neck slipped down to my ass, where he landed a resounding slap. "Now back to work, darlin'."

I gasped at his retreating form. "You did not just smack my ass!" I called after him. Except he did. I could feel the burn through the fabric of my jeans.

He turned to walk backwards through the vineyards, his lips curling. "I did, and I'll do it again."

"Try it, and it won't be this vine I'm pruning, Mershano." I waved the weapon menacingly, but all he did was laugh.

"Feisty," he returned.

"Cocky," I threw back. "Ass," I added as I massaged my rear end. It both stung and tingled. I'd have to return the favor later and see how he liked it.

14

SOOTHING, SEXY & SEDUCTIVE

Will was right. Nine hours of working in the vineyard gave me a new insight into his business. It also left me sweaty and exhausted.

The early evening sun winked at me as I finished my row. Bradley, one of my fellow pruners, met me with a grin and a bottle of water. I suspected Will had given the guy orders to keep me hydrated, because he kept showing up with various drinks and food at frequent intervals.

"How ya doin'?" He had dimples like Will, but less prominent, and he flashed them at me now. I'd call him a flirt, but his mannerisms rivaled the other men I'd met today. *Friendly* was a good way to describe the crowd, mingled with Southern charm.

"Good." I wiped my brow with my forearm before accepting the water. The hat was long gone. My long hair did not need the added weight. I'd tied it back into a messy bun to keep it off my neck, but that did nothing to thwart the sun. "How pink am I?" I asked after taking a long swig from the bottle.

His lips twitched. "Not pink, red."

Yeah, I thought he might say that. My forehead and nose were on fire, which never ended well for my too-pale complexion. Sarah was the one who tanned naturally. Not me. Irish and German genes ran in my family, hence my fair features. I pressed the cool water against my head and looked up at the cowboy in front of me. "I finished my row."

He scratched the dark stubble on his jaw as he eyed my work, and nodded. "Yep. You did good for a city gal."

"Lawyer lady, city gal." I shook my head in mock disapproval. "*Y'all* need better nicknames."

He guffawed at my poor use of southern slang and pressed a hand to his flat abdomen. "Do me a favor and say that in front of Mershano, 'kay?" He was still laughing as he added, "Follow me."

I fought the urge to groan. Long days were nothing new to me, but I usually spent them in the comfort of my office, not in a blazing-hot field. My hands and feet were sore, and I knew my shoulders and back would be complaining later. I'd really thought this section would be it for the day, but apparently not.

Wiping my brow again, I trailed behind him past several rows and turned when he did, only to come to a complete stop. Will stood not five yards away, shirtless, with what looked like a net rolled up in his hands.

"You ready yet?" he drawled, addressing the man in the next row. The muscles in his back flexed as he shifted his footing.

"Yeah, yeah, throw it over," his associate replied.

Will lifted his arms with a swoosh and sent the mesh flying over the vine. Something resembling the wooden end of a broom appeared as his partner helped drape it over the other side. Looking down the line, I could see most of the vines were covered in a similar fashion but were fastened at the bottom by clothespins. There were several clipped to Will's belt as well. His ass flexed in his jeans as he bent to start rolling the netting from the bottom, and I stood frozen in my fascination. No wonder the man had zero percent body fat.

Bradley chuckled beside me, and I ignored him. Yes, I was ogling. No, I didn't care. Because wow. He made it look so easy, and sure, the mesh looked light, but the speed with which he adhered everything to the vines suggested years of practice and expertise. Was there any facet of life this man hadn't yet mastered? Running a business, legal negotiations, employee recruitment and management, hard labor; he put my law degree to shame.

He lifted his hands over his head and rolled his neck before turning to smirk at me. "Enjoyin' the show, darlin'?" I watched as a bead of sweat trailed down his chest and over each defined ripple of his abdomen.

"Yep," I replied, unashamed. Because what woman would deny it at this point? At least I could blame the sunburn for the heat caressing my cheeks. He peeled off his gloves and tucked them into his back pocket as he sauntered up to me. I tilted my head back to meet his gaze, hoping he intended to kiss me. Because all that golden skin? Yeah, it would feel like heaven.

Instead, he tsked through his teeth. "We need to get you out of the sun."

"She lost her hat," Bradley explained, chuckling. It wasn't exactly a lie. I'd set it down somewhere and forgotten to retrieve it. Who knew where it was at this point.

"Oh, I just bet she did," Will drawled, eyes narrowing. "You're going to regret that later."

"That sounds like a threat." Something that should have turned me off, not on. But my body didn't seem all that interested in reason at the moment.

"No, gorgeous." He palmed my cheek and brushed a

thumb over my lips. His pupils seemed to dilate as he tracked the intimate touch. "It's a promise."

Electricity zipped down my spine. Oh, I liked the sound of that. Not that I would admit it out loud. I shrugged to loosen my shoulders. "I'm not worried."

Unfettered challenge stared down at me. "Good." That single word and the look that went with it made me weak in the knees. He brushed his knuckles over my jaw and down my neck. I shivered beneath his featherlight caress. *What will it feel like when he* really *touches me?*

"Lawyer lady did better than I expected," Joe announced from my left. "You have my compliments, Mershano."

Will's hand continued its path over my shoulders and traced my arm all the way down to my hand, where he interlocked our fingers. "She's a keeper, then?" he asked, grinning at the older man.

"Yes, sir. She's welcome to come back anytime ya like." He beamed at me. "And whenever ya return, I'll call ya whatever ya like."

I laughed. "Rachel is fine."

Both of Will's eyebrows shot up. "Just Rachel?" He looked conspiratorially at Joe. "You got off easy, my friend. She would definitely be giving me a ridiculous name to call her."

"'Your Majesty' is not ridiculous," I deadpanned. "And neither is 'All-Knowing One' or 'Goddess Rachel.'"

"Goddess?" Will repeated, his eyes dancing over me. "I think I can work with that." His low baritone was becoming one of my favorite sounds. Soothing, sexy, and seductive. *Mmm.* "But for now I'm calling you Cherry, 'cause, darlin', you're turnin' redder by the minute. Let's get you home."

He tugged on my hand, prompting me to walk alongside him, before I could form a proper reply to his *cherry* comment. Good thing, too, because I had nothing witty to snap back. He'd rendered me speechless with that delicious voice of his sprouting words laced with sexual intent.

This is a battle I'm destined to lose. From the minute Will stepped into my life, I knew he'd be trouble. His commanding presence and overwhelming confidence brought out the fighter in me, but each gesture and word chipped away at my armor, leaving more and more of me exposed. Attraction sizzled between us, hot and heavy, and as he looked at me now, I saw my impending doom.

I wanted him more than I'd ever thought possible. Maybe it was a result of going so long without sex or the fact that he stood before me in nothing but a cowboy hat and jeans. Or maybe that kiss the other morning knocked a few screws loose. Whatever it was silenced my desire to fight. I liked him. Maybe even more than liked him. All the others who came before him didn't compare, including Ryan. I'd been head over heels for that man, yet he never lit my blood on fire the way Will did. One look was all it took to melt my insides, and I was dying to know how that translated to the bedroom.

"Mmm, you wear that look well." His breath was hot against my ear. I glanced sideways, surprised to see that he'd managed to guide me all the way to the truck without me realizing it.

"What look?" I asked, throat dry.

"The one that says you're almost ready to join me in bed."

Almost? My lacy panties disagreed with him. I was more than ready.

He planted an open-mouthed kiss against my neck and opened the door. "Yes, almost," he confirmed. I must have questioned that out loud. He helped me into the truck, then stepped up to pull the buckle over my lap. His lips were a hairsbreadth from mine as he locked me in his stare. "But, Rachel," he murmured, his bare chest radiating heat. "It's going to happen, and soon."

My thighs clenched. Again with the words in that damn

sexy voice! I tried to form a snappy comeback, but my brain refused to process my request. It just kept repeating, *Half-naked Will*, over and over again. His smirk said he knew it too.

I still had nothing rational to say when he climbed in beside me.

His masculine scent washed over me as he reached into the back to grab his shirt. I inhaled deeply, luxuriating in it. A hint of soap underlay the woodsy appeal, turning me on more. Crap. Who knew a day in the field could smell so alluring? He pulled the fabric over his head, hiding that delicious abdomen from my view. It didn't help kick-start my brain. His rippled torso would be forever burned into my memory. I wanted to trace each groove and ridge with my tongue.

Will started the car, and with it the music. Oh no. If he started singing again, I'd never recover. There were only so many seductive traits a woman could take, and he'd thrown enough at me to last a lifetime.

"Thank you for helping today," he said as we started down the gravel drive through the field. It wasn't part of the vineyard but appeared to be part of Joe's property. Focusing on that recognition brought a nonsexual question to mind that I latched on to with the single thread of reason I had left in me.

"So how does this work? You own the vineyard, but Joe maintains it and grows…" I squinted at the rows of thick bushes. "I'm not sure what those are."

"Blackberries," Will replied. "They're almost ready for picking, too, if you want to come back."

I scrunched my nose and immediately regretted it. "I'll need sunscreen."

He chuckled. "And your hat."

"Because that worked out well the first time," I muttered. Before he could tease me about it again, I shifted back to my safe topic. "Okay, so do you own the blackberries too, then?"

"It's complicated." He turned onto the main road before continuing. "Mershano Vineyards started with the property I live on today. I used my last name to apply for the loans I needed while also taking a little out of my family trust for the down payment, then spent three years cultivating the land and hiring a small team. I wanted to master the field work for several reasons, but mainly so I could earn the respect of some of the local winery owners."

"Like Joe," I inferred.

"Yes, exactly. It helped me develop a trusting approach rather than a smarmy salesman one. But before all that, I developed a business strategy. I knew my vineyard had promise, had seen it in its full glory as a kid, and wanted to return that potential to the land. It also served as a tribute to my mother since it was her favorite vineyard." His grin was sad while he spoke, tugging at my heartstrings.

"Anyway, I worked hard to restore the fields and the winery, taking out loans to replace rusty equipment, barrels, and other crappy machinery, and made two types of red wines. Meanwhile, the business-savvy part of me worked through the permits and legalities and started soliciting contracts for sale. It probably won't surprise you, but Mershano Suites was my first customer. Evan offered me an advance to help with wine production, but my fields only sustained a certain percentage of his needs."

I could see where this was going. "So you started soliciting partners."

"Exactly." He relaxed one forearm on the console while he spoke, his fingers drumming against the shifter. Even after all that work outside, he still had energy keyed up inside of him. Did the man ever rest?

"So," he continued, "I approached some local vineyards first, specifically the ones I knew were struggling, and offered various forms of partnerships. Some of them agreed to sell land to me outright, while others, like Joe, offered to sell their product under my brand for a fee."

"Like a franchise," I translated.

"Yep. About sixty percent of Mershano Vineyards is composed of franchise properties that sell under my name but are not owned by my corporation. Contractual agreements allow me to stop by and check in as needed to ensure the highest quality product, which is what my team of quality analysts handle. But I still like to help some of the locals when they need it."

"That explains all the types of wine," I murmured, thinking about the long list from his company website.

"Exactly. The key factors are variety and quality. I guarantee both, but there is a limit on each style, which also allows me to control price. It's a simple game of economics."

"Simple," I repeated. "Right."

His dimple peeked at me. "Well, again, it was all part of my business plan. And much to the bank's chagrin, I managed to pay back my loans in my first seven years, and now I put most of my profit into the family trust. And I was able to pay back Evan's ridiculous advance." The way he said it indicated there was a story there, but he didn't elaborate. I would have dug into it, but something else he mentioned intrigued me more.

"You didn't use family money to buy your first vineyard?" I had assumed more than once that he did. It wasn't like the Mershano family empire was short on cash. His cousin was estimated to be worth several billion, hence his well-earned nickname as "The Prince of New Orleans."

"I used some of it for a down payment, but mostly I just capitalized on my name. The banks knew I was good for the money, especially with the family trust sitting behind me, but I wanted to create my own empire. I had already used enough of my parents' money for college and business school, and I wanted Mershano Vineyards to be a product of my own work. Which it is to an extent, but my familial ties also helped. Most banks would never give a loan in that sum to an average person, but I accomplished what I could, given the situation."

I studied him in fascination. Northwestern had introduced me to all manner of wealthy men and women. Most of them enrolled because their parents required it. Ryan belonged to that crowd. His father's career as a long-term Illinois senator granted him all kinds of political connections and guaranteed his admittance into the legal program of his choice. He never once had to fight for anything in his life, nor did he have the desire to. Most of his rich trust fund buddies were exactly the same, greedily accepting everything from their silver platters and scoffing at those who had to work for it. Like me.

Meanwhile, Will admitted that his inheritance helped, but he also strived to disassociate from it. He broke all the stereotypes I'd crafted in my mind that pertained to rich and powerful men. I worked with several of them, all of whom maintained the same arrogant air as Ryan and looked at me in a way that said, *I could make you kneel at my feet with the crook of my finger.* Will possessed a similar confidence, except his left me feeling hot instead of cold. When he gave me that look, the one that said he could have me with a single flick of the wrist, I wanted to get down on my knees and beg for it.

I shook the image from my head. Ryan affected me like that once upon a time, perhaps not to the same extreme, and he'd left me crawling for his attention. He owned me so completely, so wholly, that I lost sight of myself. It was no wonder—

I jumped back to the present as Will's palm slid to my thigh.

"I've told you my life story. Now it's your turn," he said, voice soft and soothing. With a deep tenor like that, it was no wonder the man could sing.

"Uh"—I paused to clear my throat—"my history isn't nearly as exciting." An understatement.

The hand on my thigh gave a gentle squeeze. "Enlighten me anyway."

It took all my effort not to squirm as his thumb drew hypnotic circles above my knee. All my senses seemed to focus on that single point, waiting for him to do more. I cleared my throat and tried to think.

"Um, well, I grew up in Indiana with Sarah, but I always craved the city life. So I set my sights on Northwestern because it was close enough to home that it kept my parents happy and also offered the programs I wanted. Sarah applied, too, not really because of me but because she wanted out of Indiana as well, and when we were both accepted, our families agreed to let us go together." I paused to see if he was still listening.

"And then?" he prompted, grinning.

"Well, and then I took out some insane loans and went to Northwestern with Sarah. We lived together for undergrad in the dorms and eventually in a cheap apartment. I double-majored in business and French, while—"

"Why French?" He glanced briefly at me before refocusing on the road. "Sorry for interrupting, but I've wondered about that since reviewing your resume."

I bit my cheek. Leave it to Will to care about a detail few others ever mentioned.

"Um, I thought French might be useful if law school didn't work out, for teaching or something. But obviously, law school did happen. I went to Northwestern, which you already know, and I completed a dual concentration in business enterprise and international law. Baker Brown offered me a job right out of school, pending my passing the bar, which I did, and I'm still working there today."

He didn't look at all satisfied with my story, which I expected. I warned him it was boring for a reason. "You lived with Sarah during undergrad, but what about during law school?"

I stiffened. "Uh…" Fuck. I couldn't… *wouldn't*… go down that rabbit hole. "We didn't live together after our senior year." *Because Ryan wanted to live with me.* I'd been so excited and naive. I thought it was a gesture of love. But it was never about that between us. *Ownership* was a better term. I cleared my throat. "So yeah, that's me. Student loans out the wazoo, but I rent a nice apartment, enjoy my job, and yep."

"I see." His thumb had stopped moving while I spoke, something I noticed with a hint of regret. I rather liked that soothing circle he was drawing against my thigh. "I know Sarah has a twin sister, but what about you? Any siblings?"

This was a topic I could discuss comfortably. "I have an older brother, Caleb. He went into the military at eighteen and disappeared for a while, and now he does something for the government in an office somewhere. He doesn't talk a lot about it, and I only see him around the holidays."

"So you're not close?"

I snorted. "Not at all. I'm actually closer to his best friend." I bit my lip to keep from saying more. Talking about Mark could lead us to a conversation I preferred to avoid. Like why I considered him one of my closest friends despite rarely seeing or talking to him, or about his involvement in my escape from Ryan.

Will's property crept up in front of us as he navigated down the familiar drive. I'd only done this once, but it was memorable enough for me to recognize it. My thigh shivered as his palm moved from my leg to the steering wheel. I'd gotten comfortable with his hand there, perhaps too comfortable.

"Not to change the subject, but I hope you like cheeseburgers," he said as we started up the hill toward his home. "Because I'm craving them."

I laughed. "After all that work today? Yeah, I think I can handle a burger night."

"Good. 'Cause that's what we're having." He parked the truck by the front door and hopped out. I unbuckled my seat belt just as he greeted me on the passenger side.

"My lady." His eyebrows danced as he held out a hand.

I shook my head even as I accepted his help to the ground. "You do realize I'm capable of getting in and out of this massive truck by myself, right?"

He tugged me closer, invading my personal space and causing my breath to hitch. "Oh, I'm very aware. But the gentleman in me insists."

"Gentleman," I repeated, my voice softer than I anticipated. "Is that what you're being?"

Pure, unadulterated wickedness stared down at me. "For now, yes." His lips brushed mine in a chaste kiss that didn't match his darkening expression. "Don't let it fool you, darlin'. My proclivities in the bedroom are anything but gentlemanly." The ominous words were a breath against my jaw, followed by a light nibble that left me shaking with a need that felt as forbidden as it did hot. He pulled back with a wink. "Let's eat."

15
THIS ENDS NOW

I cringed at my red reflection. The flames dancing across my skin only seemed to get hotter during dinner, a result of both Will's charm and my sunburn. I'd tried to cool down with a shower after we finished eating, but the water stung in all the wrong places.

After thirty excruciating minutes, I was clean and dressed in my usual yoga pants, but my nightshirt sat on the counter. I couldn't bear the thought of covering my shoulders. Sleeping naked would be my preference in these conditions, but that seemed like trouble with Will so close.

I plucked a pale pink camisole from my suitcase. It was thin and meant to be worn underneath a blouse, but it would do. I pulled the light fabric over my head and didn't bother with a bra, then gently combed my hair. Normally, I would dry it, but the cool strands felt heavenly against my burn.

A chirp sounded from my purse. Voicemail. I hadn't checked my phone all day thanks to Will's unexpected field trip. Work had probably called for an update since we were scheduled to leave for France tomorrow night. Thankfully, everything was ready—or at least, we were as prepared as we could be going into the meetings. More research and discussion would be needed afterward. Janet had considered joining us, but after observing me last week during our final debriefings, she said her assistance wasn't needed. It'd been the biggest compliment of my career so far.

Hopefully, she hadn't called to say she'd changed her mind.

No.

It was worse.

Much, much worse.

My blood went from hot to cold as I scrolled over the abundance of messages and missed calls littering my screen. Two words jumped out at me over and over again.

France.

Bitch.

"Oh my God," I breathed.

Ryan had my airline itinerary.

And he was furious.

There was something about a wedding announcement and engagement pictures. All things I *never* agreed to and never would.

The messages blurred as I continued to run through them. Eighty-seven missed calls. All him. Nothing from work. They wouldn't have been able to get through with his incessant redialing. When the phone started to ring in my hand, my eyes narrowed. So, what—now he could tell when I was touching the damn mobile? My limbs shook with a mix of fear and fury as his ringtone sang through the room.

I couldn't believe this was happening again. He'd been like this right after the breakup. Constantly calling, dropping by, and checking up on me at all hours of the night. They were some of the most terrifying months of my life, but eventually he backed off. Not entirely, and never for long periods, but he gave me space. He started dating other women, something he enjoyed flaunting in my face. I only cared because I feared for them, but he was never with the women long enough to *own* them. Not in the way he owned me.

The ringing stopped.

I waited.

And it began again.

He'd texted a few times throughout the week and called once, but I'd never replied. Mostly because he had messaged me when I was with Will but also because I didn't feel that immediate pull to respond.

Something about being here had emboldened me enough to ignore Ryan. That had to be a first. I hadn't even really thought about him all week. Will consumed my every moment, and I'd actually felt relaxed. Happy, even.

Seeing Ryan's name flash on my screen was a shock to my system, but it lacked the usual punch. Instead, something else flared inside of me. A long-buried annoyance that I could no longer contain.

His ringtone started singing for the third time.

A scream tightened my throat, but my lips refused to let it loose.

No.

No more.

Maybe it was my week with Will that bolstered my confidence, or the terror ripping through my veins at the very real proof of Ryan spying on me. Or maybe I'd finally reached my breaking point and my mind had cracked. Or perhaps all of the above.

My finger hovered over the answer button.

What would he do? Waltz into Will's house and beat me? Show up in France unannounced and drag me home to an impromptu wedding? He couldn't wait for me at my apartment. I had no return ticket scheduled yet. Just a one-way booking to France. We would be staying at a

Mershano Suites, of course. Ryan could follow me there, and then what? He was in the middle of gearing up for a Senate run. A public disturbance in another country wouldn't bode well for his political career. Even insane, he had to know that.

My jaw clenched as a fresh text rolled across my screen. *Pick. Up. The. Fucking. Phone.*

I rolled my shoulders and waited. When his number flashed again, I answered.

"You fucking—"

"No," I snapped, cutting him off. "You do not get to call and scream at me for no fucking reason. This ends now, Ryan. I'm done. *We* are done."

Silence. This tactic always unnerved me, but not tonight. I felt elated. High, even. I couldn't believe all those words had spilled out of my mouth, and with such fervor too. I didn't necessarily raise my voice, but my tone brooked no argument.

I'd just called off our wedding. *Again.*

And it felt amazing.

"Stop calling me," I continued, the words tumbling out before I could think them through. "Stop texting me. Just, stop."

His blue eyes were undoubtedly storming right about now. That right hand clenched into a fist. His brow pinched. I could picture it clearly. Ryan Albertson was an attractive man, with his aristocratic features, artfully styled hair, and broad shoulders. I'd been drawn to him immediately. But beneath that flawless skin lay a monster, and I knew from experience that it was clawing to the surface right now.

You're safe here, my conscience whispered. The rolling in my stomach settled at the certainty in that thought. Ryan couldn't touch me. There would be hell to pay later, but I'd worry about that when the time came. Which would, hopefully, not be soon.

"Okay, Rachel." His neutral tone sent a chill down my

spine. Oh yeah, I'd well and truly pissed him off. "We'll talk soon."

I opened my mouth to repeat my comments about not calling me anymore, but the line went dead before I could utter a word. The phone slipped from my hand and bounced on the bed. My throat convulsed.

I'd done it.

I'd stood up to Ryan.

The room spun as a foreign sensation settled deep in the pit of my stomach.

"It's done," I whispered to no one in particular.

A laugh escaped my throat, part mad, part elated. I couldn't believe it. For the first time in years, I'd talked back to Ryan. It'd been so long since I dared to try, too terrified of the repercussions. But even though I knew he'd punish me later, I couldn't bring myself to react. Fear lingered on the precipice of my thoughts, looking for a weak point and finding none.

For the first time in a very long time, I felt untouchable. Strong. Daring. Confident.

The curtains at the open balcony door fluttered in the night breeze, beckoning me forward. And in that moment, I knew what I wanted. *Whom* I wanted. I'd fought it from the moment I met him. I was terrified to acknowledge the undeniable attraction radiating between us, scared of allowing myself to fall for a powerful man, and worried I might get him hurt in the process. But not anymore.

It was as if courage had finally found me again. I felt light, exuberant, and stronger than I'd been in longer than I cared to remember. Like I could conquer the world, or maybe just a sexy-as-sin millionaire.

I started walking before I could talk myself out of it, slipping out onto the balcony and over to his open door. Soft light spilled through the curtains. *This is it.* I knocked against the glass to announce my presence before entering. Will stood next to his bed, right where I wanted him, and turned with a knowing grin. He'd expected me to come to him. That should have irritated me, but it didn't. His confidence drew me to him like a moth to a flame. Influential men were my kryptonite. That's why I avoided them.

"Hmm, I thought you might stop by." He patted the oversized mattress. "On the bed, darlin'. I'll be back."

He didn't look to see if I would comply, just sauntered off towards his bathroom in nothing but a pair of low-slung gray sweatpants. My throat went dry at the sight of all that tanned muscle on display. The man was a god and he knew it.

"Bed," he repeated before disappearing through the French doors. The single-word command was uttered without him even looking at me. He knew I was ogling him instead of complying. What would he do if I refused the demand? I shivered. Maybe I would test that query another day, but not tonight.

I sat on the quilt with my legs hanging over the side and waited for him to return. The bottle in his hand surprised me almost as much as the towel in his other. I eyed the items curiously, wondering what kink he had in mind for our first time. He set the towel beside my hip as he came to stand in front of me.

One knee slid between mine, followed by a second, forcing me to spread my thighs wide to accommodate him between my legs. The dominance in that single act sent a rush of wet heat to my center. My chest rose and fell in anticipation of what he intended to do next. The bottle clicked open. It wasn't labeled, so I had no idea what to expect, but the sweet aroma calmed my nerves. Will squeezed a quarter's worth of off-white cream onto his palm before setting the lotion aside.

"Close your eyes and don't move." His low voice slid over me in a hypnotic caress. *Oh, yes, please.* My lids fell shut. "Now, I warned you about your hat, darlin'. Just remember that."

I frowned. "Wh—"

Something blessedly cool touched my forehead, cutting me off. A tingling sensation ignited as his skilled fingers massaged circles over my eyebrows and up into my hairline. It felt amazing, until it didn't.

"Whoa." I jerked back, eyes flying open, to find him shaking his head.

"I foresee bondage in our future."

I ignored *that* particular comment and focused on his torture bottle. "What the fuck is that?"

"It's cocoa butter blended with aloe vera. The sting is the moisturizer, which you need right now." He squirted more onto his hand and cocked an eyebrow. "Now, are you going to stay still, or do I need to tie you to the bed?"

Oh, shit.

This was not going to end well.

16
TAKING IT SLOW

"You can't be serious." No way would he really tie me down.

"I'm always serious, darlin'. Now close those gorgeous blue eyes and let me finish. I promise you'll thank me later."

"You seem to be confusing the term *thank* with *kill*," I muttered as I closed my eyes. I only agreed because the soothing sensation had returned and I wanted more.

"No moving." The command in his voice touched me in all the right places. I had no doubt he really would tie me to the bed, and a depraved part of me wanted to see him try. The rational part of me, however, rolled her eyes.

"Yes, sir," I replied sarcastically and regretted it immediately. His chuckle filled the air between us as his fingers returned to my face.

"Oh, I do love the way that sounds."

"Don't get used to it."

Sharp teeth sunk into my bottom lip, shocking the hell

out of me. "You've said those sexy words twice in my bed this week, gorgeous. I will hear them again, and with less sarcasm."

"Twice?" I repeated, incredulous. "Try once."

"You said them the first time you were in my bed, after I told you not to move, while we were discussing your adorable stockings."

"I don't remember…" Okay, actually, I did recall those words coming out of my mouth. "But if it happened, I didn't mean it."

"So you say." His fingers moved to my cheeks where the stinging was less prominent. The burn on my forehead must have been worse. "Are you regretting losing your hat yet?"

My nose scrunched as he applied the lotion there. "It was too hot on my head."

His chuckle was low and warm. "That's the city girl in you talkin', but we'll get you there."

I snorted. "Trust me, the cowboy look works much better on you."

"Does it?" His thumb traced my jaw, massaging the ointment in as he went. I couldn't tell what I enjoyed more—his touch or the way it soothed my sunburn. When he pulled away, I nearly groaned in disappointment, but then I heard the cap pop again. I peeked up at him through my lashes and found him studying my shoulders.

"Next time I'll remember sunscreen." Amusement flirted with his features. "Since you have an aversion to hats." He squeezed a healthy amount onto his palms and rubbed them together before reaching for my neck. I flinched when his thumb touched my throat, a place I associated with weakness thanks to Ryan. Will lifted his hands, his eyes searching mine intently. He'd obviously felt my reaction. Damn it.

"Too much?"

I swallowed and shook my head. "No, you just caught me off guard." A truth mingled with a lie. "Sorry." God, I hated Ryan. He'd trained my body to react to the dumbest movements. I knew Will wouldn't hurt me.

You used to think that about Ryan too.

But no, that wasn't exactly true. My ex had swept me off my feet, made me feel like the luckiest woman in the world, but the signs were always there. In the possessive way he handled me, the control he exuded in every situation, the way he alienated me from my friends and family… He never let me win arguments and always found a way to place the blame on my shoulders. Will's dominance felt different. *Protective.*

He studied me for so long that I worried my emotions were showing on my face. Then, ever so gently, his touch returned. But rather than go for my throat, he started at the back of my neck and massaged the lotion into the base of my scalp. His clever fingers pressed deep, making my jaw go slack.

Oh. My. God.

That felt amazing. My head fell forward against his abdomen, eliciting one of those alluring chuckles from him. I couldn't bring myself to care. All my tension seemed to melt away as he continued his ministrations along my shoulders and down my arms. He paused every now and then to add more lotion, but by the time he was finished, I felt like Jelly.

He swept my hair over my shoulder and traced my upper back. "Lie down on your stomach for me."

I groaned because that required moving. My forehead had created the perfect pillow against his six pack, and I planned to stay here forever. It wasn't the softest pillow, but I rather enjoyed the heat radiating from him.

His fingers brushed my jaw before gently taking hold of my chin. He tilted my head, forcing me to look up at him. My mouth went numb at the fierce emotion emanating from his gaze. Tension sizzled in the air between us, burning a path straight to my center. I couldn't look away. His expression hypnotized me, leaving me powerless to his will. My hands went to his shoulders when he grabbed my hips and lifted me. His movements were effortless as he repositioned me in the center of the mattress, with one of his knees between my legs on the bed. "Roll over, darlin'."

Right. He wanted me on my stomach.

He shifted as I moved, and straddled my thighs. His finger traced a line down my spine, over my tank top, and stopped at the hem. When his thumb slipped beneath the fabric, I shivered. I expected him to try to remove it, but instead, both hands slid under my shirt and began massaging my lower back.

"Oh…" I couldn't hide the moan as he worked magic over muscles I hadn't realized were sore. All those hours outside had affected me more than I expected. Pruning was an exercise my daily runs had not prepared me for, not to mention I hadn't been on one of those daily runs in a few weeks thanks to the long office hours. I pressed my face into the pillow and used it to muffle my groan.

"Mmm, I think that might be my new favorite sound." He pressed a kiss to my shoulder as he moved his palms higher. I didn't even care that my tank top was sliding up with his hands. As long as he continued touching me like that, he could strip me bare. I never wanted this to end.

"Your hands are magical." The words slipped out of their own volition. Whatever. His ego couldn't get much bigger anyway.

He nuzzled the back of my neck. "I think you'll find my mouth to be just as pleasant." His hot breath against my sensitive skin scattered goose bumps down my arms. Excitement and exhaustion fought for purpose inside of me. On the one hand, I'd never been more comfortable in my life. But, on the other, I'd never been this turned on before. My condition worsened when he tugged the straps of my tank top down, exposing my upper back. The fabric felt heavier than I remembered it being, and I had the sudden urge to rip it over my head.

But Will had other ideas. He pulled the bottom back to its rightful place before pressing the heel of his hand into my shoulder blade. I squirmed beneath him, unable to handle the conflicting sensations rallying inside me anymore. Heat pooled between my legs as the tension unfurled along my spine. It was a delicious mix that left me shaking. If this was his version of foreplay, I approved.

"How do you feel?" he asked.

Hot. On edge. Needy. None of those answers sufficed, and neither did the one that escaped my lips: "Good." Oh, I could do better than that. "Amazing." Still not enough. "I'm never leaving."

He returned my straps to my shoulders with a chuckle. "You're welcome to stay as long as you'd like, darlin'."

When I felt his thighs tense, like he was about to leave, I rolled beneath him. He stared down at me in surprise, as if he hadn't expected me to be able to move that fast. Well, that made two of us. But my body required me to act. I felt like I was going to explode. He set me on fire in a way I never thought possible, and I *needed* him to extinguish the flame. There was only one way to do that.

I went to my elbows, eyes locked on his. "Kiss me." When he didn't immediately react, I cocked an eyebrow. "Isn't this what you've wanted? Me willing and begging in your bed?"

He brushed his thumb over my lips and tracked the movement with his eyes. "Is this you begging?"

"Is that what you want?" Because I wasn't above it at this point. The man had me all sorts of hot and bothered. It took considerable effort not to shift my hips upward and seek the friction I so badly needed. "Please, Will." I tried to grab his shoulder and found my wrist caught in his big hand. He lowered it to the pillow beside my head as he stretched himself out lazily over me. When his arousal settled between my thighs, I nearly wept with joy.

"You're not ready for me yet, Rachel." The words against my ear did not match the actions going on below.

"Oh, I'm more than ready." I rotated my hips upward to show him what I meant and sighed when his hard length touched the place where I needed him most. I already knew from our interlude on the balcony that the man was well endowed, but to feel him throbbing so intimately against me really drove the point home.

That's going to be inside me...

"No, darlin'." He placed an open-mouthed kiss against my pulse. "We're going to do this right."

"Safely." I agreed. "Condoms." Ryan never allowed them, but I always wanted to use them. I shoved the memory away with an inner grimace and refocused on the moment. "You have one, right?" Because I didn't pack one.

He chuckled against my neck. "I do, but you're not listening." His free hand went to my hip, stopping me from rotating them upward again. "We're not having sex tonight."

What? "Are you serious?" Wasn't that his end goal? To get me in his bed?

"Very."

His lack of an elaboration had me freezing beneath him. "I don't understand." This game of hot and cold needed to end. He either wanted me or not.

"You're not ready," he said, repeating his words from a few minutes ago. I'd mistaken them to mean something else entirely. This time I understood what he meant, and it sent a wave of rage through my system. I'd fought off male advances for almost two years, and now that I'd finally given in to one I actually wanted, he was rejecting me. Because *he* thought *I* wasn't ready. Fuck. That.

"Who the hell are you to decide what I want?" I tried to shove at his shoulders, but he caught my hands with an ease that further infuriated me. When he pushed both of them into the pillows on either side of my head, I lost it. "You've got to be fucking kidding me! You had your chance, Will. *Now* I'm not ready." I knew on a mature level

142

that my reaction wasn't rational, that it was born of him rejecting me, but I couldn't help it. "Get the fu—"

His lips captured mine in a kiss that stole all fight from my lungs. Holy hell, that wasn't fair. He couldn't just silence me with his mouth and expect me to cooperate. When I tried to tell him that, he took advantage and slid his tongue between my lips. For half a second, I considered biting him, but my body refused. Despite my claim, I still wanted him.

My hormones overrode logic, quieting the anger inside me and rekindling the fire deep in my belly. I shook with a need I couldn't control and hated myself for it. Hated him. How could he be so hot and cold? Wanting me one minute, denying me the next, and then devastating me with his mouth? Because, Lord, the man knew how to kiss. He was right about his mouth rivaling his hands. He was a work of art, and he had me so hot and bothered that I couldn't think straight.

I ground my hips against him, and he pressed down even harder. My back threatened to arch off the bed, but his big body wouldn't let it. When I tried to free my hands, his grip tightened—a subtle control that left me conflicted. Part of me loved the idea of surrendering to him and letting someone take care of me for once. It was exhausting always being in charge, but that sense of control was what kept me sane, what kept me safe. And my hesitancy made me uneasy, took me out of the moment, and left me blinking in confusion.

Will pulled back, desire shining brightly in his gaze as he stared down at me. "You don't trust me yet," he whispered. "This is not a question of whether or not I want you, because it's pretty damn obvious that I do." He pressed his arousal into my lower belly to punctuate his point. "It's a matter of *how* I want you. Trust, Rachel."

I trembled. Was he right? Did I not trust him? I knew he wouldn't hurt me. Everything I'd learned about him pointed to him being a good man. I'd so severely misjudged him in the beginning, but he'd slowly chipped away at all the stereotypes I'd unfairly assigned to him and showed me what lay beneath the hefty bank account.

"I want to trust you," I said, realizing it was the truth.

His grin was sad. "I know, but you're not there yet."

"I might never be there," I admitted.

He finally released my wrists and pressed his palms to my cheeks. "I'm a patient man, Rachel. And you're worth the wait." His lips brushed mine and lingered. I loved the way he tasted on my tongue. Like wine and peppermint. It tingled my senses, leaving me breathless and yearning. "But," he continued, his mouth still touching mine, "I'm also observant. And I know someone hurt you."

I stiffened at his words. He must have felt it, because he kissed me again, softly. His mouth coaxed mine into submission with tentative strokes that stirred emotions deep within my soul. When his tongue entered to dance with mine, I couldn't deny him. This time he let me wrap my arms around his shoulders and run my nails over the smooth skin of his back. He felt so hot and hard above me. So safe.

"You will trust again, Rachel." His words were a whisper against my lips. "You're too strong not to. But we have to do this right. Because I want more than a night with you."

I swallowed. "How many nights do you want?"

"Oh, darlin', I want them all." He kissed me again before I could react to that proclamation. Which was good because I had nothing. I'd only just accepted the possibility of a whirlwind affair, but something long term… Was I ready for that? How would it even work? Telling Ryan off tonight was only a temporary solution, a minor reprieve. He was still very much a part of my life, and I knew from experience that this little setback wouldn't last long. He'd find a way to plow back into my world and ruin everything.

He could hurt Will…

"Shh," Will murmured against my lips. "Turn that beautiful brain off and just feel." His tongue entered my mouth as he palmed my breast. The move was so unexpected that it tore me from my thoughts and threw me into the present. He tweaked my nipple with those skilled fingers, and my bliss scattered all my thoughts.

"More," I moaned as my back came off the bed.

"Yes, ma'am." He bent to nibble my hard peak through the fabric while his hand trailed down my belly to the apex between my thighs.

"Fuck," I panted, eyes closing. "Are we… ?" My voice faded into another groan as he massaged a circle against my most sensitive point.

"I said no sex," he replied, following the question I hadn't finished. "I never said anything about fondling, darlin'."

"Unfair," was the only word I could get out as he increased his assault. Then he pulled his hand back, and I cried out in frustration.

"You'd like me to stop?" he asked, his tone deceptively innocent.

It took me a moment to catch my breath. All the foreplay and emotions had left me far closer to climax than I ever could have imagined. My panties were soaked, and my nipples ached with need. I palmed his cock through the sweatpants and squeezed, which earned me a hiss from him. *Yeah, two can play this game, Mershano.*

"Don't start something you can't finish, darlin'." The warning in his voice sent a rush of heat through me. I *liked* that tone. And I showed him just how much by stroking him, hard, through the fabric. "Fuck."

I grinned at his small slip in restraint. I managed one more caress before he caught my wrist in his hand and put it beside my head again. I expected him to hold it there, but he surprised me by letting go and palming my core again. He gave me no time to react before his lips captured my nipple through the tank top. My resulting scream was

LEXI C. FOSS

part surprise, part need. Because, oh my, he'd only been teasing before. *Now* he was touching me with purpose. His thumb found my sensitive nub through the yoga pants. I only had a second to recognize how impressive that was before he pressed down and sent pleasure racing through my veins.

He switched breasts, sucking my nipple hard into his mouth. God, how would that feel on bare skin? I wanted so badly to rip the damn tank top over my head, but my limbs were locked down by my mounting arousal. It built low in my abdomen, coiling so tightly it almost hurt, and I couldn't help the whimper of need escaping my lips. This was so much better than my midnight sessions with my vibrator. Hell, it was better than any of my previous physical experiences. I'd never felt so pent-up in my life. All I wanted was to explode, and I could feel it, taste it, on the edge of my being.

Taunting.

Waiting.

So close.

"Come for me, gorgeous." The words were hot against my lips and followed by a sharp pinch to my clit. It was so unexpected, and startling, that it snapped my restraint in half and sent pleasure spiraling through my lower belly and into my limbs. Will swallowed my scream with his mouth and continued applying pressure where I needed it to prolong my orgasm. It shook me so hard, so deep, that it almost hurt. And then I was kissing him. Hard.

My emotions took over, demanding I worship him, thank him, for whatever it was he'd just done to me. But as I tried to reciprocate with my hands, he gently grasped them and held them between us.

His mouth was relentless against mine, returning my kiss with a fervor I felt throughout my being. I had no idea how long it went on—minutes, hours?—but eventually the urges subsided, leaving me more exhausted than I ever remembered being.

When I yawned, Will chuckled and nuzzled my neck.

"It's been a long day," he murmured, affection coloring his tone.

I curled into him, not wanting the night to end. "Just a little longer."

"For as long as you want, Rachel."

"Mm-hmm." I settled my cheek against his shoulder, content to just be near him. Warmth cocooned me as he pulled the blankets around us. How he managed to do that while we were lying on them, I had no idea. I was too lost in the moment to care. Too lost in him.

He pressed his lips to my forehead, then to my temple. "You're beautiful, Rachel."

I smiled and tried to tell him we were past pickup lines, but it came out as a grumble instead.

He must have understood some of it because he replied, "You better get used to it, darlin'. 'Cause I'll never stop complimenting you."

Those words followed me into my dreams, where I entered a world of *what-ifs* and *what could be*. And for the first time in a very long time, I dreamt of a life without Ryan in it.

17
BREAKFAST BANANA

Male stubble tickled my neck as Will placed an open-mouthed kiss beneath my ear. "Wake up, gorgeous." His sexy murmur had me stretching against him like a contented cat. The hot arousal pressing into my ass suggested he liked that, or maybe it was having his thigh between mine that he enjoyed.

Light streamed in through the curtains, confirming I'd spent the night in his bed. I expected that to bother me, but it didn't. If anything, I felt relieved, which was bizarre. Intimacy didn't scare me, but Ryan did. Except when I thought of him, all I felt was a mild annoyance rather than fear. *That's new.*

Teeth scraped over my tender skin as Will gently bit my pulse. When he sucked the spot into his mouth, I practically purred. "Mmm, I like this. Learning your tells and finding what makes you tremble." The arm beneath my breasts tightened as his leg slid upward between my thighs. I fought a moan when he met my core, and quivered. "Just like that," he whispered.

I found myself beneath him not a second later, staring up into eyes filled with dark intent. My heart thundered in my chest at that look because I recognized it. Determination laced with desire. I was trapped and he knew it.

"Do you know what I do when I find a new subject or activity that excites me?"

I swallowed and shook my head, unable to speak. Not with him staring down at me like that.

"I master it," he murmured. His lips brushed mine in a gentle kiss that belied the heat radiating between us. "You've been warned." He rolled off the bed and stretched his arms over his head, showcasing all those delicious muscles and his impressive arousal. I wanted to rip those gray sweatpants off, trace all those hard muscular lines with my tongue, and taste every inch of him. If that bulging outline was anything to go by, he would certainly be a mouthful. *Yum.*

"We have a conference call in fifty minutes with Jeff and Janet; otherwise, I would take you up on the offer in your eyes." He gripped my chin and forced me to meet his gaze. "I'm going to take a shower. I suggest you do the same and meet me downstairs in thirty."

"So bossy," I replied, finding my voice. It came out a bit breathier than I wanted, but the words were clear.

He traced my lip with his thumb and grinned. "We're just gettin' started."

I liked the sound of that. He left me on the bed, staring after him. I couldn't help it. The man had a fine ass.

"Twenty-eight minutes," he said when he reached the bathroom. He nailed me with a look over his shoulder that sent heat rushing to all the right places. "Don't be late, Miss Dawson."

"I wouldn't dream of it, Mister Mershano." Not because of the taunt in his gaze, but because I was never late on principle.

His chuckle teased my senses as he disappeared from view. That man was doing things to me I never thought possible. Self-assurance always turned me on, but never like this. Will took it to a whole new level by adding his alpha tendencies to the mix and creating an intoxicating persona I stood no chance against. I'd fought it for all these months, determined to dissuade him, yet he'd only managed to deepen my attraction. To the point where I wasn't sure I wanted to say no at all anymore.

What would he do if I joined him in the shower?

It was so tempting. I could hear the spray against the tiles and knew he was in there naked and taking care of his arousal. I shivered at the image of him taking his hard cock into his hand and stroking himself to climax. All those muscles bunching, his full lips parting on a groan meant for me... My thighs tensed as sensations built low in my belly, curling tight with the indecent fantasy flashing behind my eyes. The urge to touch myself, just as I knew he was, overwhelmed me. He'd taken me to a high last night unlike any other, but it was like he'd lit my blood on fire. I needed more, so much more, and he'd denied it this morning.

Because of a meeting.

My eyes drifted to the clock on his nightstand to find ten minutes had passed already.

"Damn," I muttered, my libido cooling. The last thing I needed was to be late for my own debriefing with the partners. It took considerable effort to leave his bed, but my desire to keep my job proved a healthy motivator.

Every part of my body felt alive and more sensitive than usual. When I pulled off my clothes, my nipples hardened to a painful degree and my legs trembled. The water felt like daggers against my burn but massaged other parts of my body in interesting ways. Especially when it dribbled over my belly to the apex between my thighs. Will had awoken something inside of me that did not want to be put to rest, which was likely his intention all along.

Determined, insufferable man.

I soaped myself clean with light, hesitant touches and rinsed my hair. It did nothing to put out the fire brewing deep inside, nor did dressing in my charcoal-gray skirt suit. My pale blue blouse seemed to stick to my clammy skin, and my lacy bra abraded my tender skin. By the time I walked downstairs, I was a hot mess, while Will looked the epitome of sexy casual in his black slacks and white button-down. The sleeves were rolled to his elbows, and his collar was open since he'd forgone the tie. My eyes trailed over every inch of him. *Fine* didn't even begin to cover it.

"You look hungry," he murmured. "Banana?" He held up my usual breakfast of choice, but his innocent tone and gesture were not lost on me.

"Funny," I grumbled, grabbing the fruit from his hand.

"Someone needs coffee." He pushed over a fresh mug. "You were two minutes late, by the way."

"My hair wasn't cooperating." A partial truth. The hair dryer had been too hot this morning thanks to my hypersensitized skin. It'd taken an extra five minutes to finagle a solution, which resulted in the partial bun at the back of my head. "Besides, our meeting starts in fifteen minutes." Plenty of time. I peeled the banana and took a bite while he watched me over his coffee mug.

"I look forward to you doing that to my cock."

I choked on the fruit in my mouth and had to force myself to swallow. *Holy shit.* He said that so casually, like he was commenting on the weather or something.

"How are you feeling about the meeting?" he asked in that same tone, completely unfazed by my reaction or the fact that I was openly gaping at him. "Ready?"

I took a fortifying sip of my coffee while he observed in that relaxed way of his. How he managed to maintain nonchalance after saying something like that, I would never know. Because my face was on fire. He said nothing as I continued holding my cup like a lifeline and taking the caffeine into my body. Why I thought drinking a hot liquid would help was beyond me. It only seemed to sizzle my insides.

"So this is you flustered?" He sounded so amused. "It's cute."

"Jackass," I managed.

His dimples flashed. "There's my favorite lawyer. You know how much I adore our verbal sparring."

"Verbal sparring?" I repeated, my wit returning. "You mean all those conversations where you failed to understand the word *no*?"

He brushed his knuckles over my cheek. "You weren't saying *no* last night, darlin'. I believe I heard the word *yes* roll off those luscious lips more than once."

And the heat was back. Awesome. Just what I needed five minutes before our conference call. I cleared my throat, forced the banana down my gullet—much to Will's amusement—and slammed my coffee cup on the table. This meeting could make or break my career, and I wasn't going to let a little flirtation unsettle years of poised confidence. Even if I did still feel like a furnace.

"You better behave yourself, Mister Mershano. Or what you just witnessed with that banana is never going to happen to your cock."

Excitement brightened his expression, which was the opposite of my intent. "Duly noted, Miss Dawson. Shall we take the call in my office?"

I grabbed a bottle of water from the fridge—I had a feeling I would need it—and nodded. We'd spent a lot of time in his oversized home office this week, both working at his desk and reviewing all the materials Baker Brown put together for the meetings next week.

The purpose of this morning's call was to go over any residual questions or concerns Will had. It also served as a way to confirm whether or not I was ready for the meetings next week. If they sensed even the slightest bit of hesitation, I knew one or both of them would join us in

France. Mershano Vineyards was too big a client to disappoint, and we were down to the wire with our flight leaving in less than twelve hours.

I smoothed my hand over my jacket while Will fiddled with his teleconferencing equipment. When Jeff and Janet appeared on his projector screen, I smiled. It was time to knock their socks off.

18
FLYING FIRST CLASS

"So this is how the other half lives, huh?" I'd expected to fly coach to Paris, but Will had other plans.

We were in a first-class suite; a commercial airline feature I didn't know existed until today. Standard business class, sure, but this was something else entirely. There were only two other people up here, one on each side with their windows, while we sat in the middle in our own little nook that came with curtains for privacy. My seat rivaled an oversized recliner chair, which, according to the video we watched prior to takeoff, would magically transform into a full-length bed after dinner.

I sipped my second glass of champagne and fluttered my stocking-clad feet. My pumps were the first items I'd stowed in our closet, much to Will's amusement. He'd tried to convince me to wear jeans for the flight, but I'd refused. This was a work trip first and foremost, and I was determined to dress the part. So he'd worn his slacks and a button-down, saying he didn't want me to be the only formally clad person on the plane. I had smirked when a man in a business suit entered the private nook to my right, and Will had just shaken his head.

"You need to decide what you want for dinner," he said now as he passed me a five-course menu.

I handed the fancy leather book right back to him. "This is your world, millionaire. Order for me."

He arched a brow. "Now who's being bossy?"

I shrugged and continued to kick my feet. This jittery feeling had been with me all day. I thought maybe it was elation from our successful call with the firm this morning, but it went deeper than that. My body was ramped up on adrenaline, and I sensed the man to my left was to blame. It didn't help when he started conversing in fluid French with the blonde flight attendant.

She popped her slim hip against the wall in front of us and beamed at Will while he ordered dinner in French. Salmon tartare, grilled beef tenderloin, soup, salad, and a dessert. It was enough to feed a small army.

"Ce sont de très bons choix pour vous et votre femme." *All excellent choices for you and your wife.*

I opened my mouth to correct her, but Will beat me to it.

"Ah, nous ne sommes pas mariés, mais merci beaucoup." *Oh, we're not married, but thank you.*

"Vraiment?" *Really?*

"Non, nous sommes collègues. C'est un voyage d'affaires." *No, we're colleagues. This is a business trip.* His casual response surprised me. After all the flirting and teasing, I expected him to taunt me by implying we were more, but he kept it professional. I smiled. Good. It meant he considered me his legal counsel first and foremost, which would be important during our meetings next week.

"Bien compris." *Oh, I see.* Her flirtatious tone grated at the contentment I felt a second ago. When her round hazel eyes flickered to his left hand, my heart dropped to my stomach.

Okay, now hold on a second. That was not what I wanted her to take away from this conversation, but of course, Little Miss Tight Skirt had other ideas. Her grin spread as she dragged her gaze up his body in a slow caress that implied *exactly* what she thought of the winery millionaire. She launched into the next obvious question about what he did for a living, and Will, the charmer, answered with one of his trademark grins. Rapt interest radiated from the slender woman's posture and expression. I half expected her to start stripping and ask me to step out for a bit.

By the time she left, my fists were clenched and my stomach was in knots. Part of me wanted to grab Will and stake my claim, while the rest of me wondered what the penalty would be for punching a flight attendant. Both reactions frustrated me. I recognized them for what they were: jealousy. An emotion I never felt until I met the damn man beside me. Apparently, he could yank it out with a single glance, or in this case, a few casual words. Nothing about his demeanor screamed *flirtatious*, but the flight attendant made it quite clear that she was available for dessert, should he want it.

"So, *collègue*, what are our plans when we arrive in Paris?" I couldn't help the snarky tone, but if he noticed, he ignored it.

"We acclimate to the time change, do a little shopping, and drive south on Monday." He was reading something on his phone while he spoke. "Are there any sights you want to visit, or have you seen them all?"

"Uh, I haven't seen any of them in person."

That caught his attention. His dark eyes snagged mine. "You've never been to Paris?"

I huffed a laugh. "Did you miss the part about my student loans the other day? Not all of us were born millionaires, Mister Mershano." Okay, my snappy response was uncalled for, but the man had my emotions wound tight. And his casual replies were grating on my nerves.

"You majored in French and never studied abroad?"

I had wanted to, but Ryan convinced me otherwise. He promised to take me to France after law school, but we ended up in the Caribbean for a week instead. "*Ugh, I've done France so many times, baby girl. Let's just go hang out on the beach instead, okay?*" I cleared my throat, and with it the memory. "No, it didn't fit with my schedule."

The blonde flirt chose that moment to pop in with more drinks and made a point of leaning over Will to hand me a drink I didn't order, rather than walk around to my side of the cabin. She'd even undone a button on her shirt, which gave him an enticing view of her breasts. I considered elbowing the drink into his lap, but with my luck, the bitch would end up mopping it up with her hands.

"*Merci,*" I said through my teeth. She didn't even hear me. Her focus was on Will again as she asked him about where we were headed in France and how long we intended to be there.

I unfastened my seat belt with the intention of finding a bathroom to puke in, but Will's hand on my arm stopped me. He let it linger as he addressed the too-friendly attendant.

"*Je suis désolé, ma cherie, mais nous étions au milieu d'une discussion importante. Pouvez-vous nous laisser un instant?*" *I'm sorry, darling, but we were in the middle of an important discussion. Can you give us a minute?*

His words, although friendly, were underlined with an authority that made my heart race. It seemed to have the same effect on her if the faint blush staining her porcelain cheeks was anything to go by. She gave him another one of those simpering smiles and walked away with her ass waving goodbye.

"Wow, she's practically beckoning you to follow." I snapped my lips closed, but not fast enough. The sentence hung between us as Will took in my expression with an amused one of his own. Apparently, he found this entire situation funny. *Better than him being interested in pursuing her offer.*

"You have nothing to be worried about, darlin'," he drawled.

"Colleague," I corrected. *Okay, two glasses of champagne? Bad idea.* It loosened my tongue far too much. "Sorry, ignore me."

He brushed his knuckles over my cheek and down my neck to my breasts. I held my breath at the boldness in his touch.

"Would you prefer I introduce you as something else? Just say the word, Rachel, and I'll use it." He continued that descent until his hand landed in my lap, where he settled it on my thigh. "I don't want to make assumptions on your behalf, but as for me, I haven't considered myself an available man since the day we met."

I gaped at him. "What?"

"You heard me." He squeezed my leg before pulling away. "Now, tell me what you want to do in Paris. We're only there for two days, but there has to be something you want to see."

He never said what I expected, and this was no exception. Not only did he claim to consider himself off the market after meeting me, but he also wanted to know what I wanted to do in Paris. Ryan would never have bothered to ask; it was always about him. But Will? It seemed he always had my interests in mind, even with small details. I leaned over and kissed him softly, my version of a silent thank-you for caring. For being him. For not being Ryan.

His chuckle feathered over my lips. "I think I approve of this response."

"Quiet." Not wanting to risk spilling our drinks, I took advantage of my freedom from the seat belt and settled myself in his lap to kiss him again. His arms circled my waist, holding me to him as I tentatively explored his mouth with my tongue. This was my first time initiating the kiss rather than the other way around, and I relished the power of it. He lightly traced my spine as I deepened our embrace, showering goose bumps over my skin. I loved the way his simple touch affected me. It left me hot and needy and sent a tidal wave of sensation through my veins.

The clearing of a throat had me pulling back to meet the flight attendant's surprised gaze. She held two trays of what I assumed was our dinner. I considered apologizing, but I knew it wouldn't be believable. Instead, I planted one final kiss against his mouth before climbing off his lap. He followed it up with a smack on my ass that had me yelping.

"Will!" It came out on a startled laugh.

"Two can play that game, gorgeous." By "game," I assumed he meant my show of possession for the attendant. His returning the gesture made me grin.

Feel free to claim me anytime, Mershano, I told him with my eyes.

His returning grin seemed to say, *Oh, I will.*

And I hoped he meant it.

19
AIRPLANE SHENANIGANS

One bed.

A queen size, maybe smaller.

The preflight video said nothing about joining the first class seats into one oversized mattress. I expected to find two single flattened recliner chairs with blankets on my return trip from the bathroom, but the crew had other ideas in mind. Will's spicy cologne surrounded me as he rested his chin on my shoulder and wrapped his arms around me from behind.

"Hmm, I see the flight attendant has decided we're more than business acquaintances."

"So this isn't typical?" I pointed to soft white linen. "Where did that wall divider thing between the seats go?" It seemed a difficult thing to just remove, but I didn't see it anywhere now.

His stubble brushed my neck as he pressed a kiss to my jaw. "Magic," was all he said.

"Should we ask her to change it?" Even as I said the

words, I took them back. "Yeah, never mind."

The last thing I wanted was that blonde bitch to invite Will back to explore her "private cabin." She'd flirted with him throughout dinner, constantly asking if he needed anything else. I would have considered it fantastic service, but she never addressed me. Her offers were for Will, and there was more than just food and beverage on her menu. To his credit, he maintained a polite yet reserved formality with her the entire evening. It left me wondering how often he put up with women like her.

"You want to wear the pajamas?" Will asked, ignoring my comment about changing the bed. He let go of me to pick up the packages on the bed. Our names were on the outside, with European sizes beside them. Considering I never gave the airline my dimensions, it could only have been the millionaire next to me.

"This is the second time you've ordered clothes for me without asking." And from what I could tell, he'd nailed the measurements. Again.

"And I'm sure it won't be the last," he murmured. "Do you want to wear these?"

"You don't sound very thrilled by them."

He shrugged. "It's an airplane bed. Comfortable clothes won't make much of a difference to me."

I scanned him from head to toe. He would require at least two-thirds of the mattress, and his feet would hang over the edge—a consequence of being a tall, muscular man. But this was better than coach. As for the clothes... "I'd prefer not to change." My skirt suit served as professional armor. Sure, we shared a bed last night, but that was in the privacy of his home. An airplane was an entirely different circumstance.

Right. Because you've been the picture of professional so far on the plane. I bit my cheek and ignored my snarky bitch of a conscience. The only person who saw us kiss was the flight attendant. Who could she possibly tell?

Hopefully, no one...

Developing a sexual relationship with a client was frowned upon, especially for the lead attorney on a project. These international acquisitions were for his company, which made him and his organization a client, and a court of law would consider that a conflict of interest.

But the majority of the work is already done…

This trip was about finalizing the contracts and advising Mershano Vineyards as required. Will would be doing most of the talking, and I would only speak up if his business partners desired a change. Even then, I had instructions to send all requested changes back to Janet for vetting.

"What are you thinking about?" Will asked, his voice pulling me back to the present. The pajamas were gone, but I didn't see where he stashed them.

"Uh…" I bit my lip. Admitting that I was trying to mentally justify my semi-sexual relationship with him did not sound appealing. So I went with, "Work." *And how these feelings I seem to be developing for you are seriously bad for my career.* If things heated up between us much more, I'd have to tell the firm about it. And wouldn't that be a fun conversation.

Will gave me a look that said he didn't believe me, but he didn't press for details. I walked around to my side of the cabin, kicked off my heels, which I had put back on before using the restroom, and sat on the bed. It was much softer than I expected. They'd put some sort of foam mattress over the seats. Not bad.

I slid beneath the blankets and faced away from Will's side of the bed as he closed the curtains around us. The lights were already dim on the plane, but he blackened it more by cutting the reading lights overhead before climbing in beside me. There were earplugs and a face mask on the pillow, but I set them off to the side.

The constant rumble of the plane coupled with the darkness closed us off from the world in an intimate way I had not anticipated. We were alone, but not quite, and at any minute, someone could pull open the curtain and see us.

That's... kind of kinky.

His natural heat radiated behind me, but we weren't quite touching. I thought maybe he was on his back, legs crossed at the ankles, but I refused to risk glancing at him. It would undoubtedly lead to something stupid. Like me kissing him. Electricity zipped along my spine at the thought, sending shocks to all my nerve endings. I squirmed a little as they hit me dead center, vibrating the area between my legs.

Damn it. The man hadn't touched me in over ten minutes, and yet my body was primed and ready for him. My nipples scraped against my lacy bra, begging to be set free. I fidgeted a little to give them relief, but it only intensified my ache below. An ache Will created with all his sensual flirting and his thorough introduction to what he had to offer sexually last night in bed. Except it hadn't been nearly enough.

My hands curled into fists. I had wanted to caress every inch of him, but he'd kept it light. What would it be like to watch him come? To give him the same pleasure he gave me? My thighs tensed as an image of me on my knees before him flashed behind my eyes. Fuck. Why was that so tempting? I never enjoyed oral sex before, but something told me it would be different with Will. Everything about him defied expectations and experience.

"Darlin', you keep whimpering like that, and I'm going to need to find a way to silence you." His words were a breath in my ear. I'd been so lost in the sensations teasing my core that I hadn't even heard him move, let alone felt it. As for the whimpering, what did he expect? The man had me all hot and bothered without even trying.

I bit my lip and fought the urge to groan in frustration. Refusing him was an idea of the past, one I couldn't believe ever entered my mind in the first place. I couldn't ignore the way my body responded to him, something he had to have known all along. He weakened my defenses with his subtle advances and charmed his way past my mental guard. If he kept this up, my heart would be next.

The back of his hand skimmed my arm as he pressed an open-mouthed kiss to my neck. Not a full embrace, but enough to set my skin on fire.

"You're not playing fair, Mershano." It came out as more of a moan than an accusation.

"Never with you, gorgeous." He nibbled the sensitive area below my ear and flattened his palm against my stomach. "Now, come here." The world shifted as he effortlessly pulled me beneath him. My skirt bunched up my legs as he settled between them. I couldn't see his face well in the dark despite it being an inch from mine, but I sensed him smirking. "Do you need me to help you relax?"

"I don't think that's possible around you." Energy sizzled through my body, and having him on top of me only worsened my hyper state.

"You seemed to unravel quite well in my arms last night." He nuzzled my neck and placed his lips against my ear. "Though, you'll have to be a lot quieter here. Those curtains are very thin."

Exhibitionism wasn't my thing, but his reminder that we were not alone sent a thrill down my spine. He had a way of erasing the world around us and helping me forget everything and everyone. His ability to overwhelm me so completely both unnerved and excited me. I loved the pleasant cocoon he created, isolating me from all the troubles in life. He made me happy, and that alone was sexy as hell.

I drew my nails up and down his back. Taut muscles met my strokes through the fabric of his dress shirt, making me want to rip the clothes off his back. Last night he taunted me and watched me come. I wanted to return the favor—explore his reactions, learn his body the way he learned mine, and feel him in the process. With a palm on his chest, I nudged him to his side of the bed and rolled with him.

"My turn, Mershano."

"Oh?" Even in the dark, I knew he had an eyebrow raised. "Well then, by all means, Miss Dawson. Show me what you can do."

He tucked his arms behind his head on the pillow in a show of giving up control, but we both knew he would take it back in an instant if he felt like it. Which just meant I needed to get him so out of his mind that he couldn't think.

Challenge accepted.

I ran my tongue along the stubble of his jaw up to his ear. "Anything goes?"

"Sure, darlin'." So arrogant. He would regret it soon enough.

Yanking my skirt up higher, I straddled one muscular thigh and placed my palms on his hard chest. The shirt needed to go first, but his elbows behind his head made that problematic, as did the general surroundings. I loosened the fabric from his pants until I revealed a sliver of skin. My eyes were slowly adjusting to the dark, enough to see his lips curling in amusement. I looked forward to giving him a different kind of smile.

I pushed his button-down and undershirt upward to expose all those delicious abs and the bottom of his pecs. All those strong lines threatened to distract me from my mission, but I held myself in check and leaned down to kiss the center of his sternum. My tongue followed, tracing a pattern created by his muscles. *Mmm.* He tasted like sin and man and a sweet treat that was specifically designed for me to enjoy. When I reached his belly button, I looked up to meet his smoldering gaze.

Not laughing now, are you?

A light dusting of hair met my mouth as I discovered his happy trail and followed it lower to his belt. He didn't stop me as I unfastened the leather or when I popped open the button on his pants. I took both as a sign that I was free to continue my oral explorations wherever I pleased. And, oh, did I want to savor every inch of him.

With a grin against Will's lower abdomen, I pushed the slacks down to the tops of his thighs and played my fingers over the elastic of his boxer briefs. Heat radiated from his groin, seducing me to move my hands lower until I palmed his cock through the thin cotton.

Holy hotness. I knew from our prelude last night that the man was well proportioned, but having him in my hand took that knowledge to a whole new level. My mouth watered in anticipation and my sex tingled. Never before had the idea of sucking a man off turned me on, but nothing about Will fit my norm. I desired things with him that I shouldn't, and knowing that only made me crave those things more.

I nuzzled the muscular indent beside his hip and loved how it made his hard length pulse against my palm. Wrapping my fingers around him, I gave him a stroke and watched his abdomen clench in response. There was no hint of a smile on his face now as he watched me beneath his hooded gaze. But those arms were still tucked behind his head in a leisurely position that signified self-restraint. I hooked my thumbs in his shorts and carefully slid them down to join his pants. His hot member jutted upward, and I caught it with my mouth.

"Rachel..." My name sounded so perfect on his lips, so adoring, but when his fingers knotted in my hair, I knew he also meant it as a plea. It wasn't enough. I needed him to shatter, and I wanted to be the one to push him there.

My tongue circled his bulbous head as I grasped his hot member with one hand. His sweet and spicy taste coated my mouth, urging me to take him deeper.

So silky and smooth.

And, oh, how this impressive part of him deserved to be worshipped. It was long and thick and far too much for me to take in one pull, but I tried and met my fingers halfway down his shaft, then sucked hard on my way back up.

"Fuck," he breathed, his grip tightening on the back of my head. When he pushed me back down, I smiled inside. This was his way of taking control, but we both knew my mouth had all the power here.

I fondled his heavy sack with my free hand and started learning his reactions. His body subtly told me what he liked and what he loved, and I used that knowledge to drive him to oblivion with my hands, my lips, and my tongue.

His breathing grew heavy, and his grip turned nearly painful as he plunged deeper and deeper into my throat. I took every thrust, too exhilarated in his obvious fall into ecstasy to care that he was running the show now.

When his movements turned erratic, I knew he was close, but then his hold loosened almost reluctantly. *Oh, he's giving me a chance to pull away...* I sucked hard in response, silently reproaching him for even thinking I could want that, and moaned in approval when he retightened his grip. His sharp hiss lit my veins on fire, and when he followed it with a soft groan, my thighs clamped together. This was him coming undone, and I loved every fucking minute of it.

His salty essence hit my throat in strong spurts that rivaled the man himself, and I swallowed it all, surprising myself probably almost as much as him. This was usually the part I disliked, but as with everything else surrounding Will, it had the opposite impact. I loved sharing this experience with him and knowing I had brought him to this point.

My breasts were so painfully sensitive that I flinched when his knee brushed the stiff peak. His hands clamped down on my shoulders and pulled me upward so fast that my head spun and it took me a minute to realize he'd put me under him again. My mouth was suddenly too occupied by his to voice any sort of reaction to the abrupt shift. His tongue tangled roughly with mine, vying for dominance. I succumbed quickly, too turned on to deny him, and jolted when he tweaked my nipple.

He silenced my cry with his lips and grinned. "And now it's my turn."

His palm went to my thigh and drifted upward beneath my skirt to the place I wanted him most. He drew his finger along the middle of my thong, from my entrance up to my most sensitive point, and applied pressure slowly but firmly. I clutched his arms for support as shock waves exploded through my body. Not an orgasm, but pretty damn close, and it felt oh-so-good.

"You're soaked for me," he whispered against my neck. "I fucking love that." He slid my underwear aside to touch my flesh and slid his finger through my slick folds. "So hot, too. I can't wait to be inside of you, Rachel. To thrust so deep that you feel me for days." His masculine rumble had me quaking with a deep-seated need to see those words come to fruition. He pushed a finger inside of me while his thumb massaged my clit in delirious circles.

"I'm going to take you gently at first, to memorize your moans of pleasure and to introduce you properly to my bed." He demonstrated with his hand below, lightly prodding, and added a second finger. "Then, once you're comfortable and ready, I'll fuck you senseless." He shoved both digits into me hard to punctuate his point and accepted my moan with his mouth. Sensual vibrations shook my nerves all the way down to my toes as he continued his pleasurable assault below.

He hovered over me on his elbow and slid his fingers into my hair to angle my head for a more intense kiss. His tongue mimed his hand below, softly stroking me inside and mounting my pleasure with each seductive caress.

My body moved, seeking more friction from his thumb, and he replied in kind, pressing down hard and circling in a way that had me seeing stars. I dug my nails into his shoulders as tension curled in my lower belly, tightening and quivering.

Oh…
Too much…
So close…
Can't take it anymore…

The orgasm hit me so soundly, so perfectly, throwing my head back and bowing my back off the bed. His palm covered my mouth, silencing the noises I couldn't seem to stop as my body spasmed uncontrollably beneath him. It was even more intense than our first time together, and with it came a storm of unexpected emotion. The gravity of it paralyzed me, leaving me breathless beneath him.

I liked him.

Well and truly liked him.

Which was pretty fucking obvious considering I'd just let him put his hand up my skirt, but this went deeper than physical attraction. My draw to him went beneath the surface, to the heart of the man hovering over me. He lifted his fingers to his mouth and sucked them clean with a groan of approval, then kissed me so hard that I forgot how to think.

"Mmm, I can't wait to properly taste you later," he whispered against my lips. "You're delicious."

Those words should have made me laugh, except I felt the same way about him. I could easily become addicted to his beautiful cock, if I wasn't already.

Will silenced my thoughts with another kiss, drugging me with his affections and luring me out of my head and back into the moment. It was so easy to follow him, to allow him to pull me under his spell and forget everything else.

He took me to a place where liking him was safe.

Where I didn't have to worry about my past or my career.

Where I could be happy and enjoy my life.

Will's world was a place where I could just be me.

I closed my eyes sometime later with a smile not only on my lips but in my heart. There was no question. I liked him. And for the first time in a very long time, I wasn't afraid to embrace it.

20
ORIENTAL LILIES

"Okay. This is amazing." I slipped out of my heels to twirl around the giant living area and skipped over to the floor-to-ceiling windows overlooking Paris. First class had been a treat, but Will's presidential suite took my awe to a whole new level.

"I'll be sure to pass your compliments on to Evan," he replied from the foyer.

I spun around to meet his amused gaze. "We need to explore. Now, please."

"Yes, ma'am." He tipped his nonexistent hat and winked. "Just as soon as I shower and change."

I groaned and waved at the windows. "But Paris."

"It's only eight o'clock in the mornin'. We have plenty of time to sightsee and shop." He kept mentioning that last word—shop. I still didn't know why he insisted on it, but considering I only had a few outfits left, it seemed appropriate. I'd left all my dirty laundry at his house in a basket, waiting for me to take home later, which left my

171

suitcase very empty. Thinking of my bags made me frown.

"Where are my suitcases?" His were by the door.

"In your room," he replied as he pulled a key out of his pocket. "You're across the hall."

"Oh." Right. Of course. I'd followed him in here without even thinking. I held out my hand for the card but somehow found myself in his arms. He tilted my head back for a kiss that melted me from the inside out. This man certainly knew how to use his mouth.

"You're welcome to stay here, but I reserved you a room in case you preferred it, and also for business purposes." He nuzzled his nose against mine and smiled. "There isn't anything in the contract that forbids us from being together, but I'm guessing Baker Brown frowns upon their employees seducing clients."

I snorted. "I'm not the one doing the seducing here, Mershano."

"Those adorable stockings of yours and I disagree, Miss Dawson." He sucked my bottom lip into his mouth and let it go with a pop. "Now I desperately need a shower and to change. Your bags are in your room, but getting ready over there doesn't necessarily mean you'll be sleeping there tonight."

I shivered at the promise in his words. "Tease."

He chuckled darkly. "Oh, I can't wait to redefine that word for you later." He gave my ass a squeeze before picking up his bag and heading up the stairs to what I assumed was the master bedroom. Mershano Suites was known for opulence, but this took elegance to a whole new level. I'd have to ask Sarah later how she was dealing with this lifestyle. Something told me she was surviving it just fine.

An uncharacteristic giggle escaped me. This couldn't be my reality. It seemed too fantastic, too happy, to be my life. Shaking my head, I slipped on my pumps and picked up my purse. My room was directly across from Will's, just as he said, and I realized with a start that between the two of us, we owned the entire floor.

"Filthy rich," I muttered as I opened the door to a room that rivaled his own. "Ridiculously rich." I knew the Mershanos had an insane amount of money, but to experience it was very different from just recognizing the family wealth. This was how Will grew up, yet he'd chosen to invest in a vineyard and a relatively modest home when he could have inherited a superior position with Mershano Suites and lived somewhere like this. Knowing that only made me respect him and his accomplishments more.

I picked through my bags, leaving them near the door since I would most likely put them in his room later, and started toward the stairs. That's when I noticed the giant vase of oriental lilies sitting on the foyer table. Odd. Will didn't have that in his room. I set my clothes down on the bottom step and moved forward to investigate. Maybe the firm sent them? Or Will? But why? And how did they know my favorite flower? Were these even produced in France?

A card sat elegantly beside it. I picked it up and froze at the familiar scrawl.

Thinking of you, baby girl.
Enjoy Paris, and good luck this week.
Yours,
Ryan

I read it over and over and over again. He knew my hotel room and number. But worse than that, this card was handwritten by him. I would recognize his elegant script anywhere. Did he have it flown here with the lilies? Or worse... was he in Paris too?

My legs gave out beneath me as I crumpled to the floor. What if he was staying in this hotel? Did Mershano Suites usually include a delivery receipt? Or a notice of being in the room? Was he here now, watching me react? My gaze darted around feverishly, and suddenly the suite felt far too big. He could be anywhere. In the bedroom, waiting for me, the bathroom, a closet…

Fear paralyzed me, making it impossible to move, to even begin searching. Had he really tracked me down to Paris? Showing up unannounced at my apartment was bad enough, but this was full-blown obsession. How had he gone from leaving me alone for months to stalking me to another country? Did he suspect my feelings for Will?

"Oh God," I whispered.

The first man I dated after Ryan was on inactive duty for only two months when he received a call requesting his return. I didn't know much about the military, but I knew that wasn't a coincidence, especially when Ryan left a note under my door saying, "*What a shame. And I hear Afghanistan is particularly brutal right now.*"

My second date was more of a random one-night stand. A week after, I found a newspaper sitting on my coffee table with an article circled. The headline read, "Man Mugged near Millennium Park," and the picture showcased the man I'd picked up from the bar. He was alive but hurt. Because of me.

And now Will…

Tears streamed down my cheeks. No. I couldn't let anything happen to him. Not because of knowing me. It wasn't fair. I clutched my stomach as sobs wracked my body so hard that I couldn't breathe. I hated Ryan more than I ever had in that moment. More than the first time he hit me, or all the times he choked me until I submitted, or even the one time he knocked me out. The emotional torture was his worst punishment, had changed me irrevocably, but the fear of him hurting Will nearly killed me.

I don't just like him; I really like him, I realized. *Maybe even love him.*

It hit me suddenly, so wholeheartedly, that my tears temporarily halted. I knew I liked him and cared for him, but it went so much deeper than that.

My affection for him lived in a place inside me no one else had ever breached, even Ryan. Will had fought for me to trust him, to give myself to him wholly, and somehow he'd captured so much more of me than either of us expected. Or maybe he knew. Maybe he even felt the same. He'd more than proven that this was no simple game of affection for him; otherwise, I would have ended up naked beneath him two nights ago. And his comments in his bed and on the plane hinted at his unflinching commitment.

My hands trembled as I pressed them into my temples and rocked on the floor. It didn't matter how Will felt at this point. What mattered was how I felt and what I was willing to do to protect him.

The obvious choice was to flee, to run back to Ryan and beg forgiveness. If I groveled enough, maybe he would let this mishap slide. I'd have to give up my position at the firm, and essentially my life, but it would keep Will safe. Love was about sacrifice, and I would make the ultimate one by giving up all semblance of happiness. But love could also be about strength and unity and trust.

Trust.

"*You will trust again, Rachel.*" Will's words from the other night radiated through my heart. He said them with such conviction, such promise.

He believes in me.

But could I believe in myself?

My tears dried as I lay there searching for the strength I needed. Reaching out for help always left me feeling inferior, like I couldn't do it on my own and had to rely on others. But there was something to be said about recognizing when a situation went beyond one's control and required assistance.

Those flowers lurking above my head were an indication of just how out of control this situation had gotten already. Knowing that he might be in France, or in this very hotel, watching me? It was insane. He'd lost his ever-loving mind. Going back to him with my tail between my legs would only validate his actions. I couldn't do that. I wouldn't survive it.

I looked around the room, half expecting to see Ryan standing victorious over me, but found myself alone. My purse sat forgotten in the foyer near my suitcase. I crawled over to it, not caring at all how it destroyed my stockings. The card I wanted sat where I left it three years ago. I had no idea if the number still worked, but knowing Mark, it did. My hand trembled as I keyed each one into my cell. The call would cost a small fortune, being as it was overseas, but I had no other choice. I needed help, and something told me he knew this day was coming.

It rang once before someone picked up without a greeting.

"Mark?" Was that my voice? I sounded so broken. So scared. "Please tell me it's you." Because I wasn't sure I had the strength or courage to make this call again.

"Where are you?" His deep rumble had me weeping all over again.

"Paris."

"Are you in immediate danger?"

I looked around the empty room and shivered. "I d-don't think so." If Ryan were here, he would have come out of hiding already.

"Give me five minutes," he replied and hung up.

21
COURAGE TO TELL ALL

Will probably wanted to know what the hell was taking so long, but he didn't press when I told him I needed another half hour. When Mark called me back precisely five minutes later, it was from another number I didn't recognize. He let out a low whistle now after I finished telling him about the last month and the supposed wedding. I also told him about how Ryan handled my previous dates, and everything from the last few years.

"I don't know what to do," I whispered. "I can't let him hurt Will."

Mark was quiet so long that I thought I'd lost him. But a glance at the screen showed our connection was still active.

"I'm going to need to do some digging," was his vague reply. "In the meantime, you need to tell Mershano what's going on. If that psychopath is in Paris, which is a very real possibility, then he needs to be aware of the situation. You can't keep all this to yourself anymore, Rachel." He delivered that last line with reproach and served as the only indication that he was disappointed in me for keeping this to myself for so long.

"He's going to think I'm crazy." Or worse. He could find me weak for dating Ryan.

"No, he's going to think you're brave," Mark corrected. "You're asking for help instead of running back to Albertson like a coward."

His statement made me flinch. He and my brother were never ones to mince words, which I supposed was why they were best friends.

"You were wondering why he's upped his pursuit over the last month," he continued. "Easy. His long-term-senator father is about to step down, and Ryan wants the job, but he needs a wife first. The voters love their family values, and his running as a bachelor isn't going to look great. You're a political move for him, and one he thinks he can control."

"Because I've let him control me all along," I finished for him, wincing.

"Yes, and no. Men like Albertson enjoy a good challenge. The minute you cave to his demands, he'll get bored, but he also needs to rein you in and the clock is ticking, hence the desperation. And that makes a power-hungry man like him dangerous. You need to tell Mershano. He has the resources at his disposal to keep you safe; otherwise, I'd be on the next flight out."

"That's asking a hell of a lot from him. I mean—"

"No, it's not," he cut in. "You don't seem to realize who you're dating."

"But we're not dating. We're—"

"You're dating. Stop making excuses and talk to him. That's an order, Dawson."

I scoffed at that. "You're as bad as Caleb." He used to boss me around all the time as a kid, and come to think of it, Mark did too.

"No, I'm much worse than your brother. Now go talk

to Mershano. I'll be in touch when I learn more." He hung up without further explanation. I jumped as someone knocked at the door not a second later. My heart raced in my chest, beating a static rhythm that drowned out my hearing. What if it was Ryan? I hadn't bolted the door. If he had a key, he could enter.

My fears were realized as the snick of a card penetrated my ears. I started to scramble backward, when I heard Will's deep baritone call out, "Hello?"

A squeak escaped my mouth as relief undid me on the floor, followed swiftly by mortification. *Oh God. Talk about seeing me at my worst...*

Mark's confidence that Will would find me brave crumbled at my feet. I had to look half-crazed lying here with torn-up stockings, my hair half-undone, and clothes crumpled. Not to mention my face... I tried to hide in my arms and tucked my knees tightly to my chest.

"Jesus, what the hell happened?" Will's hands were on me a second later, causing me to flinch on instinct. He immediately withdrew, which only made me want crawl further into myself and bawl.

"Rachel," he murmured. "Talk to me, sweetheart. Are you hurt?"

I shook my head and bit my lip so hard I tasted blood. Opening up about this to Mark had been hard, but this felt like breaking open my chest. Where could I even begin? What if it changed the way he felt or the way he acted? Seeing pity in his eyes would destroy me. It was the last expression I ever wanted to see from him. All the pent-up heat and insinuating looks and comments were what I enjoyed. They would disappear once he knew the truth.

Stop making excuses and talk to him, Mark's demand repeated in my head. He was right. I needed to tell Will, not to ask him to help me, but so he could help himself. Warning him about Ryan was the best way for me to protect Will. He couldn't guard himself against an unknown threat, but he could potentially stop a known one.

I blew out a long breath and fought for the courage I needed to explain. My hands shook so hard I had to clasp them tightly together to keep my arms from vibrating.

"Please talk to me, Rachel," he whispered. The pain in his voice hammered my rib cage hard, piercing right through my heart. God, he thought this was about him. Of course he did. What else could set me off in such a short time? I nearly laughed at the absurdity of it. But it was his deep breath, followed by a shaky sigh, that did me in. To shatter his confidence so irrevocably that he not only feared touching me but also refrained from speaking? No, that wasn't fair to him at all. He deserved better, so much better.

I swallowed thickly, my throat convulsing around invisible cotton balls. It took two tries to clear my throat before I could start, and even then, my voice cracked. "I need to t-tell you about my ex."

Will remained silent while I told him how I met Ryan, when we started dating, how things began as a fairy tale and ended in disaster, and then how he refused to accept that we weren't together. I detailed what happened to the only two men I associated with after our breakup, explained why I stopped dating, and then showed him the texts on my phone from the last few weeks.

"And now, I think you might be in danger too," I concluded with a gesture to the flowers and the card on the floor. He stood and strode over to read it. I hadn't realized how close he'd been to me on the ground until his body heat disappeared, leaving me shivering. He'd sat beside me with his back against the wall, arms folded over his drawn-up knees, listening with an unreadable expression.

The pity I expected never came, which helped steady my emotions. My eyes burned from the aftermath of crying so hard, and I likely resembled a drowned cat, but at least the blubbering had stopped.

"I'm so sorry for dragging you into this," I whispered. "I'm so, so sorry." I bit my lip to keep it from trembling. No way would I break down again.

Will set the card on the table and stalked toward me with an emotion I never wanted to see directed at me. Fury. I deserved it for putting him in this situation, but it hurt nonetheless. At least it wasn't pity. My eyes fell to my hands as he crouched in front of me. It was cowardly, but I couldn't bear to watch what came next. *Accusations, yelling, guilt...*

"Rachel." His soft tone did not match the thunderous expression I'd seen only seconds ago. Nor did the featherlight touch against my hand. "Don't apologize on his behalf ever again."

That was not what I expected him to say at all. Confusion mingled with my unease, creasing my brow. *What?*

"You didn't drag me into anything, and none of this is your fault." He gently tipped my chin to meet his gaze. It was less stormy than I expected, but anger colored his features and tightened his lips. "Thank you for telling me. For trusting me."

"You're not mad?" I asked, incredulous.

"Oh, I'm furious, but not with you." He cupped my cheeks and stared deep into my eyes. "You're a strong woman, Rachel. To tell me what you just did? I know that wasn't easy. If anything, I'm proud and floored by your courage." His thumbs swept beneath my lashes as he placed a tender kiss against my forehead. "Do you think he's in Paris?"

I cleared the emotion from my throat. "I don't know. Mark is researching for me."

"Mark?"

Right. I hadn't gotten to that part yet. "Remember how I mentioned being closer to my brother's best friend than to my brother?" At his nod, I continued. "His name is Mark. He's the one who helped me escape Ryan the first time." I shivered at the memory. The pain. Will settled in front of me, his knees braced on either side of mine like a protective cage, shielding me from my past. I pressed into him, craving his gentleness.

"I told you he, R-Ryan, preferred emotional over physical pain, but the day I left…" I coughed again to settle the uncertainty stirring inside. *I'm safe.* "That, well, that was the first and only time he knocked me out." I cradled my stomach on instinct, and Will observed the move. "He slapped me first, forcing me to the ground, and then he kicked me so hard that he cracked my rib and knocked the wind out of me. Then he…" I rubbed my neck.

"He choked you," Will murmured.

"Yes. It was one of his favorite forms of… of… pain. But this time he didn't let go, and when I woke up, he was gone." It'd been the most horrifying experience of my life, not being able to breathe and seeing that dead look in his eyes that said he had no intention of ever letting me go. I thought he was going to kill me that day. And when he didn't, I vowed never to be in that situation again.

"I can't even remember what set him off, something about me working too many hours, but I'd never seen him so angry. I called Mark that night, told him I needed help, and he picked me up. He never asked any questions, but he knew, and he offered me his apartment as a safe haven. He's with the FBI, or so he says, and travels a lot. It worked for a few days until Ryan found me. I still don't know how, but I suspect he followed me home from work."

I shook my head, not wanting to digress. "Anyway, I've told you the rest, about how he has never accepted that we're not together. And as you can see, he still feels I'm his." I waved to the flowers again.

"And Mark is checking to see if Ryan is in Paris?"

"Yeah. He has access to certain resources, hence why I think his FBI cover story is bullshit." Not that it was relevant to this conversation—well, not much anyway. "I called him when I saw the flowers. He gave me a card with this mysterious number to call if I ever needed him after what happened three years ago, and I didn't know what else to do, so I used it."

"It was the right thing to do, although I'm still not quite sure what he's going to do."

Despite the direness of our conversation, I had to smile. "I never know what Mark's going to do, but I trust him."

Will considered me for a long moment and nodded. "Then I'll trust him too."

"What?"

"If you trust him, I trust him." So simple, so earnest. "Now, what else did he say?"

"Uh, he ordered me to tell you because you have resources, and he felt comfortable enough with that to not be on the next flight here." I frowned on that last bit. I'd been so caught up in the "Tell Will" part that I hadn't considered his flippant comment about hopping a flight to France. Such a Mark thing to say.

"I like him already," Will murmured. "And he's right. I need to make a few calls, but I want to go about our day as if none of this happened."

I started. "Excuse me?"

"If Ryan is in Paris, then we need him to assume it's business as usual between us. It'll keep him calmer, and, hopefully, rational, which is a term I use lightly in his regard." The face he made would have provoked a laugh from me if it weren't regarding Ryan. "We'll keep our routine," he continued. "We'll go shopping, do a little sightseeing, and maybe have dinner somewhere. He's not going to make a public scene, because he's a politician who knows better than that. So we enjoy our day, the best we can, and don't let him spoil your first trip to France."

"You're serious."

"Very."

"You want me to pretend like I don't have an insane stalker of an ex hunting me down?"

"Yep."

"And if he pops up?"

"You let me deal with that."

I started to shake my head. "You don't understand, Will. His family has connections to all sorts of people and government organizations, and I don't think they are all legal." Some of the family friends I met while we were dating did not strike me as the type of friends Ryan made in the Boy Scouts.

He leveled me with a look. "You think I'm afraid of an influential family?"

Right. Okay. "But the Mershano family owns an international business. Ryan's entire livelihood is built on the back of politics, which isn't the same. They don't fight fair."

Will snorted. "Trust me, they're more alike than you realize. I'm not afraid of him, Rachel. He might have a slew of friends, but I do, too, and, darlin', when it comes to you, I'll never fight fair."

The look in his eyes when he said those last few words was so fierce that I couldn't move, couldn't breathe. Holy shit. I couldn't decide if I liked that look or if I should fear it. Intensity poured from him as he continued to study me, letting me see the harder side of him that hid beneath a veneer of charm. This was the man groomed by an influential empire, the one who ran in similar circles to Ryan.

I swallowed. That look served as a reminder of how alike they could be and also demonstrated how different they were from one another. Ryan luxuriated in his family money and hadn't worked a hard day in his life, while Will fought for everything he owned despite having access to an easy way out. One opted for politics, while the other chose to challenge himself to try something new.

"Okay," I agreed.

"Okay to having a normal day?" he asked, clarifying.

I nodded. "Yes, as normal as it can be."

His dimples flashed for the first time since he entered my room. "Oh, I fully take that as a challenge, darlin'. I promise you won't be thinking of any man except me by the end of the day."

Only Will would find a way to turn this situation into something bordering on amusement. I almost smiled, but I wasn't quite there yet. The fact that I was so close, however, told me he would have no problem fulfilling his promise. Still, I couldn't let him win that easily. "So cocky."

"Confident," he corrected. "Now, how about you come over to my suite to shower and change while I talk to a few of *my* friends." He stressed the word *my* so I knew what that meant. *Ryan isn't the only one with contacts.*

He pushed to his feet and held out a hand to help me up. I went without hesitating.

Trust, he had said the other night. I hadn't understood what he meant, but I did now. He knew all along that I was hiding something, that I was on the verge of opening up—but withdrawing—and now all my barriers were down. No more fighting, no more hiding. It was time to live again. Freely.

22
FASHION SHOW

I studied the dress in the mirror and frowned. Will was right about shopping being a good distraction. I walked out and narrowed my eyes at his relaxed form on the couch. Because yeah, apparently, this designer boutique he'd dragged me into had a formal waiting area for wealthy men.

"No." I had to say it on principle. The dress was lovely; it clung to my curves in a subtle way that still made it business appropriate, and the blue popped against my skin. It even hit at my knees, making it a respectable length. But it was in no way worth the price tag.

He looked me over with keen interest. "Oh, yes."

"Tell me again why this is better than my skirt suit."

"Because it's French."

"Still not following that logic."

"Fashion and appearance are a staple in France, and even more so in business." At my raised eyebrow, he continued. "The French associate dress with status and

186

success, which means we need to show up in style. Hence…" He waved a hand at my dress.

I pursed my lips. "Surely there are less expensive stores."

"Of course, but in France, you buy the best you can afford."

Aha! "Well, I can't afford this." Too bad, so sad. I started to turn, when his retort froze me in place.

"Perhaps, but I can, and you're directly associated with me as my legal counsel. We're buying the dress and the two you tried on before it."

Damn it. I'd loved those, too, but I kept putting them back because of the cost.

"We'll need shoes as well, and lingerie, of course. Assuming you want more stockings?" Even without looking at him, I knew he was eyeing the ones on my legs.

"And what are you shopping for?" He had yet to try anything on or search for his own clothes. We spent the morning at a café near the Eiffel Tower, then took a long walk around it for sightseeing before we meandered this way to what he referred to as the hottest shopping area in all of Paris. What he really meant was "most expensive." Though, the clothes were lovely.

"Are you eager for me to model some things for you?" he teased.

I looked over my shoulder at him. "Actually, yes. I am." If he wanted to distract me from the Ryan situation, he should model for me naked. No way would I be able to think of anything else with all his muscular perfection on display.

Challenge lit his eyes. "I'll model for you if you model for me."

Did I say the naked thing out loud, or did he just read that from my eyes? "But I am modeling for you." I gestured innocently to my dress in an attempt to weigh his reaction.

"Lingerie," was his single-word reply. My cheeks heated.

"That's hardly a fair trade."

He arched that arrogant brow of his. "You didn't ask what I would be modeling in return, gorgeous."

"And what are you offering?"

His elbows went to his knees as he leaned toward me. "Whatever you want, clothing or otherwise. Your choice."

"Anything I want?" I repeated. "Are you sure you want to play that game with me, Mershano?"

"Absolutely, because I'll be the one selecting the lingerie you model." My lips parted at his boldness. His gaze ran over me hungrily as he added, "Don't worry, darlin'. I'll pick out stockings for you too."

When he said he wanted to forget what happened this morning, at least for the day, he wasn't joking. I expected all sorts of awkwardness between us, but he treated me just as he usually did. Sexy as always. I considered his offer. There were some ridiculous outfits in the first store we went to. Seeing him in one of those would be more than worth a few poses in lingerie sets for him.

"You're on," I said decidedly. If anything, it would be a fun way to spend our afternoon, and I was determined to do just that.

After reflecting on this morning's events, I concluded that Ryan was trying to manipulate me. He wanted to ruin this trip for me, and he knew the best way to do that was to scare me into submission through a creepy romantic gesture. Ignoring the flowers in my room and enjoying my day was the opposite of what he wanted. Leaving the hotel today with my head held high loosened a notch of Ryan's control because, rather than wallow in fear, I decided to live. I suspected Will knew all of that already, which was why he suggested we venture out today.

He paid for the dresses and asked for a courier to deliver them to his room at the hotel. We hadn't given up the one in my name, but we had no intention of using it.

Before we left this morning, Mershano Suites confirmed that the flowers were delivered to the reception and they carried them up to the room. Will gave the staff a photo of Ryan and asked them to notify him immediately if they spotted anyone resembling my ex wandering the grounds. I wasn't there for the discussion, but I saw the reverence casted his way as we left. He might not be involved in the management chain for the hotel, but they knew who he was and respected him for it.

"How about here," Will said as we walked by a boutique that catered to men. A peek in the windows showed an array of fun options for his future fashion show.

I opened the door while replying, "Oh, this will be fun."

Thirty minutes later, Will headed off to the fitting area with a shake of his head while I made myself comfortable on the plush couch. A sharply dressed tailor stood nearby, ready to assist Will with any suits he intended to purchase. I picked a few, mainly because the man looked amazing in them, but I also threw in some random colorful outfits and scarves just to tease him. Then he walked out in one of the odd combinations, and my jaw dropped.

No. Fucking. Way.

"That's not fair," I whispered. The pink-and-orange combination had looked ridiculous on the mannequin, yet it somehow worked on him. He tucked his hands into the pockets of the tight jeans and did a slow twirl that drew my attention to his fine ass. "I'm going to need you to stand just like that for at least ten minutes."

He met my gaze in the mirror. "Turnabout is fair play, darlin'."

I scanned his backside. Admiring this view in exchange for modeling lingerie in a similar fashion? "Worth it." If I had my phone, I would have snapped a photo, but I left it at the hotel with my purse. The last thing I wanted was a way for Ryan to track me down.

Will must have sensed the turn in my thoughts, because he did a little jig that would have made me laugh if those jeans weren't so damn tight. Instead, my throat went dry.

"You need to buy those."

He snorted. "They're impractical."

"I wasn't going to recommend you wear them while working in the vineyard, Mershano."

That eyebrow went up. "Yeah? Come here for a second."

"Uh, why?"

"I want to show you something."

I so did not trust that innocent look or tone. He was up to something. I unfolded myself from the plush couch and moved to stand before him. Will asked the tailor for a glass of champagne in French, which I translated to mean he wanted a moment of privacy. The elder gentleman gave a nod and disappeared, leaving us alone in the dressing area.

"Take them off." His deep baritone hit me in all the right places.

"Your jeans?" A stupid question. That's obviously what he meant, but he couldn't be serious. I took in his dilated pupils and expression and swallowed. Okay, yeah, he wasn't teasing. "Here?" It came out in a whisper.

"Yes." Still no hint of jest, and if the bulge growing beneath his zipper was anything to go by, he really did want me to remove his pants.

Not the place I expected this to happen, but the forbidden nature of his command sent a shiver of delight down my spine. A naked Will? Yes, please. I ran my hands up his thighs, loving the feel of his muscles bunching along the way. Heat radiated from him, emboldening my attentions. His hardening cock pulsed beneath my finger as I traced the impressive length up to the gold button. It flicked open with ease, and I drew the zipper down to reveal his navy briefs.

A glance down had me licking my lips. "I approve." Especially since it was the pair I picked out with his clothes.

"Keep going." Lust laced through his tone and

darkened his gaze. He didn't have to tell me twice. Except when I tried to push them down, they barely moved. I put more power into it and felt a surge of frustration when they still failed to cooperate.

"Problem?" he asked, voice low.

I pursed my lips as the purpose of this game became obvious. When he referred to their practicality, he meant they were too tight to enjoy the benefits. It was false advertising. *Hey, look at my assets, but good luck getting to them.* "At least they look good on," I muttered.

"But what's the point if you can't take them off?"

Oh, I could, but it would dampen the moment. Just like it did now. I narrowed my eyes up at him. "You win this round, Mershano. Next outfit."

"Yes, ma'am." He tilted that nonexistent hat at me again as he disappeared behind the curtain. I snickered a little when it took him over ten minutes to change, which was just in time for the tailor to return with the champagne. I suspected he took longer than needed to give us privacy.

Will thanked him and set his flute aside to fix the collar of his shirt in the mirror. It gave me a great view of his backside, which was as flawless as ever in his dark suit. The navy blue was almost black, and the jacket fit him perfectly, though the tailor made a few comments about arm lengths in French. They conversed for several minutes as the white-haired man measured the inseams of the pants, his arm, and a few other interesting places. When he finished, Will looked over his shoulder at me.

"Fishing for compliments?" I teased. Not like his ego needed it.

"Always."

I rolled my eyes. "You look amazing and you know it."

He smiled broadly at that. "Amazing?"

"Handsome, gorgeous, mouthwatering, delicious." I threw them all out there, each deepening the dimples at his cheeks. "Oh, whatever. We both know your ego doesn't need any more stroking."

"From you? I always welcome stroking." He winked and disappeared behind the curtain to try on several more outfits, all of them equally breathtaking.

"Well, at least you have a backup job should this vineyard thing not work out," I said after we left. He left his suits with the tailor, promising to be back in the morning for a final fitting. That kind of turnaround couldn't be typical, especially since tomorrow was Sunday, but the store seemed more than happy to accommodate him.

"Yeah, and what's that?" Will asked, referring to my backup-job comment.

"Modeling." He could easily work in the fashion industry or star in one of those male fitness magazines.

He laughed and shook his head. "I think I'll stick with my vineyards, darlin'." His arm settled on my shoulders as he pulled me into him. "But I vote we see how you measure up as a lingerie model."

I scoffed at that. "Uh, that would be more suitable for Sarah." She had curves in all the right places, while mine were too slim for that industry. I had the height for it, and maybe even the legs, but my B-cups weren't all that exciting.

"I'll be the judge of that," he said as we entered our final store. Will greeted the female storeowner and introduced me as his "lady friend" who required at least two weeks of undergarments. Everything was in French, which was on par with the rest of our trip so far, including his list of desired lingerie items. Apparently, he knew his way around women's underwear better than I did, something I didn't want to think on too heavily.

I frowned when the saleswoman started bagging all the items he requested. "Am I'm not trying these on first?" He'd already proven to know my sizes, so it shouldn't have surprised me, but I expected him to request I model them first.

"Oh, you will. Later." He nailed me with a look that left me weak in the knees. Hunger mingled with promise in those dark depths and sent my thoughts directly south. "You still owe me a modeling session, Rachel. And I intend to collect on that soon."

My lips parted, but I had no words. He couldn't mean...

"I held up my side of our bargain," he continued in that deep rumble. "Not my fault you chose the store as a location."

"Not fair," I managed in a whisper.

He grinned at that. "I warned you, darlin'. With you, I'll never play fair. Now, where should we go to dinner?"

23
SWEET FREEDOM

Will kept his promise. By the time we returned to the hotel, Ryan was the last thing on my mind. Then my phone binged as we entered the suite.

Several emotions barreled into me at once, leaving me light-headed. Panic, annoyance, and fury battled for purpose as I moved on shaky legs toward my purse on the dining table.

"Rachel?"

"I'm okay," I replied. And oddly, I found that to be true. The crippling fear from this morning fled throughout the day, leaving a simmering anger in its place. Ryan wished to remind me of his control from afar and used a tactic he knew would unsettle me to do it. He wanted to ruin this experience for me, and potentially my career in the process. Without Baker Brown, I would have nothing. What did he expect? That I would turn to him for help? I'd sooner move home to Indiana.

I picked up my phone and thumbed through the

myriad of text messages with a growl.

Glad to see your flight arrived safely. Love you.

Did you get my flowers?

Where are you?

Why are you ignoring me?

The messages went on and on. I read them in a daze until a random photo message appeared from a private number. A short note accompanied it.

He's still in Chicago. —MK

I studied the photo of Ryan and showed Will. "That's him outside his building. He's not in Paris."

"Did Mark send that to you?"

"Yeah." I had no idea how he captured the image, but if he said Ryan was still in the United States, then I believed him. "That doesn't explain the note." Which left me a little uneasy, but at least my insane ex wasn't lurking in Paris somewhere.

"You're sure it's his handwriting?"

"Absolutely." His penmanship haunted my nightmares. "He wrote it." I scrolled through the rest of the messages, looking for anything work related, and turned it off when I found nothing. Not responding to Ryan felt right. He hated it when I ignored him, and usually ramped up his efforts in contacting me as a result, but he couldn't touch me here. At least not anytime soon. Or maybe ever.

Telling Mark and Will this morning about Ryan was one of the hardest moments of my life, yet confiding in them had changed me on a fundamental level. It hurt at first, a lot, but as the pain subsided, a sense of lightness came over me. My conscience was finally clear, and for the first time in what felt like forever, I wasn't alone.

I met Will's gentle gaze and felt the final piece of ice crack deep inside of my chest. This man, this stubborn, confident man, had set me free. He managed to chip away at my chilly demeanor with his calm consistency. I may have started as a challenge for him, but somewhere along the way, this bond between us grew roots and created something beautiful.

His thumb wiped a tear from my cheek that I hadn't felt fall. "Rachel…"

I pressed my finger to his lips. "Don't say anything. Please. I need this. I need to feel." Because I'd gone so long without it. Ryan had terrified me into a level of submission I never quite escaped, until today. Until I picked up my phone and called Mark. Until I confided in Will.

It felt like a lifetime ago even though it was this morning. But this change was a long time coming. The process started when I called off the engagement, but then I sat in a stagnant state until I met Will. He challenged me on a level no one else ever had, and then he'd patiently waited for me to *see* him. To understand what could be between us, if I let it.

Despite his endless flirtation, he never pushed me into anything I didn't want, and was even willing to walk away from me and the firm when he sensed his meddling had gone too far. It pissed me off at the time, but his relentless pursuit relit the fire in my soul, reminded me of who I was, and gave me something worth fighting for. And with it came the courage I needed to finally break Ryan's control. Because that's what happened this morning. His initial attack shoved me to the ground, but I picked myself up and decided to help myself instead of wallow, and earned my freedom in the process.

And now, I could feel again.

Wholly.

Completely.

Endlessly.

I wrapped my arms around Will's neck and went up onto my toes to kiss him. Everything I felt, all the happiness, sadness, fear, anger, and pent-up passion, went from my mouth to his, and he accepted it all. His hand slid into my hair, holding me to him as he returned the favor with his tongue, telling me without words that he understood.

He lifted me off the ground and set me on the table. My knees spread as he stepped between them, bunching my skirt up along the way, and devastated me with his mouth. It hadn't taken him long to take control, not that I minded. Caving to his commanding touch felt right. He knew what I wanted, what I needed, and I trusted him to take me there.

My legs tingled as he trailed his fingers up the hem of my stockings to the garters. He didn't unfasten them, but he explored them thoroughly. The brief strokes against my inner thighs weren't enough. I craved friction several inches higher, and my breasts were begging for release. Too many clothes separated me from him. I needed to feel everything he had to offer.

I hooked my calves around his thighs to force him closer and ran my hands down his back to his firm ass. When I squeezed him, hard, he chuckled.

"Feeling impatient?" he teased.

I bit his lower lip in response and slid my palms to his lower abdomen. He said nothing as I unbuttoned his dress shirt and pushed it from his shoulders. That left him clad in a tight white undershirt that showcased all his delicious muscle. I groaned in frustration when he caught my wrists and planted them on either side of my hips against the wood.

"My turn." The words were spoken against my neck as he started to kiss his way down to my blouse. His eyes held mine as he deftly unfastened the first button with his teeth.

Holy wow, that's hot. He continued his descent all the way down my abdomen, never faltering. When the last one popped open, he released my wrists and slipped the fabric down my arms before tossing it to the floor.

His wicked mouth played along the neckline of my camisole, nipping and licking and driving me crazy. I tried again to remove his undershirt, which he let me do this time, and my top joined his, leaving me clad in a lacy black bra.

"Mmm, for the record, you still owe me a proper modeling show." His smoldering gaze snagged mine. "But I wholeheartedly approve of this preview."

I played my fingers over his abdomen, exploring each hard ridge and divot. "You're not the only one who approves." I pressed an open-mouthed kiss against his pec and licked a path up to his neck. He tasted like sex, spice, and sin all wrapped up in a masculine bow. "Take me to bed, Will," I whispered. "Please."

He gripped my hips and dragged me to the edge of the table so my sensitive center aligned perfectly with his hot arousal. I squirmed against him, but he held me still as his intense gaze captured mine.

"I want to, but if we do this, we do it right, and we fight for it." His lips whispered across mine in a soft caress that left me yearning for so much more, but he wasn't done. "We do this, Rachel, and you're mine. Just as I'm yours. There will be no one else. Do you understand?"

Mine. I liked how that sounded. It wasn't so much possessive but rather a promise he wanted us to make to each other. "You want commitment."

"Yes."

"And long-term." He didn't say that, but I inferred it from his tone and previous comments.

"Absolutely." No hesitation lurked in his voice or in his expression, though he was studying me intently. I couldn't blame him. We both knew that, a week ago, I would have flat out refused. Hell, two days ago, I would have said no. But Will's incessant hammering shattered the wall surrounding my heart, setting it free to feel for the first time in years.

And it only seemed fitting that he was the one I wanted. The one I felt comfortable enough with to try having a relationship again. The one I trusted not to hurt me.

I swallowed the words battering for purpose in my

mouth. There was so much I wanted to say, so much I needed him to know, to understand, but nothing could convey the feelings kindling deep inside me. Showing him was the only option. I kissed him and unleashed all my inner chaos, my anxiety, the innate fragility of my trust in him, and the overwhelming emotion overtaking my soul. It came out of me like a storm, and my tongue was the vessel. He accepted it all, his mouth answering in kind, as he swallowed my darkest fears and reaffirmed my place at his side.

Our embrace started as a flurry of passion that evolved into something darkly intimate as he lightly drew down the zipper of my skirt. It left my lacy black thong exposed at the back. He traced his fingers over it and groaned.

"Your penchant for lingerie slays me, darlin'." He lifted me off the table by my ass and set me on my feet. A wiggle of my hips sent the skirt to the ground, and then I was in the air again with my legs around his waist. His lips captured mine again, picking up right where he left off, as he carried me to the bedroom. My heart kicked up a beat at the show of strength and confidence, then it went into overdrive when he dropped me onto the bed. I lifted onto my elbows to admire the view as he removed first his belt and then those sexy slacks. His tight black boxer briefs barely contained his erection.

That's going to be inside me soon... I squeezed my thighs together with a moan as the image assaulted me. *All those muscles working as he moves over me...* "Fuck."

He chuckled and moved over me on the bed. "That's three times you've said that while in my bed. I'm about to take you up on that offer." His lips closed around my nipple through the lace, causing me to arch into him. I'd never been more turned on in my life, and we weren't even naked yet.

"Will..." It was part plea, part annoyance. The foreplay was killing me.

"Patience," he murmured, switching breasts. I needed

the bra off. Now. It abraded my tender skin in a near-painful way. I unsnapped the clasp at my back and quickly found both my wrists captured in one of his hands above my head. He tsked. "That's the opposite of what I said, darlin'."

I wrapped my legs around his waist and rubbed against him. "This is me not listening. Fuck me, Mershano."

Molten chocolate stared down at me, and my thighs squeezed in anticipation. Shit. Will on a good day was gorgeous, but this? So. Incredibly. Hot. I wanted to weep with joy as he slid my bra away from my breasts and up my arms. Then I felt him tying my wrists together with the lace. A glance upward showed him securing my hands to the headboard. With my own fucking bra. I tugged on instinct, but the fabric didn't budge.

"What are you doing?"

"Finishing my exploration," he replied with a nip against my neck. "No squirming, gorgeous." With him lounging over me like some predatory cat? Yeah, right. But when I tried to shift my hips to meet his, he stilled me with his hands on my thighs, and then he sucked my nipple deep into his mouth.

"Oh!" That skilled tongue of his drew circles in the most delicious of patterns. *To feel that against my clit...* My legs shook with the thought. "More," I begged.

He ignored me and licked a path to my other breast to restart the sensual torture. I was a quivering mess by the time his tongue trailed downward over my belly to the top of my thong. Those damn hands kept me from tilting upward like I wanted, and when he skipped over the place I needed him most, I growled. His teeth scraped my inner thigh in response, followed by open-mouthed kisses that I wished were a few inches higher.

"Mmm, I'd like to keep this on," he murmured as he nibbled just north of my garter. "Which means," he continued, his hands sliding up to grasp my lace thong at the sides, "these need to come off."

I gasped as he gave them a tug and snapped the elastic in half. My ruined thong disappeared in a careless toss over his shoulder.

"You…" My complaint died on a moan as he licked my exposed flesh all the way up to the point I needed him most.

"You taste amazing." His intimate murmur left me aching in the neediest of ways. "Hang on, Rachel. I'm going to devour you."

He led with his tongue, and, oh, that mouth of his did not disappoint. He gave my warm center the same treatment as my breasts, except this time he licked deep and used his teeth to draw out my shudders.

Tension built low in my body, straining my limbs and bringing tears to my eyes. It felt like he'd teased me forever with his endless games of anticipation, and now all that emotion culminated deep inside.

His name was both a blessing and a curse on my tongue, until, finally, I felt it—that elusive sensation of bliss unfurling and tingling my nerve endings. Just as I teetered on the edge of explosion, Will pulled away, making me scream in frustration and desire. My vision went black with the insanity of it, and when I finally refocused, it was to find him kneeling over me. Naked.

And, wow, was he a specimen to behold. I hadn't seen the whole picture on the plane, and now that it was laid out in front of me, I couldn't breathe.

"Mmm, hold that thought, darlin'." He rolled on a condom that came from God only knew where, all the while watching me in that knowing way of his, and then he lowered himself to his elbows on either side of my head. His hot member rested against my aching core as he kissed me with a reverence that left me a quivering mess beneath him.

He released my hands, and I immediately wove my fingers into his hair. Part of me wanted to tug at the strands, furious that he left me hanging, while the other part needed to be closer to him. I rubbed against him wantonly until his palm grabbed my hip. My lips parted, a protest ready on my tongue, and then his thick head prodded at my entrance.

"Still with me?" he breathed against my neck.

"Yes." I wrapped my stocking-clad calves around him, urging him forward, but he held himself there for a long, agonizing minute. Then his hand slid off my hip to the top of my sex and down to fondle my sensitive nub.

I bit my lip to keep from crying out at the unexpected touch. The tension he initiated with his tongue just moments ago slammed back into me with a force that knocked the wind from my lungs. I felt tightly wound, ready to burst, and his tongue tracing my lips wasn't helping. His muscular chest felt like heaven against my hard nipples, and having his arousal so close to mine fired electric jolts through my veins. Violent shudders wracked my body as sensations overwhelmed me to a painful degree, and then his mouth was at my ear.

"Let go, Rachel." His stubble against my neck, coupled with his words, punctured my restraint and sent me crashing over the edge into an endless pit of ecstasy. He drew out the sensation with his thumb and captured my moans with his mouth. Pain mingled with the pleasure as he seated himself inside me, and my body spasmed again in confused bliss. All thought scattered as he started to penetrate me deeper than I ever thought possible. His palm slid to my ass and angled my hips upward to meet his powerful thrusts.

"Don't stop," I panted, pleading. Already I could feel a second orgasm brewing from deep within.

"Never, darlin'." His lips were at my ear. "I'll never stop."

That spot, oh, *that spot*. He hit it with each flex of his hips, and when he increased his speed to stroke it over and over again, I thought I was going to pass out from the erotic vibrations. I moved with him, seeking friction and pressure and *needing* more. He picked up his pace, slamming into me with a force that left me breathless, and showed me just how well he could put all those muscles to use. The way he moved, so fast, so hard, so powerfully, undid me in a way I didn't know was possible.

"Touch yourself," he demanded. "Now."

I reached between us and thrummed my clit with shaky fingers and moaned. That was exactly what I needed, but my brain hadn't given the command. He squeezed my ass and upped the tempo to a rate I couldn't match and drove me into oblivion. My screams could no doubt be heard throughout the hotel, but I wasn't ashamed. Will deserved all the praise in the world.

The hand on my ass clutched me to him as he carried me through my climax, never ceasing that moment and drawing out every ounce of my pleasure. I scored my nails down his back, luxuriating in the aftershocks, as he found his release deep inside of me.

"Fuck..." His groan vibrated the sensitized skin of my neck where he'd dropped his head. The elbow he had used to prop himself up tensed, and I suspected he was using every last ounce of his energy to keep from crushing me. I had just enough sense left in me to wrap my arms around him and force him down. His weight on top of me felt right.

"You're never allowed to move," I said, my voice raspier than I expected. He really did make me scream during all that.

His chuckle lacked depth, which I assumed meant he'd worn himself out. Knowing that made me smile.

"You'll want me to move again at some point, darlin'." He gave a shallow thrust to strengthen his point, and it sent a rush of tingles through my lower body. Okay, yeah. I'd like him to move again. Eventually.

Unfortunately, that moment came all too soon as he rolled off the bed to dispose of the condom. When he returned in all his naked glory, I went to my elbows to take him in. Every inch of him was perfectly proportioned and confirmed that he had close to zero body fat. All those long hours in the vineyard had certainly paid off.

"Keep lookin' at me like that, and I'll be tempted to start all over again."

I glanced at his semi-hard member and grinned. "Is that a promise?"

His hand closed over my ankle and yanked me across the bed, causing me to fall to my back. I squealed when he kissed my inner thigh, and started to scoot away, but his hands held me in place.

His eyes held mine as he unhooked my left stocking and slowly rolled it over my knee, down my calf, and off of my foot. He repeated the process with the right leg, all the while watching me under his thick lashes. It was erotic as hell and spiked my body temperature to a rolling boil. When he removed my garters with his teeth, I bit my lip.

Holy hell hotness…

He crawled over me and went to his elbows on either side of my head. "I have you right where I want you, Miss Dawson."

I swallowed. "Is that so?"

"Yep." He nuzzled my nose and cheek and trailed kisses along my jaw to my ear. "Do you still want to go to the Louvre tomorrow?"

Not what I expected him to say. We discussed it briefly on the plane after listing all the attractions in Paris. It'd been high on my list of preferred sightseeing options, and he suggested we go on Sunday so we had a full day to explore. "Do you want to go?"

"Of course." He licked the shell of my ear. "And afterward, we can stop by the store for my final fitting, and then we'll have dinner at *Le Meurice*."

My mouth popped open. This might be my first trip to Paris, but even I'd heard of that place. "You mean the restaurant at the Dorchester?" It was one of the top hotels in Paris and likely stole quite a few potential customers from Mershano Suites.

He chuckled. "Yes, and we have reservations tomorrow night."

"Isn't that like cheating on Evan somehow?"

"Hey, it's not my fault their food is better." His defensive tone didn't match the mirth tugging at his lips. "Besides, it's your first trip to Paris. Only the best will do in this situation."

I laughed and shook my head. "Well, you sure know how to sweep a girl off her feet, Mershano."

He smirked. "You think so? Wait until you see the car we're renting for our drive south on Monday."

"Another truck?" I teased.

"No."

"Something sexy, then?"

He gave me an affronted look. "My truck is sexy."

I patted him on the back. "Sure it is, darling. Now, tell me about this car. Is it fast, and do I get to drive it?" Because that's all that mattered.

"Yes, and that depends. What would you be willing to give me in exchange for the keys?" His gaze dropped to my lips, then slid back up slowly.

"I'm sure I could come up with something you'd enjoy." I waggled my brows at him suggestively.

"Such as?"

"Well, you see, I have certain oral skills, Mister Mershano, that may intrigue you."

He grinned. "Oh, I'm very familiar with your argumentative abilities, Miss Dawson. Although, I'll never complain about putting your smart mouth to better use."

"Careful, or I'll put my teeth to *better use* as well."

"I might enjoy that."

With all his biting and nipping? Yeah, he probably would. "I don't even remember what we were talking about now." All this sexy banter distracted me.

"That's okay, gorgeous. We can work out the details of our trade later." He kissed me soundly before pulling back with a smile. "You know what the French are famous for?"

"Fashion?" If he expected me to model lingerie right now, he was in for a surprise because I had no intention of getting out of this bed anytime soon.

His dimples deepened as he interpreted my expression correctly. "Don't worry, darlin'. You can model for me later. I was talking about dessert."

"I like dessert."

He brushed a kiss over my lips. "Then I'll order some for us to enjoy in bed before round two."

"Round two?" I wasn't even close to recovering from round one.

Desire dilated his pupils. "Oh, darlin', that was just our warm-up. You'll understand after we eat dessert."

24
CONFLICT OF INTEREST

I studied the photo on my phone. The dark-haired beauty wore a fashionable suit, one meant for being captured in an image such as this. Her gloved fingers were wrapped around the neck of my ex-fiancé as he bent to whisper something in her ear. His grin was one I recognized well. He used it when he wanted to charm someone, and the woman clearly approved.

The text was the last thing I expected to pop up on my screen after driving all day from Paris to Nice, but I knew something was coming because Mark hadn't contacted me since my confession on Saturday. Until now.

"What am I looking at?" I asked.

"That is Bianca Jenkins," Mark replied over the speakerphone. "Wife of Senator Jenkins."

My eyebrows shot up. Not only did I recognize the name, but I'd met the man several times. "He's one of Ryan's biggest supporters."

"Yes, and it would seem his young wife is an even

bigger supporter." His droll tone indicated his amusement at the word choice. "But it gets better." Another photo popped up on my phone of a pregnant Bianca. "Your comment about him leaving you alone for six months didn't fit his profile, so that's where I started, and guess who got knocked up around the time he stopped harassing you?"

Will let out a low whistle beside me. He had one arm slung across the back of the couch, but his focus was on the phone in my hand. Mark's text had arrived just as we walked into our new suite.

"You think the baby is his?" I guessed.

"Affirmative." His voice seemed to deepen as he continued. "This is Jenkins's fourth wife in twenty years, and none of the previous women ever conceived. Birth control is entirely possible, but I'm betting he's infertile. Plus, the timeline is right. That first photo is from a hotel security camera taken eight months ago, right about the time she got pregnant, while her husband was conveniently in another state."

"And he doesn't suspect anything?" Senator Jenkins wasn't a dense man. He had to know.

Mark snorted. "He's an arrogant son of a bitch who thinks the fourth time around is the charm, or maybe he just needed a wife who was twenty years younger. Who the hell knows, but he's not about to question it. He's too cocky for a philandering wife, which is probably why he didn't care when she asked to stay in Madison after the holidays while pregnant. Jenkins had been in DC while Albertson had been privately tending to Bianca's every, uh, need." He paused to let that sink in before continuing.

"So that's why he left you alone. He had other things to worry about, like a pregnant woman who could ruin his career. Which brings me to my second reason for believing he's the father—he pushed for her to abort the child."

I frowned. "How do you know that?"

"Physician records that were not as well scrubbed as he

thought. His name might not be on the paper trail, but there's a financial link that suggests he paid for several consults. In any case, I'm confident he's the father, and we'll know for sure in a few weeks."

"Okay." I chewed my lower lip and met Will's gaze. Just having him there put me at ease in a way I didn't know was possible. Especially when discussing Ryan. My emotional response seemed to dwindle with each new threatening message. The last one came in two hours ago, and I'd all but ignored it. Every time I deleted one of Ryan's messages, I felt empowered and gained a sliver of control back. The few times his words kicked me in the stomach, I took one look at Will and felt my resolve strengthen again. The man's confidence radiated from him, surrounding me with a comfort I'd not felt in years.

I cleared my throat. "Okay," I repeated. "So that explains his absence, but why is he bothering me again?"

"Because he needs a wife." Mark's flat answer sent a chill down my spine. "His campaign managers are riding him hard about it, too, hence the desperate feel to his actions. He's also not thrilled that his favorite possession is acting out by fucking a prime competitor."

"Mark!" I couldn't believe he'd just said that. Except yeah, actually, I could. The man was not one to mince words. But still... "Don't... I don't... Just..." My face was on fire as I shook my head, unable to say anything back to that. Because wow. Just. Wow.

"So what are you suggesting?" Will asked, speaking for the first time. His tone lacked his usual amusement and held an edge to it that I wasn't sure I liked. The hairs on my arms danced in response. *Danger.* He shifted his arm to my shoulders and pulled me closer to place a kiss on my neck that dispelled some of the tension tightening my limbs.

"I'm not suggesting anything yet, Mershano. His affair with Bianca is enough to destroy his political career, but Albertson is still vastly connected. It's his other business connections that I want to explore a bit more before I give Rachel her options."

Will ran his hand up and down my arm. "Mafia ties?" he asked.

"Something like that," he answered vaguely. "I'll be in touch as I learn more, Rach."

I was still trying to swallow the mafia comment, so all I managed was a "'Kay" in reply.

"Oh, and Mershano? Hernandez is a good hire, but don't piss him off. He throws a mean left hook." Mark hung up without a formal goodbye. Will's responding chuckle confused me almost as much as the man on the phone did.

"Who's Hernandez?"

"One of the members of our security detail in France. He's former black ops, which I suspect is what your friend is involved with because no way in hell that man is FBI."

As I already suspected the latter, I focused on the former. "We have a security detail?" He never mentioned anything about hiring anyone to watch us, nor had I noticed them.

"Yes, and Rick Hernandez is the one I hired to organize it. He has two men in the hotel whom I haven't met yet but plan to this evening."

"And they're what? Going to follow us to our meeting?"

"Yes, and wherever else we go while in Europe."

"That's a bit much, isn't it?" I understood his concern, but bodyguards accompanying us to a bunch of boring meetings felt extravagant. Ryan was obsessive, not stupid. He would never strike during a business negotiation.

"Your safety means everything to me, Rachel." He grasped my chin and forced my gaze to his. "I won't let that asshole touch you ever again. Do you understand?"

A shiver tickled the back of my neck. *So intense.* "And what happens after?"

"After?" he repeated. "After what?"

"After we leave Europe." It was something I hadn't wanted to think about these last three days, but I would eventually have to return to Chicago. To work, to my apartment, to Ryan...

"We agreed the other night that this isn't short term. When we return, we return together. We fight, remember?" Will's stern tone reminded me of that day in the boardroom with the partners. Charming, but in charge in every way that mattered with no room for negotiation. I had no intention of arguing with him, but there were things we hadn't discussed yet.

"I'll need to be reassigned to a new project, and I doubt my management team is going to take kindly to my hooking up with a client." I winced at that last part. So much for my professional reputation.

He cleared his throat. "About that... Remember when Garrett came to Chicago and we met with the partners?"

I eyed him sideways. As if I could forget the morning I woke up in Will's bed and met one of the South's best attorneys not thirty minutes later. "Yes."

"Part of our negotiations revolved around adding a conflict of interest clause regarding my preexisting relationship with you. An agreement I agreed to and signed before starting work with you on the project."

My blood ran hot as a myriad of emotions battled for purpose. "I... You... Fuck!" I couldn't decide if I wanted to be furious or relieved. Anger seemed to be winning, as my fists clenched tightly and my eyes narrowed.

"Before you blow up at me, keep in mind that my intentions regarding you have never been a secret. I wasn't about to hire your firm without protecting you. Your career means the world to you, and rightly so. I would never jeopardize that, Rachel. Ever. So you can be mad at me all you want, but I did the right thing, even if I did lie a little and say we were already dating."

"You did the cocky thing," I corrected. "Expecting me to date you? And saying we were already dating from the beginning?" Fury won against relief. His words and assessment were one hundred percent sound and accurate, but his gall grated on my last nerve.

"Oh, fuck…" That conversation I had with the partners the day after he signed the agreement took on a whole new meaning and made a hell of a lot more sense now. I'd thought they were talking about Evan's relationship with Sarah, but no. They were referring to the conflict of interest between Will and me. Because he told them we were already dating. "You're un-fucking-believable, Mershano."

His chuckle only infuriated me more. I reacted without thinking and lunged at him, only to find myself on my back beneath him on the couch.

"Okay, first? I knew it was an inevitability. And second, the agreement was worded in a way that implied my preexisting tie to you, not your commitment to me. You admitted months ago that you admired Garrett's gift for words. Trust me when I say he applied that to my agreement with Baker Brown."

"It doesn't matter. The partners inferred it the way you intended." God, I was such an idiot. They'd even offered to let me read it, but I'd naively said no.

And what would you have done? Great fucking question.

"Of course they did, but have they treated you any differently over the last few weeks for it? Because I recall Janet singing your praises on that call Friday. They respect the hell out of you, Dawson. And if you think a relationship with me is going to affect your career, then we need to work on your confidence."

I glowered up at him. "This is not so much about my *confidence* as your making assumptions."

"It was never an assumption. Our attraction to each other has always been mutual, and you know it."

I scoffed at that. "You believe what you want." I only said it because he had pissed me off, and seeing his expression change from amused to disappointment had me regretting it in an instant.

"Denying it does nothing to move us forward." His soft tone hit me right in the gut, but it was his next words that nailed my heart. "If anything, belittling our connection pushes us backward, and that's the opposite of fighting, Dawson. And not what we agreed to." He pushed off of me and left the living area.

My mouth opened and closed. I didn't know what to say. What started as a tentative conversation about our future blew up into a disagreement over his presumptuousness.

Discussing the nature of our relationship with my firm behind my back grated on my nerves, yet his reasons were genuine. He meant to save me from an even more embarrassing situation of having to talk with the partners about a sexual relationship with Will during the project.

By mentioning it up front, he kept our interactions honest and also saved my reputation. The partners probably thought Will selected the firm because of our relationship, which was essentially true. We weren't intimate until recently, but we already had a connection. One I'd just denied outright.

I palmed my forehead and blew out a breath. Controlling any aspect of my career reminded me too much of Ryan, except unlike my ex, Will did it with my best intentions in mind. The partners did treat me differently, but in a positive way. They knew my name and were directly involved in my work, and my career had never been in a better position. I always had the skills, but never the opportunity to shine, and Will had given that to me.

His overzealousness often irritated me, but it also floored me. The man bent over backward to break down my barriers and convince me to take a chance on him. Adding the conflict of interest clause also showed that he cared about protecting me from the ramifications of sleeping with my client. And it implied that he considered the long-term implications, not the short-term.

He fought for us at every turn, and I'd thrown a fit at our first hiccup. Granted, it was a big one, but not unforgivable. Will was a man who knew what he wanted and went after it, and he would never apologize for doing whatever it took to achieve it. Even if that included admitting our relationship to others before confirming it with me. Because at the end of the day, he was right. The attraction was always there from the second he stepped into my office all those months ago. It served as my primary reason for turning down his employment offers and the reason I should have requested the firm not assign me to his project.

I ran my hand over my face and stood up. His final words reverberated in my chest as I traced his path to the kitchen of the suite. He stood braced over the counter, his focus on the cabinet. A glass of amber liquid stood off to the side, surprising me. Will always drank wine. Always. The tense line of his shoulders was even more prominent in his crisp white dress shirt. He'd rolled the sleeves to his elbows, exposing his flexed forearms as he gripped the marble surface.

"I never meant to force your hand," he said in that same soft voice from a few minutes ago. "But I knew you would see it that way. I only wanted to avoid complicating your career." He picked up the glass and finished the alcohol before setting it in the sink.

I grabbed his arm as he tried to pass. "Will…"

"It's been a long day, and I need a minute before I go meet with the security team. You can berate me more when I get back." He sounded so defeated, and when he left the kitchen without even looking at me, my heart ached. The confident man I'd come to adore was nowhere to be seen. Did he think this would push me over the edge to end things between us?

The snick of the door as it closed echoed through the now-empty suite. It seemed to answer my unspoken question.

For the first time since we'd met, Will walked away.

He didn't argue in that clever way of his.

He didn't try to win me over with a flirtatious comment or a charming grin.

He didn't push.

He left.

25
FIGHTING FOR A FUTURE

Pissaladière.

That's what the Mershano Suites employee called the pizza he brought up to the room thirty minutes ago. It looked savory enough, but my stomach was too cramped to eat. Will had yet to return, and the meal only served one.

"Mister Mershano says you try this wine," the older man had said with a thick French accent. The glass of red stood untouched with the recorked bottle behind it. My fingers kept inching toward it, but I wanted my mental faculties fully charged for his return.

I paced the suite again, walking through both bedrooms and out onto the balconies overlooking Nice. The balmy air did little to warm my exposed arms. My blue dress was one of our purchases from the weekend. Will called it beautiful this morning before wrapping his arms around my back and kissing me so hard that I forgot how to move. Thinking about it gave me butterflies, which did not mix well with the nerves rattling around inside of me.

"Damn it." My whisper disappeared into the night, floating somewhere in the streets of Nice below. I wanted to admire the gorgeous view but couldn't. Not because of the lack of sunlight, but because my eyes refused to focus.

I hurt Will.

Me.

And my angry words.

Despite his meddling, he meant well, and I knew that. But in the moment, I'd reacted irrationally to a deep-seated pain brought on by years of living under a man's control. Will wasn't Ryan. I knew that on a logical level, but my wounds never fully healed.

Rattling came from the living area behind the sheer curtain, and I turned as Will entered with two suit-clad men. He met my gaze briefly as I walked in, but didn't hold it or smile like he usually did.

"Rachel, this is Beau and Sam. They'll be accompanying us to the meetings this week." His professional tone sent a chill down my spine. I'd heard it plenty of times before, but he hadn't directed it my way in what felt like forever, which was actually closer to a week.

Had we only kissed six days ago? Our relationship seemed so much older than that. *Because I fell for him the first day we met.* Now, if only I could admit that out loud.

"Rachel?" Will's saying my name had me returning from my thoughts. His furrowed brow suggested I'd missed something he said.

"Sorry, right. Hi." I extended my hand to Sam first, then Beau. They were night and day in appearance. Sam had a sly, light-on-his-feet look to him, while his counterpart exuded a quiet authority. Both flashed me a grin, and Sam's included dimples. Not sexy ones like Will's, but they were cute and added to the man's overall lanky charm.

"Rachel, I thought you might want to hear more about their backgrounds and roles in our plans this week," Will murmured. "So I'll leave you all to chat. Gentlemen, great meeting you. I'll be in the bedroom if you need me." He gave the two bodyguards a nod and left us standing in the living area.

Uh... I tried to smile at the men but failed. "Sorry, I'm not feeling like myself tonight."

"No worries, ma'am," Beau replied, his voice deep. "Hernandez gave us an overview of the situation before we arrived, so we're up to speed. We're both former Special Forces and trained to blend in with our surroundings. So if we're doing our jobs right, you won't even notice us."

"Unless you need to," Sam added with another easy grin. I sensed he was the down-to-earth one of the pair. "We're here as a precaution only, Miss Dawson. And we'll do our best to stay out of your way."

"Okay." I wasn't sure what else to say.

"Do you have any questions for us?" Beau asked, his vivid blue eyes intense.

"Umm..." My brain refused to function. All I could think about was Will's professional demeanor and easy dismissal. He'd left without looking at me again, and it left a sour taste in my mouth. As for asking these men questions, I had none. Will likely questioned them thoroughly over the last ninety minutes. "I don't have any right now."

"Very good, ma'am. Mister Mershano knows where to find us, so feel free to reach out if you need anything." Beau held out his hand again, and I shook it, followed by Sam's.

Both men let themselves out after advising me to lock up. I did as they asked before hunting down their boss. I found him leaning on the balcony outside the master bedroom with another glass of amber liquid in his hand. He didn't say anything as I joined him, and kept his forearms on the railing with his gaze on the city. I couldn't tell if his silent treatment was a result of being deep in thought or not knowing what to say. So I broke the ice with the obvious question.

"Since when do you drink scotch?" I asked. And where the hell had he found it? He never stopped in the kitchen. Was there a minibar in the bedroom?

"It's cognac, which is produced by doubly distilling white wines in certain regions of France." He finished the glass and set it aside without looking at me. "Are you okay with hiring Beau and Sam?"

I studied his profile. "They're your employees. I'm not going to give an opinion one way or another."

"They're here to protect you, Rachel." He finally met my gaze, and what I saw there stole the air from my lungs. Uncertainty mingled with hurt behind a mask of forced professionalism. "I don't want to make assumptions on your behalf, so I'm going to need your input. Are you comfortable with me hiring them, or should I ask Hernandez to send new candidates?"

His use of the word *assumptions* was deliberate, but not in an accusatory or provocative way. My reaction to his decision to sign the conflict of interest form had made him so uncertain that he needed my input now on something we both knew already had my approval.

"We both know I'm okay with it, Will."

He studied me for a minute, then nodded and turned his focus back to the view. "They come highly recommended, and interviewed well. I'll let Hernandez know." This professional facade needed to end. I laid my hand on his arm, and he tensed. His reaction kicked me right in the gut.

"Will." I had to pause to swallow the knot in my throat. "Look, I'm not happy about what you did, but I understand why you did it. And it saves me from having an awkward conversation after this business trip."

The tension in his arm didn't lessen, nor did he redirect his attention. It left me feeling alone and a little shunned. Maybe he was mad.

"Do you remember the first day we met? In your office at Baker Brown?" He ran his fingers through his hair and huffed a laugh. "Because I do. Vividly. I walked in with certain expectations, one of them being an over-and-done-with conversation where you reviewed the contract and gave Sarah the approval she needed to continue with the show, but one look at you turned my entire world upside down. I think it was your fiery blue eyes that hooked me and your mouth that reeled me in for the fight." He shook his head and let it fall to stare at his hands.

"My dad loved my mom more than everything in this world," he continued, voice soft. "And after they died, I went to live with my aunt and uncle, who have a relationship on the opposite side of the spectrum. The change was a bit of a shock, but it did teach me a valuable lesson. It taught me what I want out of life: a partner, someone to love the way my father loved my mother, someone to build a future with… It's taken me a long time to find the right woman, but my dad always said I would know, that she would knock me off my feet with a glance. And that day in your office, his words proved true."

His gaze burned as it met mine. "We've never been just friends, not in my mind anyway, and being up-front with Baker Brown was the only way I knew how to protect your career. I mean, the first day we met, I stayed the night at your apartment. Nothing happened, but they don't know that. And I've been courting you ever since. To feign only a professional interest would be a lie, and I consider myself an honest man. I've wanted you for months, and I know you wanted me, too, but it's on you to admit it to yourself. There's only so much I can do here, Rachel. Our relationship will never work if I'm the only one willing to fight for it."

Each word slammed into me with a force that left me winded. My fingers curled into his forearm for support, or maybe I just needed to cling to him, because his stature and tone said this was a pivotal moment for our relationship. He'd done everything up until this point to win me over, while I'd done everything in my power to push him away. And today, when I denied his claim regarding a mutual attraction, had finally tipped him over. I could see it in his eyes, the defeat and the exhaustion and the lurking doubt that this may never work. It was a result of my constant refusal to admit out loud what I knew in my heart.

Whatever I said next would define us. If I denied it yet again, I risked him walking away. A week ago, I would have done exactly that to protect him and myself, but things had changed between us.

Tonight, I would need to tell him everything or risk losing him forever.

26
MAKING A POINT

Trust.

I swallowed hard and gathered the strength to do this, to confide my deepest fears to a man who could so easily destroy me. It helped that he knew about Ryan, but there were other things I hadn't admitted yet. Not out loud, anyway.

"You asked if I remember the day we met." He meant it as a rhetorical question, but I figured this would be a good starting point. "I do, but it was different for me. You possessed a confidence that I immediately wanted to challenge, partly because it's in my nature to do so, but mostly because it unnerved me. I've always been drawn to influential men, but after Ryan, I vowed never to be involved with one again. Then you showed up, all sexy as sin in your expensive suit, and charmed your way into spending the entire day and night with me. Part of me hated how effortlessly you inserted yourself into my life as if you belonged there."

It infuriated me at the time but also fascinated me. My cheeks heated at the memory of it, how hot and bothered he left me without even trying. I coughed to clear my throat.

"You're right. The attraction has always been mutual, but unlike you, I haven't wanted to embrace it. I am still trying to survive the first powerful man I fell for; there is no way I can balance two of you. Not when you have so completely shattered every wall I've built to protect myself. You could destroy me, Will. Trusting you not to is taking all my willpower, but I started down that path the second I told you about Ryan." I placed a hand over my aching heart and allowed all my emotions to show in my eyes. All the pain, the fear, the love...

"It may not look like I'm fighting for us on the outside, but that's only because my struggle is in here." I tapped my chest for emphasis. "I'm my own biggest obstacle, but I'm trying, Will. I promise you that I am."

He wrapped his arms around me in a hug that warmed me inside and out. I didn't realize how cold I'd felt until he embraced me, and I immediately melted into him. "I'm sorry," I whispered.

"You have nothing to apologize for, sweetheart," he replied, voice soft. "I knew you wouldn't react favorably to my confession, but I feared it would drive you away. Especially after revealing what you did about Ryan. I'm aware that it was heavy-handed on my part, but I did it to protect you."

"I know." I kissed his jaw, then his cheek. "It was the right thing to do. Nothing about our relationship has ever been strictly professional, but I need to know something." I pulled back to read his facial reaction. "Why did you go through all the trouble of hiring me? Why not just try to date me?"

His brow furrowed. "Because you're brilliant. Why would I hire another lawyer when I could have you?" He sounded genuinely confused, which placated me a little. It meant he'd recruited me for the right reasons.

"But what about Garrett? Surely he wouldn't mind representing Mershano Vineyards."

"He manages my personal estate. I needed a corporate lawyer, and your work with Sarah's contract impressed me. Did you think I only hired you to get you into bed?" The last was said with a twinkle in his eye. "Because although that might be a benefit of working together, it wasn't part of my decision process. I would never hire a woman just to sleep with her, and I believe I've proven that I would never need to either."

I rolled my eyes. "So cocky."

"I've more than earned my confidence, darlin'." He smiled against my lips. "Or do you require a reminder?" I opened my mouth to reply, and he silenced me with his tongue. My toes curled from the sensual assault. The man possessed the mouth of a god, and he knew it. Each skillful twist set my blood on fire. I clung to him and held on for the ride as he devoured me. My legs went around his waist as he lifted me off the ground and pushed me up against the wall. I shivered as the cool air caressed my exposed thighs. Will's hands rivaled his mouth, stroking and touching me in all the right ways.

"Would you like your reminder out here or in the room?" he asked, his voice a whisper.

I shivered as he pressed his arousal into my hot center. The scrap of lace between my thighs allowed me to feel every pulse of his hard length through his slacks. We'd barely started, and already I was eager for him to take me. I fisted my hand in his hair to force his mouth back to mine.

"Here," I demanded before giving myself to him in a kiss. All the frustration from our first fight went into my embrace, culminating in a meeting of mouths that was all about confirming what he meant to me. I wanted him now and for always, and I would fight with my dying breath to make this work. He returned the emotions in kind and tore my dress over my head. It left me in stockings and a thong.

I'd not worn a bra today, something he seemed to luxuriate in as his mouth dropped to my breasts.

"You're fucking perfect." His words were filled with a reverence that left me breathless. "You still owe me a lingerie show, but I do like these." He traced the navy lace strip over my hip and down the crease of my thigh. "We'll have to replace them."

I yelped as he ripped them off of me, leaving me in nothing but my garters and silk stockings. It struck me that I was completely exposed and the only thing protecting my dignity was Will. He still wore his slacks and dress shirt, and for whatever reason, that only seemed to turn me on more. I pressed against his hard ridge with a moan.

"I need you, Will. Now."

His chuckle vibrated my neck as he trailed kisses up the column of my throat. "What are you willing to do for it?" He palmed my ass with one hand while the other drifted south of my belly button.

When he thrummed my clit, I bucked into his hand and groaned, "Anything."

"Anything, hmm?" His tone was filled with dark amusement. "Even call me 'sir'?" He pinched my sensitive bundle of nerves, making me see stars. It left me panting against him and aching with a need only he could soothe.

"I'll call you whatever the hell you want if you fuck me right now." It came out louder than I intended, but the man was driving me crazy.

"That's what I thought," he murmured. "Unbuckle my pants, Rachel."

I ran my hand down his crisp shirt to the belt at his waist and trembled as I loosened the leather from his hips. He kept massaging my sensitive nub but withheld the pressure I craved. Each sensuous caress stoked the flames deep inside me, keeping them burning hot without allowing it to boil over.

"You're killing me," I managed in a pained whisper.

"Keep going," he urged after I popped the button on

his pants. My fingers shook as I tugged down the zipper. "You know what I want you to do, Rachel." And I did, because it was exactly what I wanted. I tugged his heavy member free from the briefs and pressed him against my wet heat. He felt so smooth and hot against me, so right. I shifted up to position him where I needed him and felt him tense. When he pulled a condom from his pocket, I glared at it. Protection was important, but it always ruined the moment.

"I'm on birth control," I breathed. "And I'm healthy."

"We'll properly discuss that later." He ripped the packet open with his teeth and rolled the condom on one-handed. His other hand was busy holding me up with his palm on my ass. When his cock returned to my entrance, I quivered. "Hold on, gorgeous."

I wrapped my arms around his neck as he slammed home inside of me. No gentle prodding or exploring, just hard, fast fucking, and it felt amazing. Each thrust sent me higher, to a place only Will could take me. Knowing the city existed just over his shoulder sent a sinful thrill through me and heightened my pleasure. It felt dangerous, and wrong, and all kinds of right.

My head dropped to his shoulder with a shudder as pleasure warmed me inside. This was the part I loved, the part where I teetered on the edge of that special world created by Will. The one filled with bliss and passion and wonder. He drilled me harder, scraping my back against the wall with each thrust, and wound his fingers in my hair to force my gaze to his.

"I love that look in your eyes," he whispered. "Drunk on lust and ready to explode." He swept his tongue against my lips, coaxing me to open, and dipped inside. I moaned into his mouth as he took me even harder. He palmed my breast, tweaking my nipple, then lowered his hand to my tender point.

"Are you going to come for me, Rachel?" he asked. "I want to feel you let go around my cock. Now, Rachel."

He applied just the right amount of pressure to send me soaring. I screamed his name, not caring at all who heard me, and let go of everything. All my worries and concerns failed to matter. Erotic sensation was all that existed here, and it rolled through my body in arousing waves that Will had to feel. I buried my head into his neck as he carried me back into the suite, and startled only slightly when I felt the mattress against my back. Then it was beneath my knees as he propped me up and drove into me from behind.

"Oh God…" I couldn't believe how much deeper he was now, hitting a spot that mixed pleasure and pain over and over again, until another ripple of ecstasy crashed into me. My hands tightened on the quilt as my body spasmed from the unexpected orgasm, and I barely registered him removing his hand from between my legs to grab my hips.

"You feel amazing," he breathed. "So fucking amazing." His grip tightened as he picked up his pace, and I tried to push back against him to grant him more access, but my limbs protested. Two powerful orgasms left me weak and depleted beneath him. My name slipped from his mouth on a guttural growl, and he collapsed against my back with a tremble that I felt pulsing between my legs. He lifted my hair out of the way and kissed the back of my neck as his body continued to shake against mine.

"Mmm…" He nuzzled my ear and rolled us to our sides so he could spoon me. "I consider my point made."

I huffed a laugh. He more than proved his point with that little *reminder*. "Your confidence is well deserved, Mershano."

His teeth nipped my ear. "I thought we agreed on 'sir'?"

"I'll call you whatever you want after that, *sir*."

"One more time. Just so I remember it."

"Whatever you want, sir."

He chuckled. "That's two points made, then. Excellent."

I rolled my eyes. "Cocky, sir."

His hard length twitched inside me. "Cocky indeed, gorgeous." He pressed another kiss to my neck and rolled off the bed to dispose of the condom. His slacks were zipped and belted again when he joined me on the bed with a warm washcloth. Why was it so sexy to be naked around a fully clothed man? I jolted when he pressed the damp towel to my core, and shuddered as another aftershock hit me.

"So sensitive," he mused, rolling me to my back. His lips brushed mine while he continued to soothe me below. "For the record, I don't care what you call me. I just wanted to prove that I could convince you to call me whatever I liked."

"Uh-huh." I stretched like a lazy cat and sighed. "I hope you don't need me to work tomorrow, because I think you broke me. All I want to do is lie in bed and fuck all day."

His deep laugh warmed me. "Maybe we can plan a getaway for after the acquisition meetings and do precisely that."

I brightened at that idea. "Really?"

"Sure. We can go wherever you want after we're done this week." He kissed me on the nose and smiled. "I'm yours to do with as you please."

"Oh?" I lifted a brow. "Is that a promise?"

"Absolutely."

I liked the sound of that, but it made me wonder. "Why the condom, then? Unless... Is there a reason we need one?" The not-so-random thought soured the moment. We'd yet to discuss his previous relationships, and he definitely had experience. Females practically threw themselves at his feet. Like those women at the hotel last month.

"One of the things I adore about you is the ability to read emotions from your beautiful eyes, but I'm not sure I like the one looking up at me now." He went to his elbow to stare down at me. "I'm healthy, Rachel. My last checkup was a few months ago, and you're the only woman I've been with since. But I wasn't about to fuck you without protection in the heat of the moment, not without proper consent."

"I gave consent."

"Yes, in a pleasure-induced state, darlin'. Not the same."

I bit my lip, considering. "Do I want to know how many women you've been with?"

His sigh answered my question before his words. "No, but I can tell you a number if you need it. What matters more is that none of my previous relationships, whether brief or otherwise, compares to what exists between us. I've never felt this way about anyone except you, and I sure as hell have never tried this hard to win a woman over."

I snorted. "That's because all the others likely fell to their knees with a single command."

He smiled at that. "Maybe true, but not you. I like that you made me work for it." He palmed my cheek and kissed me lightly. "But yes, I've been with other women and I've dated, but nothing long term. None of them were right for me, and I found myself loving my company more than them. You're different. For the first time in my life, I'm with someone I value more than Mershano Vineyards. You're not just some random woman to me, Rachel. You never have been, nor will you ever be."

My heart warmed at his words. "I think you like me, Mershano."

He traced my lower lip with his thumb. "I think you like me too, Dawson."

"I do," I confirmed. "Maybe a little too much."

"That's impossible," he returned playfully. "I'm very easy to adore."

"Oh, here we go with the arrogance again."

"Do you need another lesson?"

My thighs squeezed together at the promise underlining his tone, and since his hand was still lounging down there with the washcloth, I knew he felt it. "I need to eat first," I whispered, my stomach grumbling in agreement. His thorough fucking had left me half-starved after skipping dinner. "But afterward, maybe you could make your point without a condom?"

His eyes glittered at that. "It's a promise, gorgeous."

27
UNKNOWN NUMBER

Watching Will in his element all week left me respecting the man even more than I already did. He handled each acquisition meeting with a professional poise I admired while he charmed everyone with his easy candor. It was no wonder the vineyard owner wanted to work with him. Four days of meetings, and the deal was pretty much done. I'd emailed copies of the paperwork back to Janet for her review, but so far she hadn't found any issues. If all went according to plan, the merger would move forward as soon as next month.

I jumped as Will grabbed my ass. "Mershano!" I chastised, laughing.

"In a dress like that, what the hell did you expect?"

"You picked this one out."

He waggled his brows. "I know, and I can't wait to strip it off you later."

"Mister Mershano," a deep voice called from behind us. We turned as Javier, the vineyard owner, approached in

231

the hotel lobby. My face flamed in response to what he'd just witnessed, but he didn't say anything or acknowledge it. "I was hoping to run one idea past you before you go," he said, his gaze hopeful. "It's about an aging technique I want to try, but since you'll be the one selling the product, I'd like to get your opinion first."

"Of course." Will glanced my way. "I know you need to check in with Baker Brown, so I'll meet you upstairs."

Right. Janet wanted me to call her with an update after today's meetings. It was just after eleven in the morning in Chicago, which made it a perfect time to touch base. I shook Javier's hand again and headed to the elevators with a wave. I could feel Will's gaze on my ass the whole way, which excited me for what would happen when he joined me in the suite. I had a feeling dinner would come second to sex again. His appetite was insatiable, and not just for food.

My phone buzzed as I stepped into the elevator, and I glanced at it, expecting it to be work. Instead, it was a number I didn't recognize. I snorted and hit ignore. Since I hadn't bothered to answer Ryan's calls all week, it was probably him trying on a new line. When it vibrated again, I silenced it and then did that three more times on the way to the room before something in me broke. This had to end once and for all. I was finally happy for the first time in forever, and I needed it to be permanent. That required me to reject Ryan with a finality he couldn't ignore.

When the number flashed a fifth time, I answered. "Look, this—"

"He's there. He's in the hotel."

Okay, not the voice I expected to hear. "Caleb?"

"Rachel, listen to me, he's in the fucking hotel. You need to run, right now. Go!"

His urgent tone froze me in the hallway. I hadn't spoken to my brother in months. "What are you talking about? Who—"

"Rach—"

Something hard slammed into the back of my head, causing the phone to slip from my fingers. "What the—"

An expensive leather shoe appeared in my blurry peripheral vision and stepped on the mobile, shattering it against the marble floor. Dread tightened a noose around my neck as a familiar aftershave overwhelmed my senses.

"Hello, little whore," Ryan drawled as he knotted his fingers in my hair and half dragged me down the hallway. My purse fell from my arm as I struggled to loosen his grip.

"Ryan—"

He backhanded me across the face so hard my world spun, and then he wrapped his fingers around my throat to keep me from falling. My shoulders hit the wall with a force that knocked the wind out of me.

"Shut. The. Fuck. Up," he said through gritted teeth, squeezing harder with each word. "You want to be a slut—I'll treat you like one."

He yanked me forward and started down the corridor toward the stairwell again.

Holy shit.

This could not be happening.

Where are Beau and Sam?

In their rooms.

Right. Because Will dismissed them after the meeting and said he would escort me.

Fuck.

I tried to gain purpose with my heels, to push away from him and run, but his grip on my windpipe left me too weak to fight. My feet barely held me up enough to walk as he pulled me down two flights of stairs. Black spots danced behind my eyes as I fought to breathe, and then I was sucking in sweet air as he shoved me onto the ground of a guest room that was significantly smaller than the one I'd meant to enter upstairs.

I curled into a ball as he circled me, and waited for the first kick to come. He moved slowly as his cruel gaze raked over my prone form. His snort of disgust tainted the too-silent air. "Fucking pathetic."

He dragged a chair over and lit up a cigar while he studied me in that eerie way of his. Those vivid blue eyes narrowed as he blew out a string of smoke that only seemed to add to the ominous atmosphere.

"You know, alcohol trade laws are a fickle thing." He paused to take a long drag on his cigar, those midnight eyes glowing with malcontent in the dim lighting of the room. "It would be a real shame if someone like Mershano made a mistake on one of his many filings. Could even jeopardize his little empire, or at least set it back for a few months, maybe years. Would be even worse if, say, some of the paperwork disappeared. Especially while in the middle of an international acquisition. Have I mentioned my friends with the US Alcohol and Tobacco Tax and Trade Bureau?"

My blood ran cold. "Ryan..."

His foot connected with my jaw, silencing me. It wasn't so much a kick as a stern tap and served as a warning that he could do worse if he wanted. I massaged the tender spot with my palm and fought off the tears brewing behind my eyes.

"What did I say about talking? Fuck, Rach. You're smarter than that, unless all this whoring has gone to your brain." He puffed his cigar again, his expression bored.

"Well, I thought it would be good for my career to have an accomplished woman at my side, but apparently, allowing you to work on this project has backfired. You'll be going home with me in the morning, and we'll be starting over. The first thing you'll do is quit your job. All your time will be focused on planning our wedding and the campaign anyway, so that shouldn't be a big deal. While you're doing that, I'll have your things moved back into my house. Then we'll start working on your behavioral issues and my expectations."

My stomach revolted at his words, and my limbs

tensed.

No.

I would *not* be going anywhere with him.

The woman he used to push around retreated to the back of my mind as the confident one who confided in Will stepped forward. Ryan didn't control this new version of me, nor would he ever own it. He could kick and hit me all he wanted, but I would not bow down to him. Not again.

"No," I whispered.

This time I anticipated his foot and moved away from him to put my back to the wall and curl my knees into my chest.

I narrowed my eyes at him when he stood. "Go ahead, Ryan. Do your worst."

He had likely already given me a concussion if the throbbing at the back of my head was anything to go by, and my throat would have a hand print around it in the morning, just like the last time he choked me, but my heart would be free. My mind, too. And that's what mattered.

His gaze ran over me as he set his cigar aside and stood. I expected to see anger darken his features, but instead, they brightened with lust. My throat convulsed at the sight of it. Furious Ryan I could handle, but not this. It froze me in place, so much so that I couldn't even breathe. He must have sensed my overwhelming fear, because he smiled.

"Oh, Rachel. I've always enjoyed whores with attitudes." He grabbed a fistful of my hair again and forced me to my knees. "It's so fun to fuck their mouths into submission." His free hand was on his zipper when the door flew open.

One minute my skull was on fire from his grip, and the next, Ryan was on the floor beside me, cradling his jaw. A livid Will Mershano loomed over us, his gaze on my neck. His jaw clenched at the sight, but he said nothing as he held a hand out to help me up from the floor. I managed to stand with a wince, and he immediately pulled me to his side with an arm around my shoulders.

"If you ever touch her again, I will end you." No hesitation, no anger, just an unerring threat delivered in the calmest tone I'd ever heard from Will.

Ryan spat out a mouthful of blood and stood to take his opponent's measure. They stood at an equal height, both broad-shouldered and athletic, but the man beside me had more muscle on him. My ex's lithe form was crafted from an expensive personal trainer, while Will earned his doing manual labor.

I half expected Ryan to try something stupid, like punch Will, but he was too suave for that. Instead, he smiled that damn charming smile and shrugged. "What happened to your security detail, Mershano? They seem to have dropped the ball." He fixed his tie and smoothed it with a hand. "You might want to check on that."

Will grinned. "Your connections don't scare me, Albertson. But thanks for the not-so-subtle warning." I had no idea what he was talking about but sensed something bad had happened to Beau and Sam. Ryan wouldn't kill anyone, would he?

"Well, you can't say I didn't try." My ex put his hands in his pockets, the picture of nonchalance. "Last chance, Mershano."

"As previously stated, you don't scare me. Now get the fuck out of my family's hotel."

Ryan nodded once in acquiescence, then caught my gaze for a long moment and held it. "See you soon, baby girl."

28
ALL THE FEELS

Will rolled a block of ice in a towel and handed it to me. "You're sure you don't want to get checked out?" he asked, eyeing my throat.

I shook my head. "No, the ice and painkillers are fine." The hospital would be more uncomfortable than this couch, not to mention more invasive. What I needed right now was to breathe and to relax.

I'm safe.

For now.

I pressed the cool pack to the back of my head with a grimace. It hurt a lot more now that the adrenaline was no longer flooding my veins.

"But are you okay?" Will's soft tone did not match the faint flush of his cheeks or the fury blackening his gaze. "Sorry, that's a stupid question. Of course you're not." He ran his fingers through his hair and paced the living area. "Fuck, if I'd answered my phone sooner... But I kept ignoring it..." He shook his head and went to his knees before me. When his head fell to my lap, my heart broke a little. He evidently blamed himself. "I'm so sorry, Rachel."

"Don't," I whispered. "Don't apologize for him." It was reminiscent of what he had said to me after I'd told him about Ryan... *Don't apologize on his behalf ever again.* Will's nod said he understood, but his eyes still grieved.

If he hadn't shown up when he did, who knew what would have happened. My body had frozen when Ryan started to unzip his pants, and all the fight inside of me fled. He'd reduced me to my most vulnerable state with a simple act. I'd managed to stand up to him in person for the first time in years, but one flip of a switch sent me back to my knees. Literally.

"I hate him," I seethed. "I fucking hate him."

Will's arms came around my middle as he hugged me awkwardly from the floor. We stayed like that, holding each other, without speaking, for countless minutes until a buzzing interrupted the moment. He pulled the phone from his pocket, took one look at the number, and handed it to me. "This will be for you."

"Just put it on speaker." I didn't have the energy to move, and everything hurt.

"She's okay," Will said by way of answering.

"That remains to be seen." My brother's voice knocked my brain into motion. I'd completely forgotten that he called before Ryan arrived.

"Caleb?"

"Hi, little sis." The affection in his tone floored me. He never cooed at me, not like this. "Kincaid will be there in about three hours, so just hang tight, okay? I would come myself, but he was closer."

I gaped at the phone as my mouth filled with questions. "What are you talking about? And how did you get Will's number? No, scratch that, how did you know about Ryan? And what number are you using? Where—"

"Whoa, whoa, don't go all lawyer on my ass, Rach. Look, all you need to know is Kincaid is on his way to you.

He'll explain as much as he can. Until then, stay put and I'll handle things from here. Oh, and don't worry about Albertson either. I should have handled him years ago, but I didn't want to intervene. Now he's left me no choice."

"I'm going to need more answers than that, Caleb." I told him flatly, my fire slowly returning. "How do you even know about Ryan? You weren't there the one year I brought him home for the holidays, and Lord knows we hardly talk."

The sigh that came over the line was trademark Caleb. Always brooding, always tired. I couldn't even remember the last time I'd seen my brother smile.

"We may not see each other or talk very often, but I'm always there, Rach. And I'll always be there."

The line went dead.

Will pocketed the phone and arched a blond brow. "What did you say your brother does for a living?"

"He has some desk job with the government." Whenever someone brought it up, he would shrug, spout something about it being boring, and change the subject.

"Right," Will replied with a snort. "He's the reason I found you. Not only did he figure out my private phone number and call me to say Albertson was in the hotel, but he knew what room the bastard had dragged you to. That requires a level of security access that goes well beyond the typical 'desk job.'"

"Caleb called you too?" Obviously, he did. Will just said that, and he recognized the number when my brother called him back again. Stupid question. "I wonder how he knew."

"I'm guessing he hacked into the hotel's security cameras, which, again, implies skills beyond that of a clerk. Not to mention, I don't think it's necessarily legal either."

"You think he works with Mark, then?" I'd never thought about it before, but it would make sense. As far as I knew, they were still best friends despite working in different cities and rarely seeing each other. Was it all a cover?

"Absolutely, and no way they're FBI either. From my understanding, federal agents operate inside the United States, not outside of it."

His assessment matched mine, but I didn't have the energy left to ponder it. I exhaled heavily and winced. My shoulder felt stiff from holding my hand up, which was sad considering it'd only been about ten minutes.

"Here, let me." Will slipped onto the couch beside me and took control of the ice pack. My arm fell limp to my side, thankful for the break. Everything ached. My feet, my throat, my stomach, my ego...

I relaxed into the strong man beside me and fought the urge to cry. This emotional roller-coaster ride we were on needed to end, and there was only one way to do it. But it would require all the strength I had left, and then some.

"He'll never stop," I whispered. "He'll consider this a setback and come after me again later when we least expect it."

"And I'll kick his ass." So certain, but it wouldn't solve anything. Knowing Ryan, he would frame it in a way to make Will look bad or ruin his reputation somehow. My ex held an advanced degree in manipulation and never hesitated to use it when he wanted something.

I shook my head but stopped when the room started to spin. "No, we have to beat him at his own game. It's the only way." A restraining order would just make him laugh, as would increased security or bodyguards. Which reminded me... "What happened to Sam and Beau?"

"According to your brother, Ryan fucked with their water upstairs and knocked them out cold. I don't know if he did it himself or hired someone, but either way, it shows he had access to their rooms and the bottles in their fridge."

Because that wasn't terrifying. "I warned you. He knows people, Will. It's always been this way with him." I shivered and folded myself into his warmth. "He was talking about his friends with the TTB." I knew Will would recognize the abbreviation, as his company would have filed several documents with them over the years.

Will chuckled. "He wants to come after Mershano Vineyards, does he? I'd love to see him try. He seems to be under the impression that I don't have access to similar resources, which is a fault on his part. And you call me arrogant."

"This isn't a joke, Will. He could hurt you."

He set the ice off to the side and pulled me into his lap. "Darlin', you let me worry about me, okay? I grew up with men like Albertson. He's nothing new, and he sure as fuck doesn't scare me. What does scare me is how close he came to hurting you. It was purely a power play on his part to grab you and hurt you within arm's reach of me. He knew I would find you, but probably hoped it would be a bit later. He wanted to deliver a message, and he succeeded. Except I'm not backing off. If it's a fight he wants, he better fucking bring it."

Promise and certainty underlined each word, and I could see the determination in his eyes. Ryan's warning had backfired. He expected Will to tuck tail and run, but the strong man holding me had no intention of taking the bait.

"You're amazing," I said, awed. Most men would walk away from my baggage with a muttered "Good luck," but not Will. He sat beside me, radiating strength and fury on my behalf, and knew all the words to put me at ease. I should have been a quivering mess of tears right now, but instead, I felt safe. My body ached all over, and I'd definitely be covered in bruises tomorrow, but inside, I knew nothing could harm me. Relying on another person went against the grain, and yet, that's what relationships were all about.

Trust.
Security.
Understanding.

Love.

I smiled at that last thought and let out a little laugh. Because it rang true. I loved Will. This man, this impossible, stubborn, trying man, had bulldozed over all my barriers and plowed into my heart with the speed of a freight train. I never thought it possible to grant anyone such intimate access again, but nothing about this man met normal standards. When he wanted something, he took it all, and I was no exception.

His brow crumpled as he studied me. My giggle must have confused him. Talk about the wrong time to realize how I felt. But to hell with it. He had to know, and if Ryan's threat wasn't going to make him run, neither were a few harmless words.

"Will Mershano, I've just realized I love you." There. Done. No taking it back, no running away, no hiding. He wanted me to fight, and this was it. I, too, could go after what I desired, and I craved him. Always, and forever.

His forehead smoothed as his lips curled into a breathtaking smile. "Oh, darlin', if you're just realizing that, then I have more work to do."

I slapped his chest playfully. "Always arrogant."

Those dimples deepened. "I've earned it."

"You have," I conceded and curled back into his chest. Content. My eyes fell closed on a yawn. All the commotion from this evening had exhausted me, and I knew that with Mark coming, we were in for a long night.

"Rachel?"

"Hmm?" I murmured, groggy.

"I love you too."

29
MARK KINCAID

Will called Janet from his phone since mine was destroyed in the hallway, and gave her an update. She seemed pleased with the results, then asked for our weekend plans. The way she said it confirmed Will's comments about the conflict of interest form. I'd never noticed it before, but the curiosity was always there. Now I knew why.

"So what are we going to do after this trip?" I asked as he pocketed his phone.

He tucked a loose strand of hair behind my ear and cupped my cheek. "My answer is the same from the other day. We go home together as a couple."

"Right, but you live in North Carolina. And I don't." The idea of going back to Chicago didn't appeal to me like it once did, mostly because of Ryan, but also because I liked Will's country home. It was peaceful, and safe.

A knock at the door cut off his response. "That must be Mark," he said as he walked over to check the peephole. "Tall, dark hair, and bearded?"

I snorted. "The beard would be new, but sounds right."

Will turned the handle, and Mark strolled in wearing jeans and a white shirt. And sure enough, Mark Kincaid had let his facial hair grow. It was well groomed, though, and kind of sexy on him. It lent to the whole badass appeal he had going for him already. He walked over and scooped me off the couch into a hug without saying a greeting or even acknowledging the man who opened the door. When he pressed a kiss to my temple, Will cleared his throat.

"Relax, Mershano. She's like a sister to me," Mark replied. And it was true. I'd known the man for half my life. Dating him would be weird.

"That thing on your face is tickling me," I murmured, squirming.

He let me go with a chuckle. "Glad to see your sense of humor is still in play."

"There's nothing funny about it," I said, gesturing to his square chin.

His near-black eyes narrowed. "You sound just like Caleb."

I shrugged. "We both understand how to use a razor."

"Do you see what I put up with?" he asked, his gaze on Will. "I drop what I'm doing in Dubai and catch the next flight out, just to be harassed." He shook his head and sobered. His stance changed as he crossed his arms over his broad chest, shifting his persona from big brother to bad man in charge. "I've already met with Hernandez's men. They're awake and packing, and they're aware of their dismissal."

Both of Will's eyebrows shot up. "Excuse me?"

"They've been compromised. Why would you keep them on staff? Besides, I'm here and I actually know what the fuck I'm doing." Mark settled into the armchair beside the couch and placed one jean-clad ankle over his opposite knee.

I took that as a cue to sit as well and folded myself back into my seat, and Will slid into the open space beside me. His leg pressed against mine as he wrapped his arm around my shoulders and stared Mark down. My brother's best friend didn't flinch; he held the gaze with an assertiveness that rivaled the man beside me.

All the hairs on my arms danced as testosterone thickened the air. Neither one of them would ever bow to the other, which made this battle of wills a waste of time.

"So." I cleared my throat. "Mark, this is Will. Will, this is Mark."

I'd forgotten to properly introduce them earlier, not that either of them seemed to care. They were too busy trying to win Alpha Male of the Room.

Silence.

I bounced my foot in irritation and winced. It was already bruising from my trip down the stairs. Will's warm hand brushed my leg on his way to my ankle. "Do you want more ice?" he asked.

"You might as well fill the bathtub at this rate," I remarked, annoyed not at him but at the situation. "I'll be fine. I just might need more painkillers soon." He'd already given me more than the recommended dose for my headache.

"Look at me." Mark's command caught me off guard. He squatted in front of me without touching me. I met his serious gaze and held it. "Food," was all he said as he stood and wandered over to the balcony door.

Will tilted my chin toward him and held my stare with an intense look. I swallowed, unnerved by having two very dominant men in one room. Then Mark started speaking in fluent French, ordering what sounded like dinner from a local restaurant, and broke the moment.

"Since when do you speak French?" Although it was whispered, he heard me just fine and winked at me before continuing the conversation.

"FBI, my ass." I shook my head and rested against the strong man beside me. His natural heat blanketed me in the comfort I needed. I hadn't realized my eyes were closed until Mark sighed. He was back in the chair by the couch with an ankle on his knee. His chin was propped on his fist, watching me.

"You'll feel better after you eat something," he said.

"I'll feel better when you tell me how to handle Ryan, because I assume that's why you're here." My voice was stronger than I expected. Every other part of me ached with exhaustion, but not my heart or my mind. "He's not going to go away unless I do something drastic."

"Yes, and his coming here shows escalation," Mark replied.

"It was a message," Will cut in. "He never wanted to take her; he just wanted to mark his territory so I would back off."

"Precisely." Admiration underlined that single word. "And he'll become truly dangerous when you don't, which is why we need to take action, and soon."

"What do you suggest?" Will asked, his voice low.

"Political suicide," he replied simply. "The tabloids love a good sex scandal. It seems to be the only way to destroy a career these days, and once that happens, Albertson will have a number of more pertinent issues to tend to than his errant ex-fiancée. Not the least of which being his more questionable connections, ones that are relying on him to become the next senator of Illinois."

"He's been making promises he can't keep," Will inferred before I could say the same. "But all this hinges on the child being his."

Mark shrugged, his expression bored. "Whether or not it's his is irrelevant. Senator Jenkins is not going to be happy to hear his young wife cheated on him with his protégé. He'll destroy Albertson in retaliation for harming his precious manhood, while we can sit back and enjoy the fireworks. I'm sure Senator Albertson won't be too pleased, either, not that he's an exemplary role model himself."

I snorted. That was an understatement. Ryan's father

treated all women like objects, including me when Ryan and I were dating. He kept saying how sweet it was that I wanted a law degree, like it was a hobby and not a career. "So you're suggesting we release the affair to the media," I said after both men looked at me.

"No, I suggest we post some of the footage online anonymously and let the tabloids run with it. I have a few trusted sources we can leak it to directly to make sure it's found, and the rest will take care of itself. Also, we need to do it next weekend."

"Why?" I asked.

"Because that's when he's announcing his candidacy," he replied. "If we time it right, which we will, the news story will start to flash while he's making his speech. No way he can recover from that, especially when Senator Jenkins will be sitting right next to him with his lovely wife to the left."

It sounded perfect except for one thing. "We'll be ruining her life as well."

Mark grinned, but it didn't quite reach his eyes. It never did. "I knew you would say that, which is why I did more digging into her background while I researched some of Albertson's more questionable relations." He pulled out his phone and started thumbing through the screen. "Mrs. Bianca Jenkins is a debutante who married for money and status. Not necessarily something to destroy her for, but she has a history of ruining the reputations of others purely for fun or selfish means. Let's just say she more than deserves a little public humiliation."

"The media will crucify her because she's the woman," I argued.

"Something she likely knew when she sent her best friend's sex tape to the entertainment industry in retribution for trying to seduce her former lover. That would be the man she was fucking before Ryan, while she was still married to Senator Jenkins." His flat tone suggested he wasn't impressed at all. "I won't lose any sleep over it."

I bit my lip, uncertain. This was supposed to be about taking down my controlling ex, not anyone else. But even I could admit extreme measures would be needed here. It would take a hell of a lot to force him to leave me alone, and hurting his political aspirations would accomplish it. Ryan cared far more about his career than he did me.

"Is there any risk this will make him more desperate for her?" Will asked. "I mean, taking everything away from him could have the opposite impact, yes?"

Mark fiddled with his beard, gaze thoughtful. "It's entirely possible, but I suspect he'll be too busy worrying about his political fallout to think about anything else. He's in bed with some dangerous people who have entrusted him with certain secrets in expectation that he would be useful in the future. Removing that makes him more of a liability than an ally, which will force him to find other ways to appease his various benefactors."

"So he's received funds from them for his election run," Will murmured.

"In a backward kind of way that can't be tracked, but yes, essentially his family has received financial incentives for decades. These are old relationships, ones I'm sure you're more than familiar with, Mister Mershano." The implication was obvious. Ryan and Will both came from old, wealthy families. From what I'd seen over the last few years, those backgrounds came with a certain prestige, and within that social circle were a myriad of affluent individuals who acquired their assets in a variety of ways.

Will gave a single nod with his chin to acknowledge the truth. "Albertson doesn't seem to grasp that as well as you do."

"That's because he's under the misconception that you're not as deeply tied to the Mershano empire as your cousin is, which we both know isn't true at all. You might own your own company, but your last name affords you the same contacts and resources, not to mention your bank account rivals Evan himself. Albertson doesn't acknowledge any of that, and that's his downfall." Mark pushed off the chair and stretched his lanky arms over his head. "It's been a long two days, and I need bourbon."

"There's cognac in the kitchen," Will replied as he brushed his hand up and down my arm.

"Not my preference, but it'll do," he grumbled back.

"He's charming," Will muttered sarcastically after Mark disappeared.

I smiled. "He's always been like that. Rough and to the point." It was something I enjoyed about him and my brother. I never had to worry about them judging me in private; they were too blunt for it. "So, French, huh?" I asked as the man in question strolled back around the corner with a tumbler of amber liquid.

"It's a simple language, Rach. You should try Farsi or Arabic." He grimaced. "So many grammar rules, and you break all of them. Really fucked-up shit."

I eyed him speculatively. "Right. All part of your FBI job? Because all the agents have to learn Middle Eastern languages and travel to Dubai regularly?"

This time his grin did meet his eyes. "Absolutely."

"Uh-huh. Are you ever going to tell me what it is you do?"

That sobered him a little. "I have a knack for helping people out of difficult situations, like the one you're in." He set the glass down on the table and braced his elbows on his knees. "I knew that asshole was trouble, but I didn't realize how bad he was until you called me. Now I'm going to do what I should have done three years ago when you left him. He will never touch you again."

"You can't promise that." I didn't mean it as a taunt or a warning, just a fact. No one could promise something like that, not where Ryan was concerned.

"Oh, but I can, Rachel. When I'm done with him, you'll be the last thing on his mind. He's about to face a whole new enemy, one he'll never see coming." He smirked. "Outing his affair will feel like a honeymoon when I'm through with him."

"What else can you do?" I asked, curious.

"It's better if he doesn't tell us," Will murmured. "The less we know, the less we can be implicated, which lessens the chance for revenge."

"Exactly." Mark lifted his glass again in salute. "I like him, Rach. This one you can marry."

My eyes bugged at that. "Excuse me? As if you have a say in something like that."

Mark chuckled. "As Caleb sent me here to assess the situation, I beg to differ." He looked to Will with amusement. "It's not Rachel's father you need to be worried about; it's her brother."

"Yes, I've gathered that. I look forward to meeting him."

"Oh, and you will. Soon, I imagine."

"Good," Will replied.

I frowned at the exchange. This bonding thing wasn't working for me. I preferred when the two men were having their alpha standoff. "I decide whom I want to marry, thank you."

"Of course," Mark agreed. "But Caleb could make things awfully difficult if he didn't approve."

"By what? Not showing up or calling me for months on end?" Because that was my brother's role in my life. Until today when he randomly tried to warn me about Ryan. And that comment about always being there. "He's not a government desk jockey, is he." Not a question, but a statement. I groaned and shook my head. "You two are unbelievable. Running off to join the military at eighteen, then doing God knows what for the last few years, you supposedly living in Chicago—"

"Oh, that part is true," he cut in. "The place you stayed after living with Ryan was real, and mine. I just don't see it often."

I shook my head again. "Right. And Caleb?"

"He's in Virginia, most of the time."

"Uh-huh." I looked at Will, who had stayed quiet through the whole exchange. "Welcome to the insanity of my life."

"I wouldn't be anywhere else," he replied with a kiss against my cheek. "Okay, Kincaid, tell me what you want us to do next. Because I'm guessing you don't want us anywhere near Chicago when he makes the announcement next weekend."

"Right, the farther away the better. You're done with meetings, right?"

I didn't bother to ask how he knew that. "Yes."

"Then I recommend you go somewhere remote and stay at a private villa of sorts, not a Mershano Suites. Which reminds me, you need to have a serious discussion with your cousin about his computer system, as it's been compromised." He left that hanging and cocked a dark brow.

"He's aware of the breach and would also love to know how Caleb accessed his security cameras of the hotel," Will drawled. "Not that I suppose you'll tell us."

"What would be the fun in that?" Mark asked, taunting. "But I can recommend someone to do a thorough risk assessment."

"I'll pass it along to Evan," Will replied before returning to the subject at hand. "So you want me to whisk her away somewhere while you handle the Albertson issue?" He sounded amused. "Why do I feel like I've been given the easy job?"

"Your job will never be easy, Mershano. I expect you to keep her safe, and if you don't, if you ever hurt her, it won't be just me you'll need to worry about."

"Because I'll kick his ass," I put in, irritated. "You both do realize I'm in the room still, right?"

"I'm more than aware," Will murmured, his lips against my ear. "I'm always aware, darlin'. And do tell me more about this ass-kicking. I'm intrigued."

"Cocky," I returned with a snort. "But seriously, you can't just handle Ryan for me. I want to be part of this."

"And you are," Mark replied. "I'm only here because *you* called me, and Will is here because you trusted him. *You* decided it's time to fight back, and we're your army. Mershano has the means to keep you safe, while I have other skills useful to your situation. The call at the end of the day, however, is yours, and that makes you the queen on the chessboard. We're just the knights moving to do your bidding as requested."

I gave him a doubtful look. "You've never done anything I've requested, and neither have you," I added with a glance at Will.

"But in this case, we will do whatever you want." He cupped my cheek and let me see the sincerity deep in his eyes. "If you don't want Kincaid to use the intel he's gathered, he won't. And we'll go about it a different way. The decision is yours, Rachel." So serious. So unlike my Will. But in this, he was giving me the ultimate power. As was Mark, something that couldn't be easy for him either.

I cleared my throat. "There's no other option, right?"

"There's always another option," my non-FBI friend replied. "But this is by far the best one, especially considering his recent escalation. I suspect he'll be back tomorrow or Sunday, if you're still in Nice."

"And he'll do what? Grab me again?"

"No, he'll do something much worse, and he'll do it to Mershano to get him out of the way. Albertson might be a trust fund kid, but he's an intelligent one. He knows how to maneuver his way around a chessboard better than most politicians."

Will pressed a kiss to my temple and hugged me close. "Don't worry, darlin'. I can handle whatever he throws at me. The decision is still yours."

My denial was immediate. "No, it's not. There's no choice in the matter if you're in jeopardy. You say you're not afraid of him, but I am, and he knows it. He'll use you to extort that fear. And I can't let that happen." I closed my eyes and braced myself for the inevitable. For three years, none of my attempts to thwart Ryan had worked. Not long term, anyway. If Mark thought this idea had a chance, then I owed it to myself, to Will, and to our future together to try it. I said earlier we had to do whatever it took to bring him down, and if this was what it took, then we would do it. "Okay. We try to sabotage his career, then, and pray like hell that it works."

"No prayers needed," Mark replied. "It'll work. His focus will be off you in two weeks, tops. But you two need to go on a little trip in the interim because Ryan is going to try to force Rachel to come home for his candidacy announcement dinner."

"I'll handle that part," Will murmured. "We'll borrow one of Evan's jets so we can't be tracked as easily."

Jets. As in plural? "How many does your cousin own?"

"Oh, darlin', you have so much to learn." He kissed me gently. "I might not live in extravagance, but Evan sure does. Sarah now too."

"That bitch has been holding out on me," I accused half-heartedly.

He chuckled. "We both know you wouldn't care. Now I should go make the arrangements—"

"Nope. Food first," Mark interrupted. He hopped up seconds before someone tapped at the door. "Thank fuck. I'm starving."

"How did he do that?" I asked, startled.

He held up a phone over his head on his way to the foyer. "I told the guy to text me from the elevator." When he returned, it was with three separate bags that he promptly divided between us. "This is my favorite place in Nice. Trust me, you're both in for a treat."

"Favorite place in Nice," I repeated. "Right. Because you come here all the time."

"Sure. Didn't you know the FBI loves France?" He didn't even crack a smile as he ripped open the bags. And if I didn't know he was completely full of shit, I'd say he was serious.

"One of these days, you're going to tell me the truth about what you do."

"Honestly, it's Caleb you should talk to. He has more fun than I do." He waggled his brows. "Now eat, Dawson. Something tells me you'll need your energy over the next few weeks."

30
FROM MY FAMILY TO YOURS

Four Weeks Later

"So the baby is his," I said after reading the article Kincaid handed me. Senator Jenkins required a paternity test, and someone leaked it to the press. I had no doubt it was the man sitting across from me in Will's living room.

"Oh, it gets better," he mused. "Albertson was more prepared than I expected and had a contingency plan in place. The media received a handful of incriminating photos that painted Senator Jenkins as an abusive husband, which is actually true. So now Albertson's campaign managers are busy assigning their lead candidate with the role of white knight."

"How is that better?" Will asked before I could. He stood leaning against the wall beside the couch, swirling a glass of wine. Those sinful jeans were in place, making me want to lick him. Too bad we had company.

"Because," Mark drawled, "Bianca will divorce with sole custody of the kid and immediately marry the baby's father."

My stomach twisted. "That's not better; that's worse." Ryan would destroy her, and all because… I couldn't even finish the thought. It hurt too much. I'd sent another woman to serve my sentence. How was that fair?

Will, sensing my discomfort, asked the question I couldn't articulate. "You're not concerned for Bianca?"

Mark scoffed. "Please, that woman was groomed for this. She's over the moon at winning the hand of a future senator. He comes from good breeding stock, he has money, and he has a long future in front of him. And it probably helps that he's prettier than her soon-to-be ex-husband." He flipped out his phone to show us a photo that was taken from a distance, likely by him. "Does that look like an unhappy woman?"

"I used to look like that," I whispered, taking in her doting smile and doe eyes. "Give it a year."

He shook his head sharply. "No, you fail to realize what drives a man like Albertson. You challenge him in a way that this woman never will. Honestly, he'll get bored with her before he ever lays a hand on her. I'm more concerned that he's going to come after you again at some point to fill the void, but he'll be busy maintaining the perfect husband facade for at least the next two years."

"And if you're wrong?" Will asked.

"I'm not, but on the very small chance I am, we both know you already took care of it." Respect colored his features as he added, "The wine was brilliant."

"I'm certain I have no idea what you're talking about," he replied.

"Wine?" I repeated, taking in Mark's obvious amusement and Will's emotionless expression. "What are you two going on about?"

"Your betrothed sent Albertson a clever message and

let him know in no uncertain terms that the Mershanos are an equal, if not superior, competitor in this game." He sounded impressed, which said a lot about whatever Will had done.

"What was the message?" I asked, ignoring the *betrothed* comment. "What did you do, Will?"

He rubbed a thumb over his bottom lip as if debating how much to say. I narrowed my gaze, silently demanding him to tell me everything, or there would be hell to pay later. Ryan was *my* ex, and my problem.

"Mmm," he murmured, sensing my unspoken challenge. His expression said he liked it, perhaps too much. "Let's just say I returned the favor by playing with the water in his office, and when he woke up, a bottle of Mershano Vineyards's finest wine was waiting for him."

"With a note that said, 'From my family to yours,'" Mark added. "Sorry, but that was my favorite part. Well, and the whole attacking-him-inside-his-own-home bit. Nice."

Will shrugged. "Seemed appropriate. He knocked out Sam and Beau because he couldn't get directly to me. I wanted him to know that my contacts don't lack that particular skill set."

I gaped at him. "Why didn't you tell me this?"

"Because this wasn't so much about you as about me informing Albertson that I'm not an enemy he wants to fuck with lightly."

"And now your ex will think twice about touching you," Mark said. "Because not only would he be putting his career on the line, but he would have to maneuver around Mershano. Which he now knows would be easier said than done."

My gaze flipped back and forth between them. I was torn between frustration and relief. "You should have told me, Will." If anything, just so I knew. "But I'm glad you did it." His connections should have scared me, but I knew him too well to fear him. He wasn't Ryan. He would

257

never use those contacts against me. But he would use them to protect me should I need it.

Warmth flowed from my chest at the realization that for the first time in years, Ryan Albertson couldn't touch me.

No more threats.

No more texts.

No more calls.

No more pain.

Freedom.

I blinked back tears as I studied the men before me. I worried this moment would leave me feeling weak, but it was the opposite. Strength and pride lit me from within.

Yes, Mark had done most of the heavy lifting, and Will used his influence to intimidate Ryan, but *I* was the one who asked for help. I trusted them with the darkest part of me and let them guide me to the light. *That* took courage.

It wasn't so much physical as mental, and now I was ready to begin the next step of my healing process. The part where I never allowed Ryan to control me again. It wouldn't happen overnight. Just thinking about the last time I saw him sent a chill down my spine, but someday, it would disgust me more than frighten me. Knowing he could never touch me again allowed me to start building a new wall, one that belittled his impact on me, and fortified my resolve.

"Thank you," I whispered, then cleared my throat to say it again with more strength. "I don't think I'll ever be able to articulate what you've done for me."

Will set his wine on the glass table before joining me on the couch to wrap me in his arms. I melted into him with a content sigh as he kissed the top of my head.

"I love you," he said, his lips brushing my ear. "I'll always be here when you need me."

"I know, and I love you too."

"And I've apparently chosen the wrong time to enter the room. Or perhaps the right time," Garrett mused as he joined us in the living area. His unexpected presence immediately drew Mark's undivided attention, or maybe it was an excuse to not observe my embrace with Will.

"Everything good?" Will didn't sound at all fazed by his friend's abrupt arrival. He had warned me that Garrett would be stopping by today, but I didn't realize the man would just walk right in like he owned the place.

"Other than your cousin losing his mind, sure," he replied as he smoothed a hand over his black tie. Then he trained that startling blue gaze on Mark. "I don't believe we've met."

My friend stood to shake The Devil's hand, and a moment passed between them that unsettled the room. Garrett might look fancy in that designer suit, but I sensed that a fighter lurked beneath the clothes. One who wasn't averse to a little pain, and it seemed Mark sensed it as well.

"Your employer intrigues me," Garrett finally said, cocking his head to the side. "We should talk."

"Indeed," Mark agreed.

"If you two are done flirting, I have one final question on the Albertson case." Will's voice held a touch of amusement, but his expression was bored. "Does he know we're behind the media leak?"

Oh, I hadn't thought to ask that. Good question.

"No, he assumes it's a political opponent, but his sources are digging into it. If they find anything, and that's a big if, it won't point to our meddling." He didn't sit down again, and I wondered if it was because of Garrett. Both men maintained casual stances, but neither looked entirely comfortable with the other. "As I've already stated, I'm not concerned, especially with Rachel moving in with you next month. Which reminds me"—his devious gaze swung my way—"do you need any help packing? I'll actually be in town for a bit."

"Uh…" I didn't get a chance to say anything else, as the other men in the room spoke over each other.

"Oh, for fuck's sake, not you too," Garrett said as Will

pulled away with, "You're moving in with me?"

Heat crept up my neck as I met my boyfriend's surprised expression. "Uh, no? I don't know. I put in a transfer request for the Charlotte office last week, and it was just approved this morning."

"And he knew this before me?" He pointed to a smirking Mark. The nosy man seemed quite proud of himself.

"Not because I told him," I said with a glare at the so-called FBI agent. When I looked back at Will, my throat tightened. He looked not so much mad as darkly curious. I wasn't sure if that was better. "So, uh, Janet called me two hours ago and said the relocation makes sense since I'm Mershano Vineyards's primary contact. She also said she expected the request, but it's not mandatory. I can stay in Chicago, but I just wanted the option to, uh..." I cleared my throat. "Yeah, we can talk more about this later." When we didn't have an audience.

"Oh, we'll be discussing it," Will replied, his eyes glittering. "Thoroughly."

That look captivated me. It held a dark promise, one my body craved more than oxygen. "Yes, sir," I whispered, knowing he would understand my meaning. It'd become a taunt of sorts that I used when I wanted him. He looked ready to kiss me, but voices in the foyer ruined the moment.

"I miss having an empty house," he muttered as he stood again to greet his guests.

31
A MERSHANO FAMILY REUNION

"He's right here," Evan said as he entered the living area. A glowing Sarah was attached at his side as they focused on the phone in his hand. I guessed someone's face was on the screen, and when he passed the device over to Will, his expression brightened into a smile.

"Well, hello, darlin'. You're looking tan." Affection laced his tone—not the sexual kind but the happy kind.

"Burnt," a female voice corrected over the speakerphone. "But I didn't call to talk about me. I want to hear about you."

He chuckled. "You mean you want to hear about Rachel."

He's been talking about me. That thought warmed me to my toes.

"Obviously. I finally met Evan's fiancée, or rather, saw her, so now tell me about yours," the woman said. I assumed it was Mia, even though I couldn't see her nor did I have the wherewithal to focus on it.

Then her words hit me.

Evan's what?

Fiancée?

No...

My gaze homed in on my best friend's beet-red face. That alone was a tell. Sarah Summers *never* blushed. "You're engaged?"

"Surprise?" She raised her left hand and wiggled her fingers, which of course forced me off the couch. I grabbed her wrist to better examine the gorgeous ring.

"You were not wearing that earlier, were you?" She flew in this morning with Evan, but we hadn't spent a lot of time together yet. Mostly because I spent the day working in Will's office.

She bit her full bottom lip and shrugged. "You were busy."

"I think that's the kind of thing you're allowed to interrupt me for, Sarah." I loved my job, but not nearly as much as I loved my best friend. "And this didn't just happen, so why didn't you call?"

"He proposed a few days ago in Iceland, but I wanted to surprise you in person."

My hands settled on my hips. "By letting some woman on the phone tell me?"

She grimaced. "Uh, no, not quite like that..."

"Uh-huh," I said, eyes narrowed. But I wasn't mad. Not with my best friend radiating so much happiness.

"Isn't she gorgeous?" Will stage-whispered, drawing my attention to the phone angled my way. A female version of Evan Mershano smiled back at me.

"Hello," she said. "I'm Mia."

I pursed my lips and fought the heat creeping into my features. "Rachel," I replied and coughed to lodge the cotton from my throat. "Sorry. Just surprised to hear my best friend is engaged."

"Oh, don't apologize. I'm loving this. It's all quite amazing. I leave the country, and my big brothers finally decide to grow the fuck up."

"Hey," Evan chastised, stepping into view. "Don't loop me in with Will. We both know I'm the adult in the room."

Mia scoffed. "Whatever, Ev."

"And she calls me a child." He shook his dark head and went back to Sarah's side to hug her. The way she looked at him said it all.

"When's the wedding?" I asked, curious.

"We were just talking to Mia about that," Sarah replied. "We plan to go public with our engagement in the spring, after she returns. Then we'll plan a wedding for either next summer or the autumn. Something small."

Mia's giggle had us all looking at the phone. "'Small' and 'the Mershano family' don't go together, but sure. Try it. Hey, who is that in the background, sulking by the wall?"

I glanced over my shoulder, expecting to see Garrett, but he was on the opposite side of the room, staring out the window with his hands tucked in his pockets. Tension seemed to roll off him in waves. Interesting.

"That's Kincaid," Will said by way of introduction. "Rachel's friend."

"He's cute," Mia replied.

Garrett turned at the words and arched a haughty brow but said nothing. When his gaze met mine, my breath stalled. Thankfully, he looked away a second later, refocusing on whatever held his attention outside. Because wow. Someone had issues with the woman on the phone. Had no one else noticed that? A glance around said nope, they were all smiling at Mark as he waved to Mia with polite interest.

"He doesn't smile much, does he?" Mia asked, eyes narrowed in an astute way. Will wasn't kidding when he called her brilliant. Intelligence radiated from her, even through the phone. "Okay, who else is there?"

"Garrett, but he's busy sulking by the window," Evan murmured. "He's not nearly as thrilled by our engagement as you are, Mia."

Her expression darkened with disapproval. "Shocking," she muttered. "I doubt much thrills The Devil outside of his lair."

Will and Evan exchanged a glance. "Probably not," they agreed in unison.

The conversation lightened a bit after that comment, but Garrett's shoulders remained tense. It could have been my imagination, but there seemed to be a history between Mia and her older brother's best friend. The other two men were happy to hear from her, but the third remained unmoved, his expression impassive. I'd have to ask Will about it later.

When the call ended, Sarah ran over and threw her arms around my neck.

"I'm so sorry I didn't tell you. I didn't want to interrupt earlier, and then Evan was insistent on telling Mia. He didn't want her to hear it from someone else, especially with the show airing right now." She hugged me tightly, and I returned the embrace.

"It's okay. I'm happy for you, Sarah," I whispered. "So happy."

"I'm happy for you too," she replied, equally soft. "Are you going to move?" Unlike Will, Sarah had overheard my conversation with Janet earlier about transferring offices.

"I don't know." I glanced at the man I really wanted to have this discussion with, but he was busy sharing a drink with Evan and Garrett. The latter still wasn't smiling, which appeared to be common for him. Mark had taken a position against the wall, his focus on a device in his hand. It looked somewhat like a phone, but not quite.

"You know he wants to be with you, like, for good, right?" Sarah said, drawing my attention back to her. She sounded so confident, and knowing. Like of course Will wanted me to move.

"I do." Of course I did. I could see it every time he looked at me. It wasn't necessarily so much possessive as all-encompassing. "But I don't know if he wants to live together yet." Especially after his reaction earlier.

"What are you two whispering about?" Evan asked as he entered our bubble with a glass of wine for Sarah. A second appeared over my shoulder as Will stepped up behind me. His lips against my neck caused butterflies to take flight in my stomach.

"Kincaid," Sarah replied without missing a beat. The woman should have been a lawyer. "And that thing I want him to do."

"What thing would that be?" Mark asked as he slid the device into his jeans pocket. His foot slid up the wall as he balanced on one leg and folded his arms. An odd position, but seemed about right for him.

"Okay, we all know you're not FBI, but more of a contractor for hire, right?" Leave it to Sarah to be the blunt one in the room.

"Sure," he replied in that vague way of his.

"Well, it just so happens I've come into a lot of money recently," she cast a meaningful look at Evan before continuing, "and I want to hire you for a project."

"And that's how it starts, gentlemen," Garrett drawled.

"Oh, quiet, Mister 'Knock Her Up And Leave Her,'" Sarah snapped. I didn't follow the reference but assumed he had said something like that about her at some point. And from her expression, she was not a fan.

"You were right, Evan," he murmured, unfazed. His blue gaze danced over my best friend in a way that would make most women squirm, but Sarah was not most women. She folded her arms and glowered at the too-forward man, which only seemed to amuse him. "I do like her."

"I don't think the feeling is mutual," Evan replied with a grin at his fuming fiancée. "Which I also anticipated."

"It'll make for an eventful wedding, I'm sure." Garrett lifted a glass to his lips and gave a motion for her to proceed.

"I cannot believe he's your best friend," she all but growled.

"He grows on you," Will put in.

Sarah and I shared a look. *Yeah. Right.*

"*Anyway*," she said, addressing Mark again. He'd watched the entire exchange with a bored expression. "I need you to teach my twin sister a lesson."

His brow furrowed. "That does not sound like something I'd be interested in doing. At all."

"But I'll pay you handsomely for it," Sarah said with a pointed look at Garrett. "Since I have the funds." When he didn't react, she continued her spiel. "What do you think, Kincaid? Intrigued?"

"Not even slightly," he replied honestly while examining his watch.

"What if I make things interesting?"

He gave her a doubtful look in response.

"Hear me out over dinner," she continued.

"Why?"

"Because it'll be a free meal."

Both of his eyebrows lifted. "And you're under the impression I require free food?" He sounded more amused than annoyed.

She sighed. "You're going to make me beg, aren't you? What will it take to hear me out?"

Mark studied her for a long moment, his expression flattening. I couldn't tell if he took pity on my best friend or if he just wanted to end the discussion, but he finally sighed, "Fine. I accept the dinner offer, but I'm telling you now that I'm not interested in your pet project."

Sarah brightened. "Oh, we'll see how you feel after I pitch my idea."

"I'm confident I'll feel the same."

"Ye of little faith," she teased.

Will wrapped his arms around me from behind and laid his chin on my shoulder. "Unfortunately," he murmured, "we won't be joining you all for dinner, but good luck on the negotiation. In the meantime, I need to have a chat with Miss Dawson."

I shivered against him despite being warm. "A chat?"

His scruff tickled my neck as he nodded. He pressed his lips to my ear and whispered low so no one else could hear. "I want you naked and waiting for me in my bed in five minutes."

Adrenaline shot through veins, setting my bloodstream on fire. Holy hell, that was hot. I had to force myself to swallow, to remember to breathe. When he talked to me like that, my entire world halted. Nothing else existed but Will and the visceral need he created deep within. We'd spent the last month and a half together nonstop, and I still hadn't gotten enough of him. I doubted I ever would.

It wasn't until he let me go that I remembered our company in the room. Garrett's gaze was knowing, while Sarah and Evan seemed too absorbed in a discussion about where to go for dinner to notice, and Mark had his phone out again.

"Uh, I'm going to change," I announced somewhat lamely. "Since we're not going out to dinner."

Sarah's eyebrows danced up, and I knew what she was thinking. *Rachel lives in business attire.* True. I loved my skirt suits, but Will wanted me naked. That qualified as a change of clothes, right?

"Good luck at dinner," I said before she could comment. "And we'll catch up tomorrow or later tonight."

"I won't be here, Rach," Mark interrupted as he pocketed his phone. "I only dropped by to give you an update, and I assumed in person would be better. After I turn Miss Summers down, I'll be heading home."

"Good luck with that," Evan replied as he pulled my best friend into his arms. It seemed he was as bad as Will in terms of all the necessary touching. "She negotiates brilliantly," he added warmly.

"I do," Sarah agreed.

"I'm not concerned," Mark replied. "In any case, you're safe, Rachel. Finally. And your brother and I will be monitoring the situation personally for any changes."

"Thank you," I whispered, hugging him. He kissed the top of my head, just like Caleb would, and let me go.

Will observed the exchange with a heated look and mouthed, *Two minutes*, when I didn't move right away.

Right.

Naked.

Bed.

"Enjoy dinner," I called over my shoulder.

32
THE RELATIONSHIP PROPOSAL

My suit felt heavier than normal, and restricting. I popped a button off my blouse in my haste to unfasten it, then ripped the rest of it over my head once it was loose enough. My skirt hit the floor next, followed by my camisole, bra, and underwear.

The majority of my clothes were in Will's laundry room, a result of spending the last several weeks abroad and only returning five days ago. That meant no stockings for me today, much to my lover's amusement. He'd spent half the morning admiring my exposed calves as I walked barefoot around his office.

Will appeared in my peripheral vision as I turned, his shoulder propped against the doorjamb. He held a glass of wine and observed me through hooded eyes. "You're not on the bed." His deep rumble warmed me in all the right places.

"But I am naked." That deserved at least a few points in my favor, if not more.

"Indeed you are." He didn't move from the door, just caressed me slowly with his gaze, up and down, not missing an inch of my exposed skin. His thumb swept over his bottom lip as he considered me casually. "So tell me about the Charlotte opportunity."

"Seriously?" I asked, shocked that he wanted to discuss this *now*. "I'm naked."

"Yes, and I'm loving the view, but I also want to know about your potential move."

"Do you want me to get dressed again?" I couldn't help challenging him. It was in my blood, and I enjoyed it far too much.

"Try," was all he said.

I wanted to, if only to prove that I could, but my hands refused to move. The idea of putting clothes on seemed counterproductive, and I rather liked the way he was looking at me. All heat and possessiveness masked behind an expression of benign interest. It fascinated me the way he could control his features and allow only the barest of emotion to color his gaze.

"The Charlotte office," he prompted, that thumb still tracing his lip. I wanted to bite it, but I focused on his statement.

"It's not a big deal. I just wanted to know if it was even possible to transfer, and Janet confirmed. That doesn't mean I have to."

"Not a big deal," he repeated, his tone incredulous. "Says the woman who adamantly told me how much she didn't want to move when I tried to recruit her for Mershano Vineyards."

"Yes, but things are different now."

"Why?" One word spoken with such confidence that it made my knees weak.

"Well, for one, I'm naked." Definitely had clothes on during all our previous discussions.

He grinned at that. "Yes, you are, and beautifully flushed, too, but go on." His tone had lowered to the one he reserved for the bedroom, and my body responded as it usually did. My breasts swelled and my nipples hardened, and the space between my legs ached with a need only he could relieve. "Rachel, why is it different?" he asked again when I didn't readily reply.

"Because *we're* different." God, my voice sounded strained, and he had to hear it. He knew his effect on me, and although I never told him, he also knew I loved this power play in the bedroom. I craved it. His being clothed while I stood naked before him only heightened my arousal, and it didn't help that I could see the outlines of his strong planes beneath the tight cotton shirt. "If you don't fuck me soon, I'm going to scream."

His grin bloomed into a smile. "Oh, I intend to make you scream all night, but we're not done discussing Charlotte. Do you want to live in North Carolina?"

I groaned in frustration. *Always in control.* He wanted an explanation, and he wouldn't stop until I gave him one. Fine. It wasn't like I had anything to hide, but placing all my emotions on the table didn't come easily to me. But Will Mershano didn't believe in easy; he believed in fighting. So fight I would.

"I love living in Chicago," I admitted. "But my primary reason for staying there these last few years was because I had to, and now, for the first time in what feels like forever, I can choose. And I chose to ask about relocation opportunities to the Charlotte office because I want to be close to you. The idea of living in another state doesn't appeal to me, but if you prefer a long-distance relationship, then..." His gaze darkened, silencing me.

His glass clinked against the nightstand as he set it down, and then he started toward me.

I took a step back in alarm at the intense look on his face, but he caught me by the hip and took possession of my mouth. His tongue mastered mine in a single swipe, telling me without words how he felt about that last sentence.

"Move in with me," he whispered against my lips.

"You don't think it's too soon?" Not that I had a normal measure to reference. Our relationship superseded all ordinary boundaries from the beginning. Why would now be any different?

He palmed my lower back to pull me flush against him. "Darlin', we both know you'll be in my bed every night regardless of where you live. You might as well be closer."

I punched his arm half-heartedly. "Arrogant."

"Confident," he corrected, like he always did. "Just as I'm confident you'll be naked in my bed every night as well and screaming my name."

"Promises, promises," I teased.

He nuzzled my neck and gently bit my pulse. "Mmm, absolutely." He grabbed my hips and spun me around, placing my back to his front. "Hands on the bed, gorgeous."

I shivered at the command and did what he asked. He nudged my legs to widen my stance and dragged a finger down my spine to the top of my ass. His lips trailed along the same path as he went to his knees behind me. I jolted when he nipped my bare cheek.

"So perfect," he whispered as he applied pressure to my lower back, forcing me to bend over even more.

"Oh, fuck," I moaned as his tongue slid through my slick folds. I'd expected his finger, not his warm, knowing mouth. He murmured his approval at finding me soaked for him and wasted no time locating my clit.

"Will," I whispered, conflicted. It felt so wrong for him to do it this way, yet so right. I trembled, my palms the only thing keeping me from collapsing forward onto the bed, as he continued his sensuous assault. It was too much and not enough at the same time.

I needed more.

So. Much. More.

His arm wrapped around my waist to hold me steady as he devastated me with his mouth. My legs threatened to buckle under the intensity, and I wasn't sure how much more I could take. I wanted to come, but I couldn't. Not yet. Not this way. Not without *him*.

"You win," I panted. "Fuck, you win." I had no idea what he won, and couldn't remember if he was even trying to prove a point or not, but to hell with it. "I surrender."

He chuckled against my damp flesh. "Do you?"

"Whatever you want," I half moaned. Just his breath against my most intimate part was enough to destroy me.

His tongue lashed out at me one final time before he stood again, leaving me a trembling mess. He palmed my stomach to keep me from tumbling face-first into the mattress, as my arms forgot how to function. It felt like he'd lit a fuse within me and then placed the explosion on a delayed timer.

I fisted the comforter and groaned.

"Shh, I'll take care of you, darlin'," he murmured with a kiss to the back of my neck. "Always."

Something about this felt different.

Primal.

Energizing.

Promising.

I barely registered him unbuckling and unzipping his pants, but my body came alive when I felt him nudge at me from behind. His palms went to my hips, steadying me as he thrust inside.

So deep.

So right.

So perfect.

My fingers tightened their hold on the bed as I arched back into him, needing more. But he already knew. One hand went to the top of my sex to thrum my swollen nub, while the other slid up to palm my heavy breasts. His pace was relentless and filled with purpose, and his fingers stroked me reverently.

"Every. Night." He punctuated the words with his cock, sending jolts of pleasure to that place deep within me.

"Yes," I whispered in response to both his actions and his words, and to the question he asked earlier. "Fuck, yes."

He flipped me around and onto the bed so fast that my head spun, and then he was there, deep inside me again and kissing the life out of me. *Sealing the deal*, I realized. And I sealed it right back. I wrapped my legs around his waist and urged him to move faster, harder, and he obliged in kind.

"That's it, gorgeous," he praised as my orgasm neared. The man knew my body better than I did, and when he pressed his hand to that sensitive part of me once more, I exploded around him. It hit me so hard and fast that I couldn't breathe. And then his name crossed my lips in a prayer, over and over and over again. His pacing increased, riding me through my ecstasy and sending himself over the edge to join me.

"Rachel..." My name sounded almost like a growl, and it was sexy as sin and matched the moment perfectly. Our embrace was quick and dirty, it was everything we both needed, and it was only the beginning. Because Will owned me now, and I owned him. Nothing, and no one, would ever come between that.

I hugged him tight, unwilling to let him roll off of me. I needed him to know, to understand, what this meant to me. "I love you, Will."

He went to his elbows to stare down at me. "I love you too, Rachel." He brushed the hair from my face and smiled. "So you'll come work for me?"

"Through Baker Brown," I added. "Yes."

"In Charlotte."

Not a question, but I answered anyway. "Yes."

"And you'll live here, with me." Also a statement, and said in that domineering way of his.

"Only if you promise to take me to bed every night, even when we're fighting."

"Definitely when we're fighting," he corrected. "How else will I shut you up?"

I smacked his arm. "Not off to a good start, Mershano."

"Is this considered a fight, then?" he teased. "Because I have something hard for your mouth, if you need it." He flexed his hard length inside me with his words.

I laughed. "You're unbelievable."

"Why, yes, you called me that once before at La Rosas. Glad to see things haven't changed."

"Oh, Will, I think we both know everything has changed."

"Has it?" He nuzzled my neck. "Hmm, I'll bear that in mind, then, for the future, Dawson."

"Meaning what?" I asked, curious.

"You'll see," he replied. "For now, I want to make love to my live-in girlfriend. Slowly, thoroughly, and all night long."

"Mmm, I think I like the sound of that." I relaxed beneath him, ready for him to take control again. It would be slow indeed, but I would enjoy every minute.

"Good, because you better get used to it, darlin'."

I smiled against his lips. "Yes, sir."

EPILOGUE

"Two weeks in Hawaii, huh?" I whistled. "You Mershanos sure know how to throw a wedding."

Sarah's grin brightened my phone screen. "Well, I did say I preferred a vacation in Hawaii over New Orleans, right? Seems fitting."

I laughed, recalling our conversation from last year around this time. Just before she went on the show to meet Evan. "Wow, I can't believe that was twelve, no, thirteen months ago."

"Right? Look at us now, you in your fancy office at Will's house, me talking to you from a private jet." She shook her head. "And to think, it's all Abby's fault."

I grimaced at that. "Yeah, I don't want to give that woman any credit."

"Oh, don't worry. She'll get what's coming to her."

"Did you finally convince Mark to help you?" He had refused outright when Sarah proposed her plan last fall, and again in the winter. *Teaching spoiled little girls lessons is outside of my job scope*, he'd said. *Get someone else.*

"No, Evan convinced him."

My eyebrows shot up. "Seriously?"

"Yep. I don't know what he said, but Kincaid is fully on board to help prank my twin. And it's so good. Wait until I give you all the details…"

A knock at the door had me looking up from the screen into a pair of sinfully dark eyes.

I smiled. "You'll have to fill me in later." Because I knew that look. It was the one that preceded Will's doing delicious things to me with his mouth.

"Hi, Will," Sarah said in response. She couldn't see or hear him from the camera on my phone but likely noticed my facial reaction to him.

"Hello, little minx," he murmured. "Are you keeping Evan in line?"

"In line, hmm." She mocked a thoughtful expression. "Well, if you're asking if I'm encouraging him to behave badly, then yes, yes, I am."

He chuckled and popped a hip against my desk. He wore dark slacks today and a crisp blue button-down, rolled to the elbows. All business, except for that twinkle in his eyes.

"Good," he replied. "He needs a deviant in his life."

She snorted. "Uh-huh. Bye, lovebirds." She gave a wave and hung up without waiting for a reply.

"Did she call about the wedding?" he wondered.

"Yep, sounds like we're going to Hawaii for a few weeks."

He shook his head. "So much for a small affair, not that I ever expected it. Not with this family." He placed a stack of papers on the desk in front of me. "Speaking of, would you mind reviewing this contract for me?"

I eyed the document speculatively. "What's it for?" Because it wasn't something I drafted.

"Read it," he said by way of answering.

With a sigh, I kicked my stocking-clad feet up onto the desk and started on page one, which was a list of property and assets, including a few sizable bank accounts.

"This looks like something Garrett should be

reviewing," I commented as I switched to the next page.

It was a list of promises. All words exchanged between us at one point or another, with a few additives of a sexual nature thrown into the mix. My eyes swam over the page, blurring at some of the more touching memories from the last year.

"Will, what is this?" I whispered.

"Keep reading."

I did.

The next page continued the onslaught of emotion, detailing every aspect of our relationship, spoken and unspoken, and at the end was a simple line. Not a question, because that wasn't Will's style, but there was a line for my signature. To acknowledge and accept his terms.

Rachel Dawson agrees to marry Will Mershano.

He placed a ring box beside my foot on the desk. "For your consideration," he murmured. "I know how much you enjoy saying no, but for once, I'm really hoping you'll say yes."

My hand fluttered to my mouth as the oxygen stalled in my lungs. I didn't know what to say. How to react. Whether to cry or to laugh or to jump into his arms. We hadn't discussed marriage yet, though that's where our relationship was headed.

"Will," I breathed.

"You don't need to reply now. I'm sure you would like to make some amendments, and as you already know, I'll always agree to your terms." He pressed a kiss to my forehead and started to leave, but I grabbed his hand and pulled him back to me.

I met his gaze and grinned. "Yes."

"Yes?" he repeated, his expression hesitant. Considering all the times I said no in the past, I wasn't surprised. But this time my heart and soul were in agreement.

I stood and wrapped my arms around his neck.

There was only one word left to say.
And I put my entire heart into it.
"Yes."

THE END

BONUS SCENE

Ryan Albertson leafed through the documents on his desk with a calm few men possessed, but that tick in his eye told Jax everything he needed know. It was his job to recognize even the smallest details, like Albertson's thousand-dollar shirt and the solid-gold pen sitting beside his relaxed hand. Both were indicators that the man could afford a hacker of Jax's caliber, hence the reason why he'd taken this assignment. At least initially.

The final page of the report listed the name his client wanted. Ryan's gaze narrowed as he read the last line, and his brow pinched. "Mark Kincaid. Who the fuck is Mark Kincaid?"

"He's an operative with the Alliance of Black Ops Services, sir. A private security company for hire." That's what his contact had said, anyway. He couldn't find any details on them, which was a rarity and one that intrigued him deeply. "From what I've gathered, they provide elite services with hefty price tags."

Ryan tossed the papers onto his desk with a snort. "Which means someone with adequate finances hired him to destroy me. Any idea who?"

Jax pulled a note from his leather jacket and placed it on the mahogany desk. "Does this name ring a bell?"

His icy gaze narrowed, then widened. "Interesting, and yes, it does."

"Then I believe my work here is done."

"Of course." Ryan slid an envelope across the flat surface. "I've added a bonus."

"Appreciated," Jax murmured as he pocketed the money without counting it. He knew the future senator wouldn't short him. "Best of luck, sir." He nodded as a gesture of respect and walked out the door, all the while keeping Ryan in his periphery—a habit of the job, and also why he brought more than one weapon with him should he need it.

He exited the Albertson mansion and hopped onto his motorcycle without any issues, likely because the family considered him more valuable alive. For now.

Jax carried out various evasive maneuvers on the road, just in case the notorious political family had anyone following him, and came to a stop thirty minutes later outside a local coffee house just north of Chicago. A dark-haired man with a well-trimmed beard sat waiting on the patio, sipping a cappuccino.

Jax parked and sauntered up with a grin. "You couldn't even be bothered to buy me one?"

Kincaid shrugged. "Didn't know how long you would be."

"Bastard." He kicked out a seat, swung it around, and straddled it. With his arms folded on the top, he eyed his old friend. "Albertson has some nasty connections, Kincaid. You gonna tell me what the fuck all that was about?"

"He needed a new hobby," he replied in that vague way of his. "Or rather, a new obsession. And I've just given him one."

"You."

"Yes." Kincaid set his cup down after another casual

sip and tilted his head back to admire the sky through his dark shades. "Rachel deserves a break. It's my turn to play now."

"Which is why you had me give him that random senator's name."

He shrugged. "Two birds, one stone." Which meant the name hadn't been random at all, but a solution to a separate issue. Interesting. "I'll send my feedback to Caleb regarding your candidacy." Because that's what this whole thing had been, an interview for a job, with some bonuses.

Kincaid slid a card across the table as he added, "But consider yourself hired, Jax. Welcome to ABS Operatives."

ABS Operatives — Coming 2019

Book One: KINCAID

What starts as a prank turns real as enemies from his past return for revenge...

KINCAID
An ABS Operatives Novel

A favor for a family friend.

An unusual mission.

A prank gone wrong.

I meant to teach her a lesson, a simple farce to change her prankster ways. But an enemy from my past saw it as an opportunity.

It's my fault for bringing her into this, and only I can help her out of it. I'll need her faith and trust, and maybe even her heart, to survive.

This isn't a happily-ever-after tale.

It's real.

It's deadly.

It's life.

THE PRINCE'S GAME
A MERSHANO EMPIRE NOVEL

There's only one way to get a "happily-ever-after,"
And that's by winning the game.

My twin sister thinks she's so damn funny with her pranks,
But I'm not laughing.
Entering me into a dating reality show,
The Prince's Game,
Isn't all that hysterical.

But this particular joke has quite the twist.
The billionaire bachelor, Evan Mershano, has no interest in marriage.
With his family breathing down his neck, he's desperate for a way out,
And I happen to be the perfect damsel to save this prince.

It's a simple arrangement: play to win, and he'll make it worth my while.
But what started out as a silly farce,
Just might be the fairy tale we never expected.

THE DEVIL'S DENIAL
A MERSHANO EMPIRE NOVEL

I did a bad thing.
I was young and stupid.
I thought I loved him, but he corrected that falsehood after our one and only night together.

I promised never to acknowledge him again… Until my brother's wedding left me no choice. Now I'm stuck walking down the aisle with Garrett Wilkinson and pretending he means nothing to me. Too bad the man is still as sexy and arrogant as I remember.

But he taught me how to guard my heart, and I have no intention of giving in to him again. Even if it is just for one night.

This time it's my turn to deny the devil.

ABOUT THE AUTHOR

Lexi C. Foss is a writer lost in the IT world. She lives in Atlanta, Georgia with her husband and their furry children. When not writing, she's busy crossing items off her travel bucket list. Many of the places she's visited can be seen in her writing, including the mythical world of Hydria which is based on Hydra in the Greek islands. She's quirky, consumes way too much coffee, and loves to swim. Cheers!

ALSO BY LEXI C. FOSS

Mershano Empire Series
Book One: The Prince's Game
Book Two: The Charmer's Gambit
Book Three: The Devil's Denial

ABS Operatives Series
Book One: KINCAID

Immortal Curse Series
Book One: Blood Laws
Book Two: Forbidden Bonds
Book Three: Blood Heart

Other Projects:
Daughter of Death: A Bad Girls Novel